STOLEN LIVES

Danny Sanchez Thrillers Book Two

Matthew Pritchard

SAPERE
BOOKS

STOLEN LIVES

Published by Sapere Books.

20 Windermere Drive, Leeds, LS17 7UZ,
United Kingdom

saperebooks.com

ISBN: 978-1-912786-79-4

Part I — Los Desaparecidos

1

Danny didn't need to ask directions: he could smell the place a mile off.

Literally.

What a crappy place to die, he thought, stuffing camera and notebook into a shoulder bag. He'd reported dozens of deaths over the years, but this was his first at a landfill site. His nose wrinkled as he opened the door of his battered Escort. If it smelt this bad in October, how must it be when the Spanish summer hit?

The road that led to the landfill's entrance was flanked by steep, sloping walls of red-brown earth, twenty yards high. Tin cans and fluttering trails of plastic littered the asphalt edges of the road, which ended in a heavy metal gate, the kind that slid on rollers. Beyond the gate were a two-storey admin building and a number of unloading bays for rubbish trucks. A middle-aged Guardia Civil officer in a green boiler suit guarded the gate. To judge by the look on his face, he was either angry or upset about something. Or possibly both.

Neither emotion boded well for Teresa del Hoyo.

The twenty-three-year-old had been missing a week, during which time her description had saturated the media: 5' 4" tall, nine stones in weight, a slender girl with brown shoulder-length hair streaked purple and braided on the left side; her ears, nose and left eyebrow were pierced, and she had last been seen wearing an Adidas track-suit top, slim-fit Levis and a pair of black Converse. Around 3 p.m. on Tuesday, October the 4th, she had gone to her waitress job at a city-centre bar, but had left at eight o'clock after receiving a call from a payphone. No one had seen her since.

A GPS trace on Teresa's mobile had led police to her pink VW Beetle, which had been found parked in a suburban street in the coastal town of Roquetas de Mar, the keys still in the ignition. The mobile phone lay on the passenger seat. How the vehicle had come to be there was a mystery. As far as Teresa's friends and family knew, she had absolutely no reason to have gone to the town.

The Guardia Civil had used tracker dogs and helicopters to search areas of scrubland and dry riverbeds close to Roquetas, but had found no trace of the young woman. Meanwhile, Teresa's family had made tearful appeals on the television for information, and there had been a candlelight vigil in the city centre.

Danny chatted with the Spanish journalists gathered outside the gate, but nobody knew anything beyond what they all knew: that somewhere on the landfill site the remains of a young woman had been discovered. When Danny approached the Guardia officer at the entrance, the man shook his head and uttered a terse, 'No comment'.

A television truck arrived, and the crew began setting up a camera tripod, while the presenter checked her hair and lipstick in a mirror. Danny was seeking some way to get a look at the actual crime scene when Paco Pino appeared, scrambling down a steep slope away to the right of the gate, tumbling rocks and earth as he did so. The big photographer was not the nimblest of men, and he half-stumbled, half-slid the final ten yards, cradling the two Canon 5D mk3 cameras that dangled from his neck.

'Did you see anything up there?' Danny said as the two men greeted each other.

Paco unscrewed a telephoto lens from a camera and shook his head. 'But I managed to speak to one of the workers. He said the body is way out in the rubbish, close to the tipping face.'

'How did they find it then?'

'They use a hydraulic claw to sift the rubbish once the lorries have dumped it off. They were going through one load earlier this morning, when someone spotted a human arm dangling from the teeth of the claw. They saw enough to confirm it was a woman then phoned the Guardia.'

'Doesn't sound too good for Teresa del Hoyo, does it?'

Paco shrugged and lit a cigarette. 'She's been missing an entire week. It was only ever going to end the one way, wasn't it?'

Danny thought about that as he lit his own cigarette, trying to calculate how many missing person stories he'd covered in the last 20 years that had ended happily. There hadn't been many.

'Presuming it is the Del Hoyo girl, how do you want to sell it?' Paco said, looking towards the group of journalists gathered at the gate. 'The UK nationals won't be interested, and the Spanish nationals will use their stringers. But we could try some magazines, couldn't we?'

'Do you mean *Gente de Hoy*?'

'I know you think writing for them beneath you, Danny, but no one else pays as well as they do.'

Danny puffed his cigarette. Both those statements were true.

'Let's check it's Teresa before we start worrying about how to sell it,' he said. 'I want to get a look at what the SOCOs are doing with the body.'

The two men walked a hundred metres back along the roadway and climbed a rocky hillside covered with cacti and tussocks of esparto grass. The chain-link fence at the top of the slope was only waist-high. From the other side of the fence Danny and Paco could see the entire half-mile valley the landfill occupied: off to their right were the pumping station, the weighbridge, the lorry-wash and the admin buildings; opposite and below them was the tipping face itself, which comprised acres of smeared, smelly plastic bags that were bulldozed into piles to form a huge curling lip of refuse that was covered over with earth each day.

Seagulls swooped and wheeled in the sky above, the only things that moved in the valley. Everything else had been sucked into the stasis that surrounds all crime scenes. A bulldozer lay idle among the refuse, its blade half-raised. Groups of workers and admin staff stood smoking and looking towards an area of the tipping face that was cordoned off with incident tape. A group of four SOCOs — Scenes of Crime Officers — in white plastic overalls and face masks stood knee-deep amid the rubbish, examining a hydraulic claw which hung from a mobile crane.

Paco took photos while Danny watched the forensic team through his binoculars, hoping to get some insight into how the investigation was progressing. The corpse's torso was visible between the teeth of the hydraulic claw. The skin was pale white, but the lower half of the body looked to be wrapped in black plastic.

'It's Teresa del Hoyo,' Paco said as he photographed the scene through a zoom lens. 'Look at the hair.'

Paco was right. The corpse lay face down within the claw, and the head was surrounded by long, straggly brown-red hair with a clearly visible purple streak.

'How the hell do you think she ended up at a landfill site?' Paco said.

'Someone probably dumped her in one of those big refuse containers they use in rural areas.'

'It's a dumb place to dump a body. It's almost certain to be found.'

'Perhaps they figured it would go unnoticed. This facility deals with hundreds of tonnes of refuse every day. And if it were the case, her body could have been inside the bin for days. They only collect those things twice a week.'

Paco clicked his tongue, looking thoughtful. 'I remember a story I covered once,' he said. 'A guy OD'ed and his druggy friends dumped him in a bin so the police wouldn't bust their smack house. Could be the same thing here, don't you think? The girl had a history with drugs.'

'True. But the mother claims Teresa had been clean for at least a year-and-a-half.'

The two men remained at their vantage point until the naked corpse was actually removed from the teeth of the hydraulic claw and laid face-up on a stretcher. Teresa's skin was pale white and seemed to show signs of numerous contusions. A wide and jagged rent had also been cut into the flesh of her neck, just above the collarbone.

'That's my OD theory out the window,' Paco said as he took photographs of the corpse.

An ambulance came and Teresa del Hoyo was zipped inside a body bag and taken away. The two men walked back to Paco's car.

You could tell Paco worked in journalism by the mess inside the boot, a chaotic jumble of old newspapers, magazines, empty Coke bottles, crisp packets and camera cases. A sleeping bag and pillow were shoved into the space behind the wheel arch.

'What do we know about Teresa's background?' Paco said as he poured himself coffee from a thermos.

Danny flipped his notebook open. 'All that stuff about her troubled youth checks out: she ran away at least twice as a teen and has two prior arrests for drug possession. And she was sectioned for three months in 2009.'

'Do we know why?'

'Issues relating to substance abuse. Heroin, my source claims. Apparently, once she'd dried out, her sobriety held and she replaced drugs with activism. I've confirmed that she's a member of *Izquierda Unida*, but I haven't managed to get a clear answer yet as to what her role was in the organisation.'

Paco gave a hollow laugh. 'That figures.'

Danny stifled a smile. Paco was a staunch member of Spain's PSOE socialist party, and as such felt a mixture of pity and contempt for *Izquierda Unida*, the left-wing political coalition that was home to the modern day Spanish Communist Party.

'What about your sources?' Danny said. 'Have you heard anything?'

'Bits and pieces. I have it on good authority that Teresa rarely slept alone, if you catch my drift. And rumour has it she's had an abortion.'

'What the hell has that got to do with anything?'

'Nothing. But you know how the right wing media is going to dress the story up once it's confirmed she's dead: the druggie communist baby-killer has paid the inevitable price for her libertarian ways. And if she was putting it about as much as my source claims, there's a chance she could've made someone jealous. You know what it's like with cases like this, Danny: 99% of the time, the killer is someone the woman knew.'

'Where did you get this info?'

'My cousin used to play football with one of Teresa's ex-boyfriends. I got an email address for him.'

'And naturally this bitter ex-boyfriend has no reason to lie about her, has he?'

Paco shrugged. 'I didn't say it was true. But if I've managed to speak to him, others will. It's going to get into print sooner or later.'

'Has this ex got an alibi?'

'You mean besides his being in Australia?'

'What about the current boyfriend? Got anything on him?'

'His name's Samuel Herrero. Again, he's got a cast-iron alibi. He's a sound engineer and was working some concert in Madrid the night Teresa disappeared. They met through the communist youth.'

'OK, I'll swing past the *Izquierda Unida* office in Almería city. I'll see if I can get Pepe Juarez to meet me there and give me some quotes.'

Paco tipped the remains of his coffee away. 'I'll head over to the bullring in Roquetas and take some shots of where they found Teresa's car. And I'll see if my police contact can let me into the pound where her car is being held. Why don't you get onto the Del Hoyo family?'

Danny shook his head. 'I've already tried and they're not answering the phone.'

'So go to the flat and doorstep them.'

'I swung past on my way here. There were already three reporters camped out by the entrance to the building. There's no chance I'd be able to speak to them alone.'

Paco rummaged in his pocket and withdrew a scrap of paper. 'Try this then. It's the number for the sister's private mobile. She's been doing most of the talking, so you might as well find out what she's got to say.'

'From what I've seen of Carmen del Hoyo, she doesn't seem the sort that's going to appreciate a surprise phone call.'

Paco frowned, as if he'd been expecting Danny to say that. 'If we want to sell the story as an exclusive, we can't worry about the family's feelings,' he said, glancing suspiciously towards the pack of journalists still gathered outside the gates to the landfill. 'We've got to move fast on this. We won't be the only ones looking for magazine sales.'

Danny pocketed the number. Paco was right: Teresa del Hoyo and her death were a commodity now. Whoever was quickest to bundle together pictures and details would get sale of the exclusive. The others would have wasted their time.

'I'll try the sister,' Danny said. 'But if we're going to sell it to *Gente de Hoy*, I don't want my name appearing on the article.'

'Fair enough. But what about *Sureste News*? Won't you have to cover the story for them?'

'I'll cobble something together later on. The newspaper's no longer my priority.'

Paco patted Danny on the shoulder. 'That's my boy. And talking of priorities, Marsha was on Skype with Lourdes for more than an hour last night.'

Danny rubbed the back of his neck.

'What were they saying?'

'No idea. They spoke in English most of the time. But from what I *did* hear of Marsha's Spanish, it's coming on in leaps and bounds. Surely that's a good thing, isn't it?' Paco said when Danny did not reply.

'Yeah. Of course it is.'

'Your expression says otherwise.'

'Look, we've got work to do. I don't want to get into the whole Marsha thing now.'

'You never do. But if you ain't going to go to her, she's going to come to you. It's as simple as that. She's a great girl, Danny.'

'I know.'

'Then show some damned enthusiasm,' Paco said, punching him on the arm. 'Anyway, moving in together is the fun part. After that, you get married and have kids.'

'Jesus, give it a rest, will you?'

Paco laughed as he climbed into his car and pulled the seatbelt over the bulge of his gut. He leant his big, bald head out of the window as the vehicle pulled slowly away.

'I used to waste a fortune on haircuts and fashionable clothes, Danny. Then I had my two girls, all my hair fell out and I put on four stone. You've got all this to look forward to, *amigo.*'

2

The province of Almería enjoys an average of 300 days of sunshine each year, but today wasn't one of those days: the noon sky was the colour of watered milk, and the wind whipped grit into Danny's face as he walked the narrow streets in the centre of Almería city. He'd had no luck phoning Carmen del Hoyo. The first three times he'd called, the phone had rung and then gone to voicemail; the fourth time, the phone had been turned off.

Danny stifled a yawn. He'd been working every hour God sent for more than fourteen months now.

It all began the previous year, when the editor of *Sureste News*, the British newspaper where Danny worked, went on sick leave and never returned. Danny would have been the obvious choice as a replacement, but instead of promoting him, head office had decided to do without an editor *and* to reduce the paper's staff to Danny and three others, all of whom were to be employed as freelancers, which meant they lost paid holiday and sick pay.

The only positive factor was that Danny no longer felt obliged to bring his stories to *Sureste News* first, and he and Paco were now doing at least two stories a month for an agency that sold to Spain's *prensa rosa*, as the lurid gossip magazines sold at supermarket checkouts are known.

Danny was used to doing tabloid work, but magazines like *Gente de Hoy* really pushed the envelope. Marsha thought he should be aiming his sights higher — a non-fiction book on Spain, or a correspondent job for one of the UK nationals —

but then Marsha was always full of ideas about how Danny could improve his life.

Pepe Juarez met Danny at the door to *Izquierda Unida's* youth building. As usual, the middle-aged politician seemed to have picked his clothes with a notion of looking smart, but had given up halfway: his tie was worn askew and stained with coffee, his shirt was rumpled and patched, and the wind blew his grey hair into wild, wispy patterns.

Juarez showed Danny upstairs into a large room that held sofas and tables. The walls were decorated with posters bearing the red hammer and sickle logo of the PCE, the Spanish Communist Party. A group of young men and women were sitting on sofas in the middle of the room, talking in low voices, drying tears and comforting each other. They looked up expectantly when Juarez introduced Danny as a reporter.

'Is it true what they're saying?' a young man with cropped hair and flesh tunnel earrings asked. His eyes were red from crying, but his tone was angry. 'Have they found Teresa dumped at a landfill site?'

'It's too early to say.'

'But they said on the radio it was the body of a young woman. Is that right?'

'I'm sure the police will make a statement later on today.'

'Don't you write anything bad about Teresa,' the young man said suddenly, fists balled as he held Danny's gaze.

'Why would I do that?' Danny said.

Nobody answered, but as Juarez led Danny towards the office where Teresa worked, one of the young men hissed, 'Fucking vulture'.

Danny let it go. Experience had taught him there was often a moment like this with missing person stories, a moment when the mundane business of reporting on the disappearance —

the interviews and quotes, the press conferences and deadlines — collided with the real human cost of what had occurred. It wasn't the first time the bereaved had chosen to vent their grief on a reporter.

Danny followed Juarez into a small office which held two desks. Like the building's other room, the walls of the office were covered in posters with slogans about organising and resisting.

'Which desk did Teresa work at?' Danny said.

Juarez gestured towards the desk by the window. Then he looked at Danny. '"Did?" Surely you mean "does", don't you? Or do you know something for definite?'

'I didn't want to say anything in front of the others — it's not my place to confirm or deny anything — but it doesn't look good.'

Juarez removed his glasses and began to wipe them clean with the end of his tie.

'I'm sorry,' he said, sniffing away tears. 'It's just the thought of poor Teresa being dumped in such a wretched place. If you don't mind, we'll talk about her in the present tense until the police confirm things.'

Danny put a hand on his shoulder. 'I'm sorry, Pepe. I didn't mean to be so tactless. What sort of work *does* Teresa do here?'

'Lots of things. She is a very special young lady, a real asset to the party. It's quite amazing how she has managed to turn her life around after all the problems she's had.'

'What's the most recent thing she's worked on?'

Juarez pointed towards one of the posters on the wall. It held a loose collage of grainy black and white photographs of men's and women's faces. The poster bore the slogan *¡Las monjas no son las únicas mártires de El Cerrón!* — The Nuns are not El Cerrón's only martyrs! — emblazoned across its lower third in red letters. Spatters of blood had been Photoshopped across the faces, and the fluttering red, yellow and mulberry flag of Spain's Second Republic was printed at the top of the poster.

'In the last six months Teresa has been very active in the campaign to locate the bodies of the Republican politicians that were murdered by the *fachas* in 1939 and buried in a mass grave outside the town of El Cerrón.' Juarez pointed to one of the men's faces on the poster. 'That man there was her great-grandfather's brother, so her interest is personal. I take it you know the story of what happened there?'

Danny nodded to show that he did. The last thing he wanted was to get bogged down with the civil war. More than seventy years had passed since the conflict ended, but Spaniards were still quick to man the old ideological barricades — and none more so than Pepe Juarez, hence his use of the word *facha*, a pejorative for Franco's supporters that dated back to the 1930s.

A battered old computer and CRT monitor occupied most of the space atop Teresa's desk. Danny asked if he could look through the desk drawers.

Juarez nodded. 'The police have already looked through them. Having said that, they didn't seem to look very hard. They were far more interested in Teresa's private life.'

'Really? What did they ask?'

'Did she drink a lot? Did she take drugs? Was she sleeping with anyone?'

'What did you say?'

'I told the truth. I said that Teresa had been a bit wild when she was younger, but that she had settled down and had been drink and drug-free for at least a year. And that with whom she slept was nobody's damned business but her own. But they kept asking about the times she had run away as a youngster. I got the feeling the police thought she had simply done a disappearing act again. It wasn't until Teresa's car turned up with her phone inside that they started to take things seriously.'

The bottom drawer of the desk was empty. The top drawer was stuffed with papers, pens, files and folders. The top folder was orange and had the words El Cerrón — New Project written on it in biro.

Inside was a photocopy of a black and white photograph. It showed two men and a woman standing outside a large three-storey mansion house. The building's front was flanked by tall conical towers and clumps of palm trees.

The man and woman in the centre of the picture were dressed in forties-style clothing. Their proximity seemed to indicate they were a couple, although there was little warmth in their body language: they stood close but not touching, their hands hanging by their sides. The woman was in her mid-twenties but had a worn, broken-down expression that belied her youth. The man looked to be older. He stared straight into the camera, his expression stern, as if uncomfortable at being photographed.

The second man was standing on the right of the picture. He wore the white military uniform of the Falange, the Spanish fascist party. His jacket collar was buttoned right up to his neck and leather straps crossed each breast. He had his arms folded together in front of him and was resting his weight on his back foot, his head thrown proudly upwards. His hair was slicked back from his forehead, his mouth creased with an expression of faint amusement. It was not an expression that made you warm to him: Danny had the distinct feeling he would have been the sort of man who would have enjoyed laughing *at* rather than with others. The words *Santa Cristina, Almería, España, 1949* were written below the image.

'Is this Teresa's handwriting?' Danny asked.

Juarez nodded.

On the back of the sheet of paper was a name, Gordon Pavey, and the number for an Almería landline, also written in Teresa's handwriting.

'What is this Santa Cristina place?' Danny asked. 'And who is Gordon Pavey? The name sounds British.'

Juarez shrugged. 'The photocopy must be from something Teresa was working on. But I've no idea who this Pavey chap might be.'

Danny pointed at the second desk in the office.

'Who works there?'

'Lidia. She might know something, but she's not here at the moment.'

Danny asked if he could make a copy of the picture. Juarez took him to a photocopier in the room outside and promised to find Lidia's telephone number when he got a free moment.

Danny was back on the street when Paco Pino phoned.

'I've just had word from a police contact. They've taken the landfill body to the *Instituto de Medicina Legal*, and the Del Hoyo family is going there to identify it. You'd better get down here.'

It was raining when Danny got to the *Instituto de Medicina Legal*. The Del Hoyo family arrived in a police car a few minutes later. The mother looked small and frail as she crossed the pavement, leaning on her husband's arm. Teresa's sister, Carmen, brought up the rear. She shook her head contemptuously as Paco Pino took shots of the family arriving, her hand raised to cover her face.

The doors closed behind them. Danny and Paco went to stand beneath the awning of a bar across the street, watching the rain fall. Danny knew they had time to kill, so he phoned the number for Gordon Pavey.

It went straight to an answer phone: 'You have reached Allen's Guesthouse,' a woman's voice said on the recorded message. 'Due to personal reasons the guesthouse will be closed until Wednesday, October 12th. Reservations can be made online.'

A guesthouse? That could mean Pavey wasn't local. Danny made a note to try the number again the following day.

It was early afternoon, but the day was dark. Danny looked up at the lights of the *Instituto de Medicina Legal*, trying to guess in which room the Del Hoyo family was.

Paco Pino wasn't the only person with police contacts. As Danny and Paco waited, a young photographer on a moped parked on the pavement opposite. Five minutes later, a car dropped off two more reporters.

The Spanish press pack was seven strong when Danny heard the ambulance siren, a distant wail echoing through the high, narrow caverns of the city centre. The sound grew louder, then louder still. Passers-by stopped and turned to stare beneath their umbrellas as the ambulance pulled up on the pavement outside the *Instituto de Medicina Legal*, its lights casting pools of blue neon on the wet tarmac.

The Spanish journalists made a beeline for the paramedics, bombarding them with questions as they unloaded a stretcher trolley and headed inside. Every reporter there began speaking into mobiles. Ten minutes later, the front doors banged open and the stretcher trolley was wheeled out with Teresa del Hoyo's mother on it, an oxygen mask strapped to her ashen face. Behind the stretcher came Teresa's father and sister.

Danny jostled with the photographers and reporters as he tried to get his questions heard, but Carmen del Hoyo held her father's shoulders and pushed him through the scrum. As they neared the back of the ambulance, one reporter got too close, and Carmen del Hoyo shoved him backwards so that the reporter fell heavily and landed in a puddle of water. The ambulance doors slammed closed and the vehicle raced away, siren wailing.

'Was the mother dead?' one reporter asked.

'Nah, she was definitely still breathing.'

'She picked a good place to collapse,' a photographer said, laughing and nodding towards the *Instituto de Medicina Legal* sign on the wall. 'But she's lucky they didn't whack her straight on a slab and start doing an autopsy. Did you see the fucking colour of her?'

There were days when Danny loved the job of journalism.

Today wasn't one of them.

3

When Carmen del Hoyo had locked the toilet cubicle door, she opened the top four buttons of her blouse, pulled the fabric to one side, and examined the red rash on the backs of her shoulders with a powder mirror.

It's just like last time, she thought: I'm coming out in hives.

And then it struck her that it wasn't like last time, because this time Teresa hadn't run away or spent days drugging herself insensible.

Teresa was dead.

Carmen sat down on the closed toilet lid. Her hands hung limply as the enormity of it all washed over her.

Her little sister was gone. Nothing now would ever be the same.

Her vision misted as tears welled in her eyes, but she shook them away. Tears would do her no good. Someone in the family had to be strong, especially now *Mamá* was so ill. As usual, it had fallen to Carmen and there was still so much to do: first, she had to take Teresa's certificate of death to the Civil Registry, then she needed to go to the funeral parlour and agree on the precise wording for the lapidary stone. After that, Carmen would have to rush over to the mortuary and begin the arrangements for Teresa's burial. Tradition dictated that the body not be left alone until it was interred, but the burial could not take place until the following afternoon, which meant she and the rest of the family were in for another sleepless night.

She massaged her temples. The last week had sapped something deep and vital from her. She'd lost weight, but in a way that made her look haggard and old. One of the doctors at the hospital had offered to prescribe her something to help her sleep, but she'd made a point of refusing him with curt civility: drugs were not the answer to any of life's problems.

God knows, the Del Hoyo family had learned the truth of that.

The week before, when Carmen's mother had phoned to say that Teresa was missing, Carmen had tried to calm her and reminded her of all the previous occasions that her sister had disappeared. But the next day, when Teresa's abandoned car had been found with her mobile inside, Carmen had made the 10-hour drive down from Barcelona to Almería.

She had barely slept since. There had been too much to do: police interviews, phone calls from the media, the organisation of an internet poster campaign and a candlelight vigil. Her parents' flat had been filled with family and friends twenty-four hours a day, all of them desperate to help, as if by maintaining a perpetual frenzy of activity they could somehow ensure Teresa would return to them alive.

Carmen had done a lot of praying during that time. At first, she had prayed novenas to Saint Jude and asked that Teresa be returned to the family safe and sound. But as the length of Teresa's disappearance increased, she had found herself whispering other prayers: that her sister had not suffered, and that her end had been quick and painless.

It did not seem that her prayers had been answered. When the family had gone to identify Teresa's body at the *Instituto de Medicina Legal*, the pathologists had made a point of showing them nothing but Teresa's face. The experience haunted Carmen. What horrors had they been hiding beneath the white sheet that covered the rest of Teresa's body? She had to know, and had insisted on seeing a copy of the autopsy report as soon as it was ready.

But she would never forget that wretched place, the way it looked and smelt. She knew now that Hell was not a place of fire and sulphur and noise: Hell was white and cold and sterile, a place of blood-stained porcelain and polished metal, where whispered words of unimaginable pain mingled with the stench of ammonia.

And to think that Teresa's soul might spend eternity in such a place...

Tears welled up again, but this time anger accompanied them. Carmen had loved her sister, but there was no denying how selfish and duplicitous Teresa had become once the drugs had taken hold of her life.

It would be interesting to see what the autopsy's toxicology report said. *Mamá* claimed Teresa had been attending her Narcotics Anonymous meetings right up until the moment she disappeared, but it was clear to Carmen what had happened: Teresa had relapsed. The first time Carmen spoke to the police, she had made it perfectly clear to them that drugs would be at the bottom of the entire matter. No one knew better than Carmen the depths to which Teresa could fall.

Anyway, even if Teresa had been going to her meetings, they couldn't have been of any use. Carmen had read about NA on the internet, read all about that twelve step nonsense, with its talk of self-acceptance and freedom from guilt. How could that ever work? Guilt was the physical manifestation of sin, and there was no possibility of redemption without it. Only penance and contrition could assuage the pain.

Carmen had said as much to Teresa the last time she saw her, told her that the church had drug and alcohol programmes staffed by priests who were specially trained. If she was serious about her sobriety, why trust it to well-meaning amateurs? Teresa had listened and then she had laughed that contemptuous little trill of a laugh she reserved for conversations about religion.

Carmen had thought a lot about the argument that had followed. Had she failed her sister? Would she have been more persuasive had she kept her temper? Perhaps. But then keeping her temper had never been one of Carmen's strong points, especially when her beliefs were being mocked.

She took a pot of moisturising cream from her handbag and began to rub it into the inflamed skin on her shoulders. She thought of the words from the book of Isaiah — *fear not, for I am with you; be not dismayed, for I am your God; I will strengthen you, I will help you, I will uphold you with my righteous right hand* — and tried to think positively.

At least the prognosis on *Mamá* was favourable. The doctors said she had suffered a minor stroke — a result of the extreme stress she had been under for the last week — but had been infuriatingly vague as to what the after effects would be. What if *Mamá* could no longer walk? Or if she lost the use of an arm? She wouldn't be able to cook, and that would mean Carmen would have to give up her life in Barcelona and move back to care for them both. *Papá* wouldn't be any help. Earlier in the week, Carmen had seen his attempt at boiling an egg, and the kitchen still smelt of burnt metal and charred eggshell.

The heavy door to the women's bathroom creaked open and Carmen heard footsteps outside the cubicle. Someone knocked on the cubicle door.

'Are you OK in there, *hija*?'

It was a nurse: Carmen could see blue trousers and white plimsolls beneath the cubicle door.

'Yes, I'm fine,' she said.

'Why don't you come out? Your priest friend is outside looking for you.'

Priest friend? Carmen shook her head at the nurse's ignorance. Then she smiled. She was glad Monsignor Melendez was there.

It was an act of true Christian charity that such an important man should have taken an interest in the family's suffering — Carmen had seen some of the paperwork inside his briefcase and it had born the stamp of both the archdiocese and the Episcopal Conference — but Monsignor Melendez had explained why Teresa's death was so important to him: he had been a close friend of Father Javier, Carmen's diocesan priest before she moved to Barcelona. Poor Father Javier had died the year before, and so the monsignor had made a special trip to comfort the family. He said it was the least he could do in such a trying and challenging time.

Carmen checked her hair in the bathroom mirror. Then she returned to the waiting room outside the UCI Intensive Care Ward.

Monsignor Melendez was a tall, broad man in late middle-age, and wore a Roman collar and a suit of dark cloth. Physically, he looked the way Carmen liked her clerics to look: stern and yet serene, a man whose depth of wisdom inspired confidence and certainty.

'There you are, Carmen,' he said, handing her a cup of coffee and a sandwich. 'I've taken the liberty of bringing you some victuals from the cafeteria. How are you feeling?'

'A little better.'

'And your mother?'

'She appears to be doing well. My *papá* has popped home to have a shower, so I'm here holding the fort.'

'That is good news. I have made you all the focus of my prayers these last few days.'

'That was kind of you, monsignor.'

'It was no trouble at all, child. When will you bury your sister?'

'Tomorrow at two o'clock. Will you be able to attend?'

'I would like to, but I fear my duties will prevent me from coming.'

They sat down together on the plastic chairs. Carmen drank the coffee but only nibbled at the sandwich. Melendez's expression became grave when he saw that Carmen was not eating.

'I see that you are still troubled, Carmen.'

She put the sandwich back into its packet.

'I'm sorry, monsignor, but I simply cannot stop thinking about my sister and where her body was found. Do you think it was a judgement upon her that her mortal remains were tossed in among the refuse? What does it mean for her soul?'

Melendez sighed, as if he had been fearing this question.

'I, too, have given thought to the fate of your sister's soul.'

'And?'

'As you know, at the end of every human life, a person is faced with the four last things: death, particular judgement, and then heaven or hell. Do you remember the conversation we had about the concept of concupiscence?' he said. 'It is a legacy of the wounds created by the Original Sin. It undermines our will and allows our emotions to slip the moorings of our intellect. Your sister was obviously prey to this failing. But Teresa was baptised. I think her soul will currently be in purgatory.'

'But how long will she be there?'

'I think that will depend upon the depth of the scar upon her soul…'

Melendez let the words fall into silence. Not for the first time, Carmen had the feeling he was holding something back.

'Are you talking about her drug use? Please, monsignor, if there is there anything that I can do, do not hesitate to tell me.'

He made a face, as if regretting having mentioned the matter.

'There *is* something. But I did not want to bring this up with you at such a sensitive time.'

'Please, monsignor. You've already done so much for me. Tell me what it is.'

He rearranged himself in the chair, and took Carmen's left hand between both of his.

'As we have previously discussed, your sister had many ill-advised friendships. Some of these led her to indulge in physical vices: drugs, alcohol, carnality.

'But there were among her coterie a number of people actively involved in trying to damage and denigrate the Holy Catholic church. I have been told that your sister was friendly with a man named Vladimir Lopez. I doubt the name is familiar to you, but he comes from a long line of church-haters.

'If Teresa had fallen under this man's spell ... well, there's no telling what wickedness he might have caused her to do. As you know, save obvious crimes such as murder and rape, there is no purer definition of wickedness than attempts to undermine and undo the work of an institution dedicated to the betterment of mankind's lot upon this earth.'

Carmen listened open-mouthed. How could Teresa have been so stupid?

'What must I do, monsignor?'

He smiled good-naturedly. 'Would that I could suggest a specific course of action to you, child, but I fear you must seek the answers yourself. First, I would suggest you try to determine how deeply Teresa was involved in these intrigues against the church. Speak to her friends. Look to her private papers, her correspondence. Or perhaps look on her computer and see if it holds any clues as to what she was involved in.'

'And if I find anything?'

He squeezed Carmen's hand a little harder between his hot, dry palms as he said, 'If she had been involved in such wicked intrigues, it would be of the utmost importance that you told me of them straight away and before anyone else. The fate of your sister's soul might depend upon it. God's Mercy is infinite, but his wrath can be a terrible thing.'

'I'll do whatever I can.'

'I know you will. You are a person of good faith, Carmen,' he said, patting her hand. 'A true believer. A *good* Catholic. It could be that it is enough to save your sister from eternal damnation.

'But while we are discussing such matters, I must also talk to you about the press. I'm sure I don't need to tell you that the media are jackals: they seek only to profit from others' grief and they will twist your words to suit their own ends. If you find that Teresa had been trying to spread calumnies about the church, you must not give them the slightest hint of it, no matter how persistent they might be.'

'Don't worry, monsignor. If they bother me, I'll give them a blast with this.'

She opened her handbag with her right hand and withdrew a small red aerosol can.

'And what is that?' Melendez said.

'It's pepper spray. I bought it from the internet. A young woman doesn't live alone in a city like Barcelona without taking precautions.'

Melendez looked at the aerosol can and smiled.

4

Danny Sanchez lived in a half-acre *cortijo* on the outskirts of one of the small rural communities that surround the city of Almería. The location offered him the best of both worlds: he could sit outside at night, surrounded by olive trees and the chirrup of cicadas, safe in the knowledge that the nearest shopping centre and multi-screen cinema were only ten minutes' drive away.

He awoke early, made coffee and sat on the patio. There would be snow in the nearby mountains soon, but coffee outside with his breakfast cigarette was a daily ritual, no matter the weather. Today, he took his flamenco guitar outside with him, his head angled so that the cigarette smoke did not go into his eyes as he played a number of rapid *falsetas* then slipped into the swirling, hypnotic pattern of a *bulería*. He loved to play flamenco: when he did so, it was like holding Spain's fluttering heartbeat in his hands.

Danny would be forty soon. The imminence of another of existence's spurious milestones had caused him to do a lot of thinking about his life: what he wanted from it, where he was going.

Paco Pino claimed he worried too much. 'There are only four things in life that are really important: family, friends, food and football — and not necessarily always in that order.'

The analysis had made Danny laugh, but he knew the formula wouldn't work for his own life: sport had never held any interest, food was something he usually stuffed down while doing something else, and it was difficult to decide whether the presence of his mother in Spain really constituted a pro or a con.

And then there was Marsha.

Danny had been with her for a little over a year now, a long distance relationship that began while Danny was in England covering a serial killer story. As a girlfriend, she ticked all the right boxes: clever without feeling the need to show it, cultured without being pretentious, and possessed of a sense of humour that appreciated Danny's jokes and could make him laugh in turn. Hell, she even liked *Black Sabbath*, and that was a first in a girlfriend.

Of course, it wasn't all perfect. Danny's habit of eating handfuls of cereal straight from the box had been an early source of conflict, as had Marsha's decision to "tidy" Danny's office one day while he was out at work, thereby destroying a cluttered but effective filing system Danny had spent years perfecting.

And it didn't help that Marsha had become firm friends with Paco's wife, Lourdes, a long-time advocate of Danny settling down. Lourdes had decided from the moment she first clapped eyes on Marsha that "she was the one" and recently whenever Lourdes saw Danny she barracked him with lines that had obviously been fed to her by Marsha: 'This one is a keeper, Danny'; 'Love her or lose her, Danny.'

Marsha always laughed them off when Danny mentioned them to her, but they seemed now like smoke signals rising from some hidden part of Marsha's psyche. So far, the relationship had trundled along quite nicely with Danny in Spain and Marsha in England — they saw each other for a week out of every six and spoke every two or three nights via Skype — but Danny knew the whole *where-are-we-going?* conversation was long overdue.

At 08:00, Danny started work reviewing the newspapers. Teresa del Hoyo's murder was the lead story in all of them.

Paco Pino had been right. While Spain's left-leaning newspapers concentrated on the discovery of Teresa's body at the landfill site, right wing publications tempered their coverage with mentions of Teresa's drug abuse and her "prominent role in quasi-legal protests" and "anti-establishment activities". Many of these papers ended their coverage with reminders that the 14 Republicans killed in 1939 had been legally executed by military tribunals due to their involvement in an earlier massacre of nuns and right-wingers.

At 08:15, Paco Pino phoned. 'The *Gente de Hoy* article is a definite runner as long as we get plenty of stuff about her private life. I took some photos of the interior of Teresa's car yesterday. The driver's seat had some blood spots on it, but the blood type doesn't match Teresa's. My police source reckons someone else drove her car to Roquetas and dumped it there, someone who had been wounded somehow. There are fingerprints on the steering wheel and dashboard, but the police haven't got a match on them yet. How'd you get on with Pepe Juarez yesterday?'

When Danny told him, Paco interrupted.

'Whatever you do, don't get bogged down with all that crap about the mass grave and the dead nuns. Remember this is *Gente de Hoy*, so we only want stuff that is easily digestible with a double-digit-IQ.'

'Does your police source know how Teresa died?'

'Apparently the prosecuting judge is a real hard arse, so he daren't tell me any actual specifics, but he did say it was, and I quote, "deeply unpleasant". The judge has ordered a press blackout on the details of the case, so there must be something significant about what the autopsy found.

'But he did mention something of interest: the autopsy gave them a DNA trace for the attacker and they're running the details through the database. If the perp's got previous, it's only a matter of time until they make an arrest. See what your forensic guy makes of the photos I took yesterday of her body.'

Professor Juan Cassella taught forensic pathology at a British University. Danny had made his acquaintance years before, and Cassella had always been generous with his time and expertise.

'Have you had a chance to look at the photos I sent you last night?' Danny said when Cassella answered.

'Did you say the woman disappeared last Tuesday night?'

'Yes.'

'Well, there's no way she's been dead seven days. I'd say that when your photo was taken, she'd been dead four days, tops.'

'So someone might have held her captive first?'

'Given the details of the case you sent me, I'd say it's a strong possibility. If I were performing the autopsy, I'd be looking for ligature marks on the wrists and ankles, or other signs of her having been restrained.'

'What else can you tell me?'

'Judging by the photos of the body on the stretcher, decompositional changes had begun to occur. There was definite evidence of swelling from gases, and it looked like bodily fluids had begun to leak from the orifices, a process known as purging.

'But what intrigues me is the marbling of the skin, or the relative lack of it. Marbling is caused by bacteria in the blood from sulfhaemoglobin which is bluish in colour, in place of haemoglobin which is reddish. As you can see from the photographs, this marbling is only present in the upper torso, the arms and the head, whereas the colour of the legs is quite insipid. Given that wound to her neck, I would guess that she died from exsanguination, and that the head was below the legs while she bled. If her jugular was cut, the blood loss could have been immense in a very short period of time.'

'So she was bled to death?'

'It's a strong possibility. But more than that I can't say from photographs.'

Danny thanked the professor and put the phone down. Bled to death? What the hell had the young woman gotten herself involved in? Afterwards, Danny phoned Carmen del Hoyo's mobile number. This time, it was answered almost immediately.

'Yes?' a woman's voice said.

Danny started to explain who he was, but Carmen del Hoyo cut him off.

'How the hell did you get this number, Señor Sanchez? Won't you jackals give us a moment's peace? Don't you know that I am to bury my sister later today, while my mother is fighting for her life in intensive care? Whatever I have to say, I said to the television cameras last night. Don't you dare phone this number again.'

Danny went inside, switched on the television news and lit a cigarette while he waited for Carmen del Hoyo's interview to cycle around again. He didn't have to wait long.

Carmen del Hoyo was clearly a very different type of woman from her sister. Physically, she was broader and thicker, and she dressed conservatively, her hair cut into a style that would have suited a woman twenty years older. Frumpy was the word Danny would have used had he been feeling uncharitable. Carmen lived in Barcelona, so she hadn't appeared in Almería until the Friday after Teresa's disappearance, but since then she had taken over as the family's spokesperson.

Carmen's television interview really consisted of a statement read directly to camera while her tearful father stood behind her, displaying that slight air of deference working-class parents in Spain often have towards their university-educated kids. Carmen's statement covered the basics and little more: that the family needed their privacy in this time of grief and that they had full confidence in the police's ability to track down Teresa's killer.

Then Danny tried the number for the guesthouse at which Gordon Pavey had been staying. This time, an Englishwoman answered.

'This is Allen's Guesthouse, Ms Allen speaking. How may I help you?'

Danny introduced himself and asked if she remembered a man named Gordon Pavey having stayed there.

'Are you another of his wretched friends?' Allen said, her voice rising in irritation. 'I've told you before, I have no idea where he's gone, but I'll warrant he's drunk somewhere and paying for it with the money he stole from me.'

'Are you at home this morning, Ms Allen?' Danny said. 'It sounds like we need to talk.'

San José is a small fishing village in the heart of the Cabo de Gata natural park. Sally Allen's property sat atop a hill that overlooked the crescent-shaped bay, where a stiff westerly wind was blowing six-foot breakers against the beach.

'Trust, Mr Sanchez,' Sally Allen said. 'That's what this is about: *trust*. I mean, you expect the youngsters to bugger you about, but not a man like Gordon Pavey. It makes you ask what the world is coming to.'

'So you're sure that Mr Pavey did a runner without paying?' Danny said, hoping the woman would actually answer him this time. Communicating with Allen was like shouting into a high wind. Ironically, that was precisely what Danny was having to do, as she had insisted on sitting outside.

Allen was a big-boned, outdoorsy woman in her early sixties, and had the sort of accent that immediately conjured images of waxed jackets and wellingtons. Perhaps she'd dressed that way in England. Today, she had opted for flip-flops, khaki shorts and a fisherman's jumper.

'Absolutely positive,' she said. By way of emphasis, she waved her mug of tea towards the guest house opposite, a large white building divided into four apartments. 'I've been in this business long enough to know a moonlight flit when I see one. There are buggers like him all the way from Marbella to Majorca living the good life at the expense of honest people.'

'Do you know why Mr Pavey had come to Spain?'

'I think he was researching a book or something. At least, he seemed to spend a lot of time reading things on the internet. And I know he was interested in gaining access to some historical archive or other. But I think Pavey used it as a smoke screen to convince me he was staying longer than he intended.'

'What makes you so sure?'

'He turned up on Wednesday the 28th of September and paid a 200 Euro deposit. I asked him how long he wanted to stay and he said he didn't know, so I told him the daily rate was 100 Euros, to which he agreed. He came and went on the Thursday, Friday and Saturday. Then on Sunday morning he went out in his hire car and I never saw him again.

'By Monday evening I'd started to get suspicious, so I went into his apartment and do you know what I found? A tatty old bag and some clothes. But his passport and wallet were nowhere to be found. Now, tell me, Mr Sanchez, what sort of conclusion was I supposed to draw from that? By that time he owed me 600 Euros in rent.'

'Did you contact the police?'

She dismissed the idea with a wave of her hand. 'And have it spread round town I'm a soft touch? No fear. That police station is the central sorting house for gossip.'

'But surely you must have Mr Pavey's credit card details?'

Her eyes became wary for a moment, then her bluster returned. 'That's what I was referring to by trust. I don't lock people's passports in a safe. I don't force them to pay in advance. I *trust* them,' she said, rolling the word's r, 'trust them to pay what's owed me when they leave. Of course, when people rent whole weeks and months I'm more careful, but off-season you have to take what you can get. A few days here and there are better than having the place empty. I'm sure you understand.'

Her smile begged sympathy. Danny smiled back and put a tick next to a question he'd noted earlier: *charged cash-in-hand?* That also explained her reticence to go to the police: Pavey's rental hadn't been going through the books.

'Besides,' she said, 'it seems Mr Pavey is already in trouble with the authorities. At least, that is what the priest intimated when he came here.'

Danny's pen stopped. 'The priest?' he said. 'What priest?' The woman's habit of jumping from one topic to another was starting to irritate him.

'Yes. Monsignor something-or-other. He made a point of mentioning his title, as if it would impress me. I told him straight off the bat that I'd been raised C of E and was proud of it.'

'And what did the monsignor want?'

'Apparently, this Pavey fellow had stolen documents from the historical archive and the priest was looking to get them back.'

'How did the monsignor know to come to the guesthouse?'

'Apparently, Mr Pavey had given my contact details to someone or other at this wretched archive.'

'When did the monsignor come here?'

'The Thursday after Pavey disappeared.'

'And what did he say?'

'He started off all smiles and formality and unctuous politeness. But when I made it clear Pavey was no friend of mine, he became less circumspect and asked to look at the room he had stayed in. I said he could please himself, but that there wasn't anything to see. Then I showed him Pavey's bag. That's when we had a falling out.'

'Really?'

'As I mentioned, the priest was all smiles at first, but when I wouldn't give him Pavey's possessions, he became a positive shrew. His face pinched up and he intimated that there might be legal consequences were I found to be in possession of church property. Then he started quoting the bible at me. I told him that Pavey's bag was mine and that I was immune to all his papist mumbo-jumbo. I've never had much time for the RCs.'

'Could I have a look at Mr Pavey's bag?' Danny asked.

Sally Allen stomped inside and returned with a canvas sports bag. Inside was a collection of clothing, some showing signs of having been worn, others still freshly folded. There was a zip up section at one end of the bag. Danny opened it. Inside was a photo pasted to a piece of crumbling, yellowed card and a folded receipt.

'That picture and the receipt were what Melendez wanted to take away. They had something to do with Pavey's research,' Allen said when Danny took them out.

Yes, that makes sense, Danny thought as he looked at the old black and white photograph: it was the original of the photocopy he had seen in the drawer of Teresa del Hoyo's desk. On the back of the card were written the same words Danny had seen on the photocopy: Santa Cristina, Almería, Spain, 1949.

'And you're sure Monsignor Melendez wanted to take this photo away?' Danny said.

'Yes. As I say, he claimed it was church property. I told him that was nonsense.'

'Why?'

'Because Pavey came straight here from the airport, and that photo was the first thing he showed me. He wanted to know if I recognised the building. Then he showed me that receipt.'

The receipt was for 80,000 pesetas, VAT included, from a marble company in Almería city, *Mármoles y Granitos Dario Paniagua e Hijos S.L.*. It was dated September 3rd, 1995, and was made out to a customer named H. Naseby.

Danny showed the receipt to Sally Allen and asked if it meant anything to her.

'Well, it's solid proof that Pavey was cracked. I mean, who wanders around with tat like that in their bags?' Then she frowned. 'Actually, that name is familiar: Naseby.' She considered this for a moment, then snapped her fingers. 'I know who it is. Last week, I had some wretched woman friend of Pavey's phoning me up, a Miss Naseby, enquiring after him. She left about a hundred messages on my answer machine, too, while I was away.'

'Apparently, Pavey hasn't even bothered to go back to the UK. This Naseby woman even had the gall to ask me to contact the Spanish police. I told her, "You come over here and report it yourself, if you're that worried".'

'Do you mean to say that someone in the UK considers Mr Pavey to be missing?'

The sudden note of urgency in Danny's voice made Sally Allen hesitate. 'I think that's what she might have intimated. I wasn't really listening.'

'Let me get this straight. The last time you saw Mr Pavey was on Sunday, October 2nd, correct? When did the phone calls from this Miss Naseby start?'

'On the Wednesday. Or maybe the Thursday. But then I went back to the UK for a dear friend's funeral. That's when she left all the answer phone messages.'

'And she's still looking for Mr Pavey now?'

'I've absolutely no idea. But I've done nothing I'll lose any sleep over,' Allen said, but the bluster had gone from her voice.

'I'd cover your bases if I were you and contact the police,' Danny said. 'I tell you what: let me take the photo and receipt away with me, and I'll keep you in the loop if I discover anything about Mr Pavey's whereabouts. Can you describe him for me?'

'He was in his mid-fifties. Bald on top, bearded. He wore a check shirt, like a lumberjack. And he had a Midlands accent.'

Danny drove to a café at the end of the street and phoned the number for *Mármoles y Granitos Dario Paniagua e Hijos S.L.*. When the phone was answered, Danny heard the screech of machinery in the background while he waited for the manager to come to the phone.

Dario Paniagua said he remembered the receipt. 'If it's the one I think it is, you're the second person to ask about it.'

'Who was the other person?'

'An Englishman. He came to the workshop a couple of weeks ago. On a Wednesday, if I remember right.'

Danny described Gordon Pavey. Paniagua said, yes, that was him.

'Do you remember the original customer? Señor H. Naseby?'

'Vaguely: 1995 was a long time ago. He was an old man and he placed the order via telephone from England.'

'Did he speak Spanish?'

'More or less. But he had a very thick accent.'

'What was Señor Pavey doing with the receipt?'

'No idea.'

'Did he say why it interested him?'

'No.'

'Can you tell me what the 1995 work order was for?'

'It was for a marble headstone and plinth with an angel and an inscription. But if it's that important to you, why don't you do what the English guy did and go to see the grave? Do you know where the *cementerio de los ingleses* is?'

5

Danny did, although he had never visited the place.

There are perhaps a dozen *cementerios de los ingleses* — English cemeteries — dotted around Spain. Most date back to the end of the 19th century when large British communities in Spain were granted permission to bury their dead according to their own traditions. Despite the name, anyone from a protestant background can be buried in them. Most of the cemeteries have now fallen into disuse as relatives prefer to cremate loved ones or fly the bodies back for burial in their home countries. Sometimes the cemeteries are entirely separate entities, but in Almería the *cementerio de los ingleses* is actually a small area set aside within the city's municipal cemetery.

There was a reception building beside the cemetery gates, so Danny stopped to ask exactly where the place was.

'I'm not the first person to ask about this recently, am I?' he said when the young woman behind the desk looked at him curiously.

She shook her head. 'Nobody's been in there for years and now suddenly we've had two different people visit in less than a fortnight.' Danny asked about the other person. The description fitted Gordon Pavey.

'Did he come on Wednesday the 28th?' he said.

'Well I only work Wednesday to Friday. And it was a couple of weeks ago. So, yes, I think that he did.'

The city's cemetery was a huge place, containing more than eighty thousand graves. A long, straight pathway lined with fir-trees led through the main body of the cemetery. The pathway ended in a stone gateway with colonnaded pillars which gave access to an older section filled with mausoleums and family vaults from the Victorian era. The English cemetery was beyond this, a walled plot of land forty yards square accessed by a metal gate.

The graves here were laid out in irregular lines on grass burnt brown by the sun. Most of the dead were either sailors from protestant countries or members of the community of British engineers that had helped to run mining concerns in Almería at the beginning of the twentieth century. All of the gravestones were old and moss-covered, except one. This bore signs of weathering, but was obviously far newer than the others.

An angel of white granite sat atop the memorial, its hands clasped together in prayer. There was a plaque attached to the plinth on which the angel knelt. Dry leaves crunched beneath Danny's feet as he crouched before it and used his jacket sleeve to rub away the thin covering of dust and sand that had gathered on the marble surface.

María del Mar Torres García

Born January 12th, 1949; Died January 12th, 1949.

Beneath it, there was an inscription in Spanish.

A la pequeña ausente, le pido perdón.

To the absent little one, I ask forgiveness.

Danny scratched the stubble on his cheek. What the hell was a newborn Spanish baby doing buried in here? It was unlikely that a Spanish family would have converted to Protestantism back in 1949. And why had someone from England paid the equivalent of more than 500 pounds to replace the headstone 46 years after the child's death?

Danny checked the names on the other graves. There were three other headstones that belonged to Spanish children. All three were stillbirths and had died between 1951 and 1960.

Danny lit a cigarette and wrote down all the names and dates of death. He thought about Gordon Pavey. Off season, there was only one UK flight to Almería, the redeye from Gatwick that left at six in the morning and arrived 09:30 local time. If the receptionist was correct, that meant Pavey had visited the cemetery the same day he had arrived in Spain. It was as if the sole purpose of his trip to Spain had been to visit the grave.

The wind was picking up. Danny buttoned his denim jacket and took photos of the graves. Then he walked back to the reception office. The young woman looked up from her computer screen as he pushed the glass door open. She gave him a smile of commiseration.

'Do you know why Spanish children are buried in that part of the cemetery?' Danny said. 'I thought only protestants could be buried there.'

'I would imagine it was because the children were stillborn, which meant they died without being baptised and couldn't be given a Catholic burial. Things were far stricter in the old days.'

'Are the burial records for the English graveyard here?'

She nodded.

'Can I see them?'

She smiled as if expecting this. 'That's the first thing the English visitor asked to see, too. But I can only show you the records that are more than fifty years old. The others aren't public information yet.'

'The records I want to see are all from before 1961.'

She went into a room filled with large, rectangular ledgers bound at the spine with red fabric. Danny opened the one for January 1949 and searched for the name María del Mar Torres Garcia. He traced his finger across to the place of death: El Cerrón, Clinica de Santa Cristina. It was the same for the other three children. All of them had died at Santa Cristina.

'Did this Englishman ask you anything else?' Danny said.

The receptionist chewed her lip, as if debating whether to speak, then nodded and leant closer, lowering her voice. 'He asked me if we'd ever found any children's graves here at the cemetery that had empty coffins inside.'

Danny thanked her and walked to a nearby bench, tapping his pen against his teeth. So, Gordon Pavey had asked about empty coffins, had he? That, combined with his visit to the grave of a stillborn child, could mean only one thing.

Empty coffins had become a depressingly familiar problem in Spain during the last fifteen years. *Los niños robados* the scandal was called in Spanish, the stolen children, a story almost too shameful for society to admit to itself: tens of thousands of children taken from their rightful parents during the Franco dictatorship and the early years of democracy and given away in illegal adoptions by doctors and the church.

According to what Danny knew of it, the process had begun in the aftermath of the civil war, when thousands of children had been left parentless due to death, exile or incarceration. But the demand for children had soon outstripped the supply, so the regime and church had begun to steal newborns from anyone unable to put up much of a fight: women with Republican backgrounds, the poor and ill-educated, single mothers.

Part of the pretence of tricking the rightful parents had involved providing empty coffins for burial as "proof" the stolen children were actually dead. Exhumations had shown the practice had occurred elsewhere in Andalusia, so why not here in Almería?

But Danny was worried. Who the hell was this Pavey? Was he a journalist? Danny hoped not. Christ, it would kill him if some bastard unearthed a major story on his home turf.

Still sitting on the bench, he took out his laptop and Googled the Santa Cristina name. The top result was an article Danny recognised: it was from an edition of *Sureste News* published about six years previously. The by-line read, *This week, Leonard Wexby speaks to Frank Dale, who shares his reminiscences of working as a cameraman during Almería's cinematic boom.*

According to the article's introduction, Frank Dale had first come to Almería as part of the *Lawrence of Arabia* film crew, and had later retired to the province. Most of the thousand-word article consisted of amusing anecdotes about the rough-and-ready conditions the film crews had endured in the '60s, and snippets of information on the stars Dale had rubbed shoulders with: Peter O'Toole, Anthony Quinn, David Lean.

There was only one part that warranted Danny's attention, a paragraph halfway down which described how in 1970 Dale had worked on *The Unearthed*, a 'God awful horror film' which had been shot at Santa Cristina, 'a spooky ruin with towers down in the south of the province'.

Leonard Wexby had once been *Sureste News's* entertainments correspondent, but he had fallen out with the paper's editor over his wild expense claims and gotten himself sacked. Leonard was English, but had been in Almería for more than forty-five years. He was a terrible gossip, but there were few who knew more about the history and folklore of Almería, and the old man possessed a huge collection of books, pamphlets, newspapers and photographs on the subject.

'Daniel Sanchez, as I live and breathe,' Leonard said when Danny phoned. 'Are you sure you high castes are allowed to mix with the pariahs?'

Leonard pronounced the r in the last word as a w. Great, Danny thought, he's been drinking.

'You might be interested to know I've been shafted by *Sureste News*, too. They've got me working freelance now.'

'Oh, I know all about that, Danny Boy. The fact you are no longer being permitted to suckle from the teat is the only reason I deigned to answer. I presume you want something, so go on and spit it out.'

'I need a bit of background for a story, Leonard. Does the name Santa Cristina ring any bells?'

'Entire peals of them. The story of what happened up there is truly fascinating.'

'Enlighten me, then.'

'I shan't.'

'Why not?'

'Because I'm sixty-eight-ruddy-years-old. These are supposed to be the Golden Years and yet here I am stuck in this ruddy house all on my tod. Are you aware that I lost my driving licence? Bloody swine Guardia pinched me twice in a month drunk at the wheel: six points each time. I told the bastards the second time, "Come round to my house later on and I'll show you what bloody drunk is".'

'Can you tell me anything, Leonard, or am I wasting my time?'

'Don't come the tabloid bullyboy with me, Sanchez. How many times have you phoned old Leonard since he was given the push? I'll tell you: twice, and both times it was to ask for information. Once life has tossed you on the human compost heap, people can't run fast enough to escape the stench. And now you suddenly appear, expecting free and easy access to the oracle.'

'OK, how about this? I'll come visit, and you tell me all about Santa Cristina.'

'Fake sympathy for use of my data banks? What a slut you are, Sanchez.'

'Deal?'

Danny heard ice cubes being dropped into a glass.

'I'll think about it. But what's your interest?'

Danny hesitated. He got on well with Wexby, but they were potentially rivals now.

'I sense by your sudden reticence that you're onto something, Danny. But it's odd how that Santa Cristina name keeps cropping up recently.'

'Who else is asking about it?'

'Now that would be telling, wouldn't it?'

'Do you know anything or not?'

'I do. But a visit you promised and a visit I will get if you expect to prise anything of consequence from me. When you come I expect you to be accompanied by two bottles of Bombay Sapphire and plenty of ice. I'll supply the lemons and tonic water. And don't bother trying to wheedle more info out of me via the telephone. If you want to hear the info I have on this Santa Cristina place you will have to come and join me at the barrelhead.'

Leonard said something else, but all Danny heard was a muffled thud as the receiver was dropped, followed by the sound of swearing. Then the phone went dead.

As Danny walked towards the gates of the cemetery, he noticed that a hearse filled with floral wreaths was passing slowly through the cemetery gates. The vehicle was followed by a curious mix of mourners: some were dressed in suits and black formal dresses, while others wore jeans, t-shirts and beach shorts.

Danny stood respectfully to one side, with his head bowed. It wasn't until the hearse and mourners drew level with him that he realised whose funeral it was: they were burying Teresa del Hoyo.

Carmen del Hoyo walked at the head of the group of mourners in formal dress, arm-in-arm with her father. She wore a black skirt suit, and her face was covered with a veil. A few yards behind came the youngsters in casual dress. They must be Teresa's friends, Danny thought. Some of them whispered among themselves as they walked, as if unhappy or angry.

Television crews, photographers and reporters loitered outside the cemetery gates, together with around 80 people who were obviously there for the funeral but had not deigned to enter the cemetery. The voices outside were respectfully low, but there was no mistaking the angry tone of many of them.

'What's going on?' Danny asked one of the reporters.

'Teresa's sister has put the cat among the pigeons by insisting on a full Catholic burial. Apparently, that's not what the rest of the family think Teresa would have wanted. You should have been at the mortuary, there was a right old ding dong.'

'Between?'

'The sister and Teresa's uncles. Apparently, there's not much love for the church in the del Hoyo family. Then some of Teresa's friends weighed in and the sister really lost her temper. She gave them a right dressing down. She even told Teresa's friends it was their fault her sister was dead. I tell you, Danny, you don't want to get on the wrong side of that one.'

6

Carmen del Hoyo watched as two cemetery workmen pushed the metal platform into place. Teresa's burial niche was a high one and they needed the platform in order to raise the coffin up to the right level.

Once the mahogany casket had been slid into the dark concrete hole, most of the mourners — those that had actually bothered to accompany Teresa to her final resting place — turned and left. An old man Carmen vaguely recognised as a childhood neighbour took her by the elbow and tried to steer her away, but she shook her head and stayed where she was.

The workmen were bricking up the entrance to the burial niche, and she wanted to make sure the marble lapidary stone and floral tributes she had paid for were correctly placed.

Besides, she was in no hurry to speak with any of her damned relatives...

The day before, Teresa's body had been taken to the city's mortuary, where it was placed in one of the building's three *velatorios*, the private rooms where family members could wait with the dead relative until the hour of the burial. Hundreds of people had come to pay their respects.

That was when the problems had started.

Carmen had always assumed that her uncles' blasphemous comments towards the church over the years had been mere bravado — the Del Hoyo family had always taken a ridiculous and misplaced pride in its working class, socialist credentials — but Carmen could not believe how they had reacted when she informed them where Teresa was to be buried.

There had been angry words outside the mortuary. Carmen had explained that, given the wicked and wanton life Teresa had led, it was essential she be buried on holy ground, but her uncles had *laughed* at her. There she had been discussing the possibility of eternal damnation for her sister's soul, and they had thrown their heads back and brayed like donkeys.

So Carmen had listed Teresa's sins for them: the drugs and drinking, the carnality, the use of contraceptives, the immoderate language. That had wiped the supercilious smiles from their faces. Then some of Teresa's so-called friends had weighed in. That was when Carmen had really lost her temper.

First, she had asked them who the hell they thought they were butting in on a family discussion. Then she had told them that it was *their* fault that her sister was dead — they and their druggie ways — and cursed them for turning up to a wake in ripped jeans and t-shirts that stank of cannabis smoke and sweat.

The funeral mass afterwards had been an embarrassment. There had been close to 150 people gathered in and around the *velatorio* when it began, but barely a third of them bothered to enter the mortuary's chapel to hear the funeral liturgy. In fact, most of them made a point of *not* entering the chapel. People had still been arguing with Carmen as Teresa's coffin was being loaded into the hearse. Thank goodness Monsignor Melendez had not attended the funeral. His reticence the day before had disappointed Carmen, but now she realised she had avoided the possibility of an embarrassing public scene.

Once the lapidary stone had been placed to Carmen's satisfaction, she went back to her car, drove to the hospital and resumed her vigil outside the intensive care ward.

An hour later, while Carmen half-dozed on one of the plastic chairs, the swing doors of the room opened and two uniformed Guardia Civil officers stepped through. Carmen recognised them: they were the family liaison officers who were handling Teresa's case.

The female officer, Matamoros, spoke first.

'We have here the details of the autopsy you requested,' she said. 'But before I give them to you, Señorita Del Hoyo, I must establish that you are *absolutely* certain you want to see this information. It could prove very upsetting.'

Carmen nodded, and Matamoros unzipped the shoulder bag she carried and handed Carmen a blue cardboard folder that contained numerous pages of printed information.

'As you'll see, the pathologist estimates your sister had been dead around four days by the time her body was discovered.'

'Why did it take that long for her body to be found?'

'We think your sister's body was—' Matamoros sought a suitable word — 'placed within one of the large bins used in rural communities. The collection of those only occurs twice a week.'

'But she disappeared on October the 4th. Where was she for the intervening period if she wasn't killed until the 7th?'

'That is what we need to establish. If you wouldn't mind, we have some questions we need to ask.'

Now the male officer, Nuñez, began to speak. 'Your sister was a vegetarian, wasn't she?'

'Yes. A vegan, actually.'

'Are you sure?'

'Yes, I'm sure. She wouldn't even eat boiled sweets because they had something-or-other in them. Why is that important?'

'As you'll see on page two of the autopsy report, the pathologist found animal blood underneath her fingernails. Dried pig blood, to be precise. Can you think how that came to be there?'

'Pig blood?' Carmen stifled a half-hysterical hiccup of laughter then pressed her knuckles to her lips. 'No, I can't think why that might be,' she said as she began to leaf through the report.

She had thought that knowing the specifics of the death would help to ease the pain, but now that she saw the cold, clinical facts of the autopsy — the remnants of chocolate found in Teresa's stomach, the ligature wounds on her ankles and wrists, the signs of vaginal and anal rape — she realised that it did not help at all. Nothing would help. Nothing could. Teresa was dead and she had suffered just as horribly as Carmen had feared.

Page four held the toxicology report.

'This can't be right,' Carmen said as she looked through the list of negative results.

Nuñez said, 'The toxicology reports showed her to be absolutely clean. No drugs, no alcohol. There's not even any trace of legal drugs such as paracetamol. It looks like your sister's sobriety held after all.

'As you'll see from that same page, we were able to take a DNA trace from semen left by one of her attackers. It could be we make an arrest very soon.'

But Carmen wasn't listening. Her eyes had flickered to the cause of death.

'Exsanguination,' she said. 'What does that mean precisely?'

7

When Danny got out of his car, he put his warm coat on. The municipality of El Cerrón stretches all the way from sierra to sea, but the actual town is at the gateway to the mountains, 376 metres above sea level. The difference in temperature was immediately noticeable.

El Cerrón's municipal archive was housed in a huge old property with weather-worn heraldic crests on its façade and a wooden door studded with iron. The archive's main door opened onto a foyer decorated with a suit of armour and 18th century portraits of Spanish noblemen. The receptionist told Danny that he needed to speak to the archive's curator, Guillermo Belasco. 'He's currently conducting a guided tour of the town's main church,' she said. 'But if you hurry, you can catch the last thirty minutes of the tour.'

The *last* thirty minutes? Danny thought. He'd seen El Cerrón's church and there wasn't anything special about it. What the hell could Belasco find to speak about for so long?

Danny realised what it was when he found the tour party in the small plaza outside the church's main entrance. Belasco wasn't merely telling the story of the church — he was including the story of what had happened *outside* the church, too.

Belasco was a podgy little Spaniard, neatly dressed in a fawn suit, wing tips and bow tie. An umbrella hung from his left arm, and he spoke with that typical tour guide tone of voice: didactic and yet vaguely disinterested, speaking with his eyes closed as he did his spiel for a dozen elderly Spaniards and a couple of tourists in pac-a-macs and hiking boots.

'The Reds launched their criminal attack on the morning of July 22nd, 1936, and they struck without warning or mercy,' Belasco said. 'Left-wing apologists still describe them as Republicans, but the simple truth is that these people were nothing more than a rabble of thugs and malcontents, hell bent on murdering their betters. With rifles and pistols stolen from the local Guardia Civil barracks, the Reds rounded up fourteen people they claimed to be right-wing supporters. Among them were five Carmelite nuns and Father Benitez, the priest from this very church behind me.

'The men were beaten with wooden flails, while the nuns were stripped and made to parade naked before the multitude as children pelted them with stones. Then the mob dragged all fourteen of them to a well that once stood beside this church and, one by one, threw them in alive. Hand grenades were later dropped into the well to silence the screams of those not drowned or knocked unconscious by the bodies falling atop them.'

There were sounds of shock and distress among the audience. Belasco allowed a dramatic pause then turned to indicate a section of the church that was clearly a modern addition to the original medieval structure.

'Once Generalissimo Franco's heroic forces had cleansed Spain of the Reds, the bodies were retrieved from the well. For obvious reasons, the water within could no longer be used, so the decision was made to enclose the scene of the vile murder within the chapel that you see here, and to bury the bodies of the priest and nuns within.

'But the Marxists still return to this shrine in the hope of defiling it,' he said as he led the tour party round to the chapel's entrance. 'Look at this,' he said, drawing their attention to the wall with the tip of his umbrella. The spray-painted message had been scrubbed out, but was still readable: *Construida Con Sangre Republicana.*

Built With Republican Blood.

'The church authorities here fight a constant battle to keep the shrine's walls free from this type of filth,' Belasco said. 'But this is not the worst of it. Do you know that these miscreants have recently sunk so low as to desecrate graves at the local cemetery?'

There was more whispering and shaking of heads among the tour party, but Danny took the comment with a pinch of salt: had graves been desecrated, it would surely have been reported in the local media. Even so, he made a note to ask Belasco about it later.

Belasco invited the tour party to enter the chapel and to join him in prayer, so Danny smoked a cigarette as he waited for them to come out and disperse. When Belasco emerged, Danny introduced himself. Belasco shook Danny's hand, but his expression became wary when Danny said he was a journalist.

'What's this about?' he said as the two men began to walk back towards the municipal archive.

'I wanted to ask about an Englishman I believe visited the archive recently. I'd like to know what he looked at.'

Belasco stopped dead.

'An Englishman? Do you mean Señor Pavey?'

'You remember him?'

'Of course I remember him,' Belasco said, his face flushing. 'I'll happily tell you all about him, Señor Sanchez, so long as you promise to print the truth about him and his wretched communist cohort, Lopez.'

'Do you mean the historian, Vladimir Lopez?'

Belasco scoffed. 'I would not use that appellation to describe him. But I can see from your face that you know the man.'

'I don't think there's a reporter in the province that doesn't know old Vladi. What's he done this time?'

'He and Pavey have stolen documents that belong to the archive.'

'What did they steal?'

'The precise extent of their theft is still being determined. I dread to think how much they might have purloined given that they were rooting around in the archive for two whole days. But I am certain that they took medical records relating to a health clinic that once operated here in El Cerrón.'

'Why would they want to steal something like that?'

'The clinic was owned and staffed by the church. Given Señor Lopez's well-publicised hatred for anything holy, I would imagine he took the documents in order to further the campaign of calumnies and propaganda he has waged against the Catholic religion for the last 30 years.'

'Why wasn't the theft reported?'

'I was all for sending out a press release when I first discovered they had taken documents from the archive, but the town council decided against it. But rest assured that the church authorities have been informed. I phoned the archdiocese myself and they have sent a monsignor to take charge of the investigation into the theft. I for one will be urging the church to seek legal action against Señor Lopez.'

They had reached the archive now. Danny asked if Belasco could give him the dates on which Vladi and Pavey had visited. They went into Belasco's office, where he opened a spiral bound ledger and drew an immaculately manicured fingernail along the rows.

'Here we are,' Belasco said. 'Señor Pavey first came on Thursday, 29th September, and requested access to the archive. I told him it was impossible, as he lacked the proper academic credentials.'

'Aren't the documents here a matter of public record?'

'Yes. But this is not a lending library. It is an historical archive. Many of the documents we preserve here are extremely fragile and require expert handling. However, Señor Pavey then returned on the afternoon of the next day, on Friday the 30th, accompanied by Señor Lopez. As you may know, I am legally obliged to grant Señor Lopez access to the archive, and he has the right to bring along an assistant. They then returned on Saturday morning.'

'And what did they consult here at the archive?' Danny asked.

'They accessed a number of boxed records relating to the health clinic that I mentioned earlier.'

'Called?'

'La Clínica de Santa Cristina.'

'Santa Cristina?' Danny said, trying to mask the excitement in his voice. 'Could you tell me something about that?'

'As I said, it was a church-run health clinic situated about a mile outside of town, on the road that leads up into the sierra. However, the building burned to the ground in 1969. The ruins remained untouched until about seven years ago, when the building and the surrounding area was sold to a consortium seeking to build a golf course.'

'So where did these medical documents come from?'

'When the developer first began clearing the ruins, it was discovered that a great deal of medical files and other documents relating to the running of the clinic were still stored in metal cases in the basement, and had survived the fire and the subsequent ravages of weather and time. Obviously, such sensitive data could not be left there, so the council arranged for the files to be transferred to the municipal archive.

'However, between the damage caused by the fire and the subsequent decades of neglect, the ruins were in a terribly dangerous state. We only managed to retrieve about half the total cache of documents before we were forced to give up. The original 19th century building was formerly the house of a rich landowner and possessed extensive cellars which extend far beyond the walls of the house. This makes the ground very treacherous, and there are numerous places where the ceiling of the cellars can give way without warning.'

'Can I see the other documents relating to the clinic?'

'I'm afraid that is impossible. As I mentioned earlier, I reported the matter of the theft to the relevant church authorities. They sent a monsignor last week, and he took charge of all the documents relating to the health clinic.'

'When was this?'

'I reported the matter on Monday, October 3rd. Monsignor Melendez arrived on the Wednesday. But don't expect me to give you his contact details. He is an important man and you've no right to go bothering him.'

'Why the wait?' Danny said, looking at the dates he'd written down.

'What do you mean?'

'If Lopez and Pavey came on the Friday and Saturday, why didn't you realise anything was missing until Monday?'

Belasco fiddled with his bow tie. He looked as if he'd said too much and had just realised it.

'I've no intention of being browbeaten by you, Señor Sanchez,' he said eventually. 'How I run this archive is none of your business. Now, if you'll excuse me, I have a lot of work to get on with.'

'One last question,' Danny said as he reached the door. 'This Santa Cristina clinic: did it have a maternity ward?'

'Naturally. I myself was born there, as were most of the children of a certain age in the surrounding area.'

Outside, Danny sent a text to Gregorio, a journalist he knew who worked for COPE, Spain's church-run media organisation, asking if he knew anything about a man named Monsignor Melendez. Then Danny returned to his car, took out his address book, unwrapped the elastic bands that held the bulging pages together, and searched through the scraps of paper and loose business cards inside until he found Vladimir Lopez's mobile number. When he rang, there was no answer. He tried it a number of times. Then he phoned Paco Pino to make sure it was the right number.

'What the hell has that sozzled old scrote got to do with Teresa del Hoyo, Danny?' Paco said.

Danny explained what Belasco had told him. 'And it makes sense now that I think about it. You know Vladi fought that court battle to get access to the archive in El Cerrón, don't you?'

'Yes, I do. But what are you doing at the damned municipal archive, Danny? Remember, we're selling this to *Gente de Hoy*, and they only pay for three things: sex, scandal or gore — and preferably all three together.'

'Don't worry, the murder article is all in hand. But it could be I've stumbled across a much bigger story.'

'One that involves Vladi Lopez?'

'Why do you say it like that?'

'Because practically everything Lopez says is bullshit.'

'Such as?'

'His gammy leg for starters. I'm sure you've heard how he was dive-bombed by a Stuka when he was a kid in Russia. Well, I have it on good authority it actually happened years later when he got knifed in the thigh by a Mexican pimp. Anyway, didn't he accuse you of being a "fascist son-of-a-bitch" the last time you spoke to him?'

'Yeah, it was something like that,' Danny said slowly, looking at the phone. He'd forgotten that the last conversation he'd had with Vladi had ended in an argument. Perhaps the old man had recognised Danny's number and was refusing to answer.

Danny put his mobile back in his pocket and walked towards his car. He would worry about Vladimir Lopez later on. First, he wanted to see this Santa Cristina place for himself.

8

Danny was on the mountain road that led north out of El Cerrón and headed up into the high sierra. It was all starting to make sense.

Those burial records at the English Cemetery indicating where the stillborn children had died were the reason Pavey had wanted to access the archive in El Cerrón. But he had hit a brick wall at the archive, as he lacked academic credentials. And so he had likely begun to search for someone that could help him to gain access. And that would have led him to Vladi.

Vladimir Lopez was a one-off, a remnant of a Spain that was now long gone. Born in 1937 — or 'slap bang in the middle of the fight for freedom,' as Vladi liked to describe it — Lopez's parents had been prominent members of the Spanish Communist Party, which explained his unusual name: Vladi had been named in honour of Lenin and was taken as an infant to Russia when the Republicans lost the civil war.

Like most of the exile community, Vladi had returned to Spain in the late '70s and become a well-known and outspoken member of the local political scene. In the '90s, he had embarked upon a series of wildly partisan history books of the post-civil war period in each of the various municipalities of Almería.

When Vladi turned his attention to the town of El Cerrón, he had been denied access to the municipal archive and was forced to engage in a protracted legal battle in order to view the documents he needed. The start of the court case had been the first time Danny met the man, and Danny had returned to the story over the years as the case dragged itself through the

Kafkaesque labyrinth of the Spanish legal system. Vladi had finally won in 2008 and been granted full access to the archive.

Articles announcing Vladi's legal victory were still all over the internet, and nearly all of them used a photo that depicted the old man surrounded by smiling youngsters standing in front of a huge hammer and sickle banner bearing the initials of the UJCE, the communist party's youth organisation.

That was probably why Pavey had gone to the *Izquierda Unida* building: he'd been seeking a way to contact Vladi and had seen the photo. But what had Vladi and Pavey taken from the archive? Had they found proof that illegal adoptions had occurred at Santa Cristina? If so, it would explain the interest of this Monsignor Melendez.

Danny dialled Lopez's number as he drove. It went straight to answer phone. He must be ignoring Danny's calls. It had been two years since they argued, but the old man had a long memory and his temper was legendary.

Vladi's book on El Cerrón — snappily titled 'Blood on the Mountain Slopes: Fascist Atrocities in the Sierra de Gádor' — had been published in 2009. Danny had written an article to mark the book's publication, which had provoked a storm of protest from both Spanish and British readers of *Sureste News*, who accused Danny of displaying a pro-Republican bias, so the very next week Danny had interviewed a 96-year-old survivor of the *División Azul*, the Spanish volunteer contingent sent by Franco to fight alongside Hitler's armies on the Russian front.

That interview had been the source of his argument with Vladi. The day after the interview was published, the old man had phoned late at night to berate Danny for having given a platform to that 'rat-fucked Nazi son-of-a-slut'. Danny had tried to argue the need for impartiality in good journalism, but by that point Vladi had been raging.

'Of course, I should have expected it from you, given the family you come from,' he'd said. 'I know all about your grandfather and what happened in Málaga, Danny. Once a *facha*, always a *facha*.'

Danny had lost his own temper at that point and begun regaling Vladi with some choice expletives of his own. He no longer remembered who had hung up on whom.

Danny was driving among the pine-covered slopes and valleys of the sierra now. El Cerrón lay below him, the dun-coloured clay roof-tiles of the old town giving way to newer areas which stretched away in five different directions, like the arms of a starfish. He followed the road uphill for five minutes, then rounded a corner and entered a long, wide valley, a mile long and perhaps half as wide, a perfect natural bowl of undulating ground surrounded on three sides by steep rock walls. The north-side of the valley was formed by a stretch of red-brown cliffs, forty yards high. The cliff-face jutted back on itself, creating vertical rills of shadow that ran across its red-brown expanse like the pleats of a rocky skirt.

This must be where they had begun building the golf course that Belasco had mentioned: lopsided topographical poles littered the area and triangular piles of stacked tree trunks lined the roadside. There was a faded billboard announcing the "imminent arrival of the Arroyo Springs golf resort", but whatever work had taken place there had happened a long time ago. Cacti and weeds ran rampant.

A metal fence ran along the edge of the land, but many of the panels had been knocked over or blown loose. Danny followed the fence until he pulled level with a white portacabin. He parked and crossed a fallen fence panel.

The windows of the portacabin were all smashed and its white walls were covered with graffiti. His nose wrinkled as he peered inside: it smelt of damp, mildew and urine. The place looked to have been a favourite with transients and youths. In one corner a makeshift bed of cardboard and plastic was laid out on the floor, surrounded by empty cans of food; on the other were empty bottles of vodka and whiskey. Danny wiped dust from a sign attached to the wall: it said *Grupo Halcón Developments S.L.*

Danny nosed around in the ruins of a desk. Pamphlets advertising the "investment opportunity of a lifetime" afforded by the Arroyo Springs leaked from one of the open drawers. The picture on the front depicted happy golfers against a background of immaculate fairways, greens and bunkers, but the pamphlet was damp-wrinkled and its colours had been faded by sunlight.

Behind the portacabin there was an advertising hoarding that had been blown over backwards by the wind. It displayed an artist's impression of the golf course, the kind a developer commissions to show how the finished product will look. The image showed the entire valley converted into a golf course with hundreds of buildings atop the cliffs at the north end of the valley: ziggurat-shaped blocks of flats, hotels, a shopping centre, a petrol station. Danny looked northwards. He could see the plateau above the valley, but there was no sign of any buildings.

When he walked back towards his car, he heard the faint putter of a motor and saw a young man riding along the road on an ancient pedal-start moped, a green crate filled with prickly pears balanced on the back.

Danny waved and the man pulled over. He was dressed in tattered jog bottoms and a t-shirt, his face and arms burned a dirty red-brown by sun and wind. An old Walkman was clipped to his belt. He removed the headphones after stopping next to Danny.

'I'm looking for the ruins of a place called Santa Cristina. Do you know if they're up there?' Danny said, pointing towards the plateau at the north end of the valley.

The man nodded. 'But I wouldn't go up there if I were you.'

'Why not?'

'It's not a good place.'

'In what way?'

The young man hesitated then said, 'There used to be a mansion house up there, but it burned down. Used to be a hospital, I heard. Lots of people died there, so nobody goes up to it anymore. Not if they've got any sense.'

'Do you mean to say it's haunted?' Danny said, trying to sound light-hearted. 'Surely you don't believe in ghosts?'

It was the wrong approach to take. The man *did* believe and resented Danny's tone of voice.

'It was the *Dama Pálida* who burnt that place down, everyone knows it. My uncle saw her once,' he said in a quick, quiet voice, 'saw her slipping between the trees at nightfall and it damned near froze his heart. She still rules those ruins. Those that don't remember that, regret it.'

Danny thanked the man and walked back to his car. When he began driving towards the plateau he looked in the rear-view mirror: the young man was sitting on his moped in the middle of the road, watching him and shaking his head.

Danny knew all about the *Dama Pálida* — The Pallid Woman — as he had written an article on it once. Local legend had it she was the vengeful spirit of a 19th century noblewoman who stole small children from their cribs and took them away to the mountains to smother them. Danny hadn't realised people still believed in it. But then the Spanish were a superstitious nation, and the older the belief, the more deeply ingrained it seemed.

The road ended in a narrow gorge, twenty yards wide. High metal fence panels had been placed across its entirety, blocking access to the road beyond. Like everything else there, the fence panels looked years old. Windblown scraps of vegetation and rubbish clogged the gaps between the wire, and a large red sign was tied to the centre of the fence panel: *¡Prohibido Entrar! ¡Peligro de muerte!* Entry prohibited. Danger of death.

The fence panels were anchored within large concrete blocks. Danny shifted one end of the fence away from the mud walls of the gorge, creating a small space, and slipped through.

The road beyond was in a bad state. The asphalt was cracked and in some places had worn right through; deep ruts showed where heavy vehicles had once passed. A square, fluted pillar stood amid the tangle of undergrowth beside the road, topped with a crouching gargoyle, its face worn featureless by time and the elements. On the side of the square column that faced back down the road, there was a rectangular plate edged with ornate scrollwork. All that remained legible were three letters: SAN.

Danny carried on walking up the road until he had reached a point where he could look out over the whole of the plateau.

The ruins of the mansion house could be seen a hundred yards distant. Time and fire had destroyed the building, but the ragged outline was still recognisable as the Santa Cristina building. One of the conical towers still stood. The other had collapsed.

He took his binoculars and examined the ruins. He could see where fire had swept through the building, leaving blackened soot-swathes fanned across the walls.

Danny thought about taking a closer look at the ruins, but then remembered what Belasco had said about the dangerous ground around Santa Cristina. He examined the expanse of scrubby wasteland that separated him from the building's remains. The patch in front of him looked solid enough, but elsewhere he could see where the ground had collapsed, leaving huge, ragged holes edged with crumbling brick-work. The closest of the holes was a mere ten yards beyond where Danny stood. Vegetation sprouted from the edges of the pit. It looked deep and dark.

A sudden shrill cry made Danny start, but he realised it was only a bird of prey that circled above him. Even so, he had to admit it was a lonely, spooky spot now that the wind was whistling through the bare-branched trees. He pulled his coat close around him and took photographs of the ruins. Then he turned and walked back towards his car.

Ghosts didn't scare Danny Sanchez much — but long falls in lonely places most definitely did.

9

Carmen Del Hoyo knocked at the flat's door for a second time then pressed her ear to the wood. It hadn't been her imagination, there was definitely someone moving around inside. She knocked again, harder this time. She was trembling with anger. She was still thinking of what the Guardia officer, Nuñez, had told her.

'Exsanguination means that your sister was bled to death. The pathologist believes the killer made a deep incision between the neck and collarbone, thus cutting your sister's jugular vein, and then hung her upside down from her ankles, presumably to facilitate the loss of blood.'

'Do you mean to say that my sister was killed the way a pig is slaughtered?'

Nuñez fiddled with the collar of his shirt. 'It would not do to dwell on such an image, especially as these are only most likely case scenarios. And it is probable Teresa was unconscious while it happened as there is also evidence she had been struck a powerful blow to the base of the skull. She would not have suffered in any way.'

'Rest assured, when we catch the bastard, we'll get the truth out of him, you have my personal guarantee of that,' the female officer, Matamoros had said, placing a hand on Carmen's arm. 'But now that you know, I think we should consider the press. Sooner or later, this information is going to get printed. It might be best to prepare your parents as gently as you can so that any lurid media descriptions further down the line do not catch them unawares.'

Carmen had nodded mutely. Matamoros had been right to mention it. The press would have a field day with the details once they emerged.

Poor Teresa. Slaughtered like a pig and then tossed into the refuse. It was the worst way she could have died, the ultimate insult. But the image had brought Monsignor Melendez's words to her mind: what clearer sign could there be that Teresa had incurred the Lord's wrath? Carmen needed to find out what the hell her sister had been involved in.

That was why she was calling on Teresa's boyfriend — if "boyfriend" was the right word to describe the casually carnal relationships Teresa had indulged in since her mid-teens — this Samuel Herrero fellow.

She banged on the door again.

The young man that opened the door looked like all Teresa's friends: scruffy and dishevelled, with piercings and tattoos in impractical places. He looked as if he'd just woken up. He squinted at Carmen from behind a mane of tangled brown hair. He had been there yesterday at the mortuary, Carmen realised. He had been one of the most vocal opponents of Teresa being buried on sacred ground.

'I'm Teresa's sister,' Carmen said. 'I want to speak to you.'

That got his attention. Focus returned to his bleared eyes. For a moment he gawped then cast a nervous glance back into the room.

Carmen didn't wait for him to invite her in. She pushed past him and headed into the living room.

The flat's décor was somewhere between a student digs and a squat, and yet the flat was in one of the most expensive city-centre properties. It must belong to the boy's parents: there was no way this feckless clown could afford the rent on such a place.

The flat smelt of stale clothes, patchouli and joss sticks. Above the sofa was a huge, garish poster of some negro guitarist from the sixties. A transparent plastic hookah stood in the centre of the coffee table, but Carmen doubted it had been used to smoke tobacco: a bamboo mat beside it was covered in ripped Rizla papers and scraps of filter-tipped cigarettes that had been pulled apart, un-smoked, for their tobacco.

When Herrero saw where she was looking he said, 'Sorry, it's a bit of a mess,' and began tidying up, stuffing all the drug paraphernalia into a wooden box and tucking it inside a drawer. When he caught Carmen's look of disapproval, he said, 'Hey, your sister never smoked any of this. She didn't even drink.'

'I'm not interested in you or your stupid drugs. I want to know what it was that Teresa was working on. I know she met you through the communist youth and that she spent most of her time campaigning for one cause or another. Had she recently been working on something to do with the church?'

'No.'

'You're lying.'

'No, I'm not.'

'Yes, you damned well are.'

Carmen felt her fingernails digging into the palms of her hands. All the pain she had felt over the past week was surging upwards within her.

'Do you know how Teresa died?' she said, her voice a hiss. 'Do you know what they did to my sister? She was hung upside down from her ankles and bled to death. The bastard slaughtered my sister the same way you'd kill a pig.

'Of course, that was after he'd kept her locked up and half-starved for a number of days, during which time he raped her

God knows how many times. Now, I'm going to ask you again: what the hell did you get her involved in?'

For a moment, it seemed Herrero's eyes strayed towards a cardboard box in a corner of the room. But then the colour drained from his face, his lips trembled and he burst into tears.

Carmen folded her arms and watched as Herrero sank to his knees in the middle of the room, sobbing, with his face pressed into the crook of his arm.

Carmen disliked seeing men cry, as they only seemed to do it when they were totally broken down emotionally. If women cried more easily and more often, it was only to avoid all this embarrassing blubbering. When she could stand no more, she gave a tut, and fished a packet of tissues from her bag.

'Here,' she said.

Herrero dried his eyes and blew his nose.

'I loved your sister, Carmen,' he said when he had composed himself. 'I loved her with all my heart.'

There was no doubting the sincerity of his words: Carmen could see some degree of her own red raw pain reflected in his eyes.

'Yes, I believe that you did,' she said. 'But that doesn't change a thing, does it? She's dead. And I need to know why. Do you know a man named Vladimir Lopez?'

Herrero looked away. 'No,' he said.

'Are you sure?'

'Yes, I'm sure,' he said with a note of irritation, the way people do when they are lying and wish to hide the fact. Carmen's anger returned. Fine, if he wouldn't tell her, she would look on Teresa's computer.

'I want to take Teresa's property away with me. My father told me Teresa did most of her work on a laptop. It's not at their flat. Is that it there?' she said, pointing to a pink Hewlett-Packard that was on a table on the far side of the room.

The change in the young man was immediate. He sniffed his tears away, and his eyes went wide as he said, 'You can't take that.'

'Why not?'

'It's … there's a lot of my stuff on there.'

Carmen put her hands on her hips.

'That laptop there is my sister's property. If there is information that belongs to you on it, I'll happily copy it onto a hard drive and bring it back to you. But I am going to find out what the hell my sister was up to before she died.'

Herrero crossed the room and picked up the laptop.

'You can't take it,' he said.

Carmen looked at him. 'I tell you what, Samuel. Why don't I phone the police and tell *them* about the laptop — tell them I think it has information on it that could help to catch Teresa's killer.' She took out her mobile. 'I can have them round here like *that*,' she said clicking her fingers for emphasis. She meant it, too, as she began searching through her phone for Matamoros's number.

Herrero blanched. He was looking at the drawer filled with drugs. 'Don't do that,' he said finally. 'I'll give it to you.'

Carmen took the laptop from him and left without saying goodbye. As she rode the lift down to the street, she realised she was trembling. It was so typical of Teresa that, even from beyond the grave, she should still be complicating Carmen's life.

Carmen had been seven years older than her sister. It had been an odd age difference. By the time Teresa became a toddler, Carmen had been old enough to be given responsibilities for her sister — nappy changes, feeding, putting to bed — while still being young enough to realise how totally she had been supplanted in her parents' affections.

As a teenager, during one of their many arguments, Carmen had once goaded Teresa with the fact that she had enjoyed seven years of undivided parental love before Teresa was born. 'True enough,' the ten-year-old Teresa had said, 'but who do you think got all the rest?'

There had been no comeback to that. There was just something about Teresa. No matter what she did, how deeply she hurt their parents, it never seemed to truly register, even when the serious problems began.

First, it had been alcohol and loud music and sex with older boys. Carmen well remembered the shock of finding a stash of pornography and a huge vibrator in a bedroom drawer when Teresa had been only 16. Then had come marijuana and ecstasy tablets and Teresa's first attempts at running away. Their parents had tried to impose limits, but Teresa had bulldozed her way through them in her endless quest for self-obliteration.

Of course, all Carmen's dire predictions had come true. Drugs were a downward spiral path, and at the bottom of it lurked the quagmire of heroin.

The second time Teresa ran away, it had taken Carmen and *Papá* 40 hours of trawling through the worst places in Almería to find her, lying unconscious on a filthy mattress in the backroom of an abandoned house in the city's gypsy quarter. Teresa had been naked from the waist down, her legs still slightly parted, and she had bruised track marks along the inside of her forearm. Three or four emaciated men lay around her in various stages of consciousness, surrounded by syringes and spoons and candle stubs stuck in tins.

When *Papá* lifted Teresa's frail body, one of the men had tried to stop him, so Carmen had taken a tin tray from the table and clouted the bastard round the side of the head with it as hard as she could.

That experience was the principal reason Carmen had decided to move away to Barcelona. She'd had enough. Sometimes, it seemed she had been the only one to see Teresa as she truly was.

She walked back to her parents' flat. *Papá* was at the hospital, so he made herself coffee and opened out Teresa's laptop.

It was time to get some answers.

10

When Danny started work next morning, he saw that Marsha had sent him a Skype message the previous night: *Are you there, darling? We need to talk.*

Here it was, the conversation Danny had been dreading: we need to talk. Nothing good ever followed a woman saying that particular combination of four simple words. Danny changed his online status to offline. Marsha was an early riser, too, and he didn't want to get into any heavy emotional crap first thing in the morning.

Outside, the weather was miserable. This was how winter announced its imminence in southern Spain. You went to bed with a stiff breeze stirring the palms and woke to find yourself in the middle of a gale: the wind howled, temperatures plummeted and any notion of Spanish rain staying mainly on plains was forever washed from your mind. It was one of the principal causes of desertification in the region, as the mini-monsoons blasted away the fertile top soil. There was something very Spanish about the irony of rainfall making things drier.

At 08:30, Danny phoned Vladimir Lopez's number one last time. There was still no answer, so Danny finished his coffee, and took his camera and shoulder bag from the table. There was nothing for it, he would have to drive out to Enix and see the old man. It wasn't far. Besides, if Vladi still harboured a grudge, Danny had a better chance of mollifying him face-to-face.

Enix is a village high in the foothills south-west of the city of Almería. Although the town is close enough to be visible from the city's beaches, it takes twenty minutes to reach via a road that snakes back and forth through mountain slopes coloured pastel tones of orange, grey and purple. With each 180° bend in the road, the view on the horizon changes: first the blue-grey waters of the Bay of Almería, then the distant peaks of the high sierra behind Enix.

Danny liked the mountains. The air here smelt clear and pure, and the people lived a quieter, more substantive life than those on the coast. Big black birds circled in the sky. Danny leant forward over the steering wheel the better to see them as they soared on the winds.

Vladi's house was located beyond the outskirts of Enix, where the village's new builds give way to older properties made of ochre stone. Vladi's house was surrounded by a high garden wall painted mustard yellow. The concrete gateposts were decorated with mosaic tiles bearing Moorish designs, and the right hand gatepost bore a sign with the property's name: *La Casa de Pavlov.*

'Know why I called it that?' Vladi had asked the first time Danny visited the property.

'Pavlov's House — wasn't that something to do with the Battle of Stalingrad?'

Vladi had nodded in approval. 'Sergeant Yakov Pavlov. He and a platoon of twenty-five held a ruined house for sixty days against everything the Nazi pigs could throw at them: 27th September until 25th November, 1942.'

Danny had given him a lopsided grin. 'And who is it that you are planning on holding out against?'

'Why, the fascist bastards who want to silence me,' Vladi had replied without any hint of irony.

Danny hoped the old man was in a less combative mood today.

Danny parked by the gate, beeped his horn and shouted Vladi's name. The gates to the property were padlocked and there was no intercom, but Vladi's battered jeep was parked on the driveway. Danny beeped and shouted again.

Nothing.

He was about to climb over the gate, when a middle-aged Spanish woman in a striped pinafore emerged from the property further along the road, drying her hands with a dishcloth. She was around Danny's age and had a broad, wind-burnt face.

'Can I help you?' she said.

'I'm looking for Vladi. Do you know where he is? His car's here, but I can't get an answer.'

For a moment the woman frowned, as if unable to understand Danny's words. Then she said, 'I'm afraid you won't ever get an answer. Not now.'

'Why? What's happened?' The woman's expression indicated it was something serious.

She placed a hand on his arm. 'I'm sorry to be the bearer of bad tidings, but Vladi passed last week.'

'Passed? How?'

'Heart attack.' She patted his arm, looking genuinely distraught at the possibility of having upset him. 'I'm sorry to drop this on you. Did you know him well?'

'Well enough, I suppose. But how come no one knew about it? When did he die?'

She looked awkward. 'Well, there's the problem: no one really knows when. He was a very solitary man and he had few visitors. The police think it was sometime last week. You see, my husband and I went away on the Sunday and didn't come home until late on Wednesday evening. It was very dark that night, so we didn't notice anything was amiss until we saw the birds on Thursday morning.'

'The birds?'

She nodded, her expression mournful. 'There was a whole bunch of vultures and buzzards hopping around in Vladi's garden. That's never a good sign up here in the mountains, so my husband jumped over the fence. Vladi had collapsed just outside the front door. Of course, it wasn't really a surprise. He'd been a heavy smoker all his life and he drank like a fish. He did well to get to 74.'

'When was the funeral?'

'Last Saturday. But it was all very rushed and last minute. Vladi didn't have any family in this country and he hated the church, so we couldn't hold a funeral service for him or have him interred on sacred ground. In the end, he was cremated and we spread his ashes in the bay. Only me, my husband and a few others from the village attended. We didn't know who else to contact. I've got the keys to the property if you want to go inside.'

Danny lit a cigarette as he waited for her to go back and get the key.

Poor Vladi. He'd been a cantankerous old goat, but Danny would have liked to have attended the funeral. Very few people deserved to die un-mourned.

But then how many times had Danny covered different versions of this same story over the years, the lonely old person that dies unnoticed, his or her remains discovered days or weeks after death? Vladi had been lucky to have died in the garden: how long might his remains have festered if he had died inside the house?

Danny thought about his own life. He, too, lived alone in a remote property and had few friends. But then Danny had always been a loner. It was hardly surprising, given the childhood he'd had: Danny had never known his father, and his mother had been a law unto herself, coming and going as she pleased, leaving Danny's grandmother, the *abuela*, to raise him. Danny found himself thinking bleak thoughts about who would attend his own funeral.

He threw his half-smoked cigarette to the ground. Then he phoned Pepe Juarez and asked him if Teresa Del Hoyo had known Vladimir Lopez.

'If she *knew* him? Why, the youngsters hang on every word he says — and given his seemingly endless supply of anecdotes about Republican exile and growing up in Soviet Russia, Vladi is more than happy to keep them hanging. If I had a penny for every time I've heard that damned story about how he got his limp…

'But now that you mention it, I think Teresa and Vladi have worked together on a number of projects for the party. Don't ask what, though. He was always very secretive around me. I think he considered me something of a reactionary.'

'When was the last time you saw Lopez?'

'Last week. Didn't you hear what happened at the meeting?'

'No.'

'As I mentioned the other day, we are making genuine progress towards finding the mass grave in El Cerrón, so we held a meeting with the descendants of the fourteen Republican victims to determine exactly what to do with the remains if and when we manage to locate them.

'As it turns out, two of the families have now decided that if we do find the grave, they do not wish for it to be disturbed, which complicates things enormously. Vladi was supposed to be giving a speech at the end of the meeting, but things got out of hand when he weighed in during the debate phase. And when the daughter of one of the victims called him a *rojo*, there wasn't really any going back.'

'What did he say to that?' Danny asked. *Rojo* meant Red.

'He said he was proud to be a *rojo*, and that the woman was an embarrassment. Then he said something about her father turning in his grave, but that he couldn't, because he was lying dead in a ditch somewhere along with 13 others. But by that time Vladi was so angry he was barely comprehensible. I think he'd been drinking before the meeting. When we asked him to leave, he started waving that damned sword stick of his around. I swear he was close to actually unsheathing the damned thing before we managed to hustle him out.'

'What date was this?'

'The 4th of this month.'

'The same day Teresa disappeared?'

Juarez paused. 'Yes, I suppose it was. I hadn't thought of that.'

'What time did Vladi leave the meeting?'

'About seven-thirty, I think.'

Danny was explaining the facts of Vladi's demise to Juarez when the neighbour returned with the key, so Danny agreed to meet with Juarez later in the day.

The gate opened onto a half-acre plot of land, enclosed on three sides by the garden wall. The side opposite the gate ended in a low hill covered with spiky cacti. The garden was a mess. Prickly pear plants grew everywhere, the huge paddle-shaped shoots covered in inch-long spikes. As the woman led Danny along the path to the house, she indicated a patch of ground.

'That's where we found him,' she said.

Danny nodded, then stopped. His attention had been drawn by the state of Vladi's jeep: two of the tyres were flat and the bodywork was covered in dust.

'He gave up driving years ago,' the neighbour said when she saw where Danny was looking.

'How did he get about then?'

'When he needed to go out, he would catch the bus.'

'What if he came home in the evening? The buses don't run then.'

'He would cadge a lift from someone, I suppose. Or phone a taxi. That was, if he'd bothered to replace his mobile.'

'What happened to his mobile?'

'He dropped it down the toilet a few weeks back. I only know as he brought the damned thing round to see if my son could fix it. The poor thing had been fiddling with it for a full minute before Vladi told him what had happened to it.'

But Danny was only half-listening. He was thinking now about the phone call Teresa del Hoyo had received from a public pay phone, the one that had made her leave work early on the night of her disappearance. According to Pepe Juarez, Vladi had stormed out of the meeting around seven-thirty. There was a chance that Vladi might have called Teresa del Hoyo and asked her for a lift home — and if he hadn't had his mobile, he might have used a payphone.

Danny rummaged in his bag and showed the neighbour a photo of Teresa del Hoyo. 'Did you ever see this girl here?'

She looked at the photo. 'I don't know. I didn't really pay much attention to Vladi's comings and goings.'

Danny then showed her a photo of Teresa's pink VW Beetle. 'What about this car? Did you ever see this around here?'

'Yes, that I have seen. You don't see many cars like that up here in the mountains.'

'Have you seen it recently?'

'Maybe a month ago. I can't really remember.'

The front door of Vladi's house opened onto the living room. The decor was exactly as Danny remembered it. A massive old wooden television with a cracked screen stood in one corner, and beside it there were bookshelves and a desk with a typewriter — Vladi had never made the transition to the digital age. Everything was grimy and dusty, and smelt of stale cigarette smoke.

'Why are all the windows open?' Danny asked the neighbour.

'I decided to air the place out. You've no idea what it smelled like inside here. Sooner or later, Vladi's Russian relations are going to turn up. I wouldn't want them walking into a pigsty.'

'What about that window?' Danny said, pointing to one that had a piece of cardboard taped over a missing pane.

'That was Vladi. The drunken old fool was forever losing his keys and breaking into his own house. That was from a couple of months ago when we found him blundering around in the garden, trying to stand a flowerpot beneath the window and crawl through — despite the frame being filled with jagged edges of broken glass. He spent that night on our couch. That's how I ended up with a spare set of keys, but after that I think he used to leave the back door open as well.'

There was a corkboard above the desk. Most of the yellowed scraps of newspaper pinned there related to the publication of Vladi's books and his fight to gain access to the municipal archive in El Cerrón.

The famous photo of Vladi taken when he began his court battle was pinned to the centre of the corkboard. It showed the old man in his black beret brandishing an ivory walking stick towards the camera as if it were a rapier. Danny knew why the old man had adopted the pose in the photograph: the cane was actually a sword-stick, as Vladi had demonstrated to Danny once by tossing the thing across the room like a javelin so that it stuck, quivering, in the wall.

The subsequent years of legal battles had involved a great deal of mud-slinging between Vladi and Leticia Encona, the mayoress of El Cerrón, and there were numerous photos of the woman pinned to the corkboard. Every one of them had been defaced in some way: devil's horns, beards, vampire fangs.

Leticia Encona was a local legend, one of those maverick right-wingers with outspoken views on everything from the iniquity of immigration to the possibility of curing homosexuality through prayer. Danny had interviewed Encona at the time of Vladi's court case. When Danny had asked her what it was she was afraid Vladi might uncover in the archives, she had been characteristically forthright: 'Shit smells worst when it's been stirred around. The same thing applies to Spanish history.'

The right-hand side of the corkboard seemed to have been recently cleared and was covered in newly printed documents. They all related to the illegal adoptions scandal. There were articles on exhumations of the graves of supposedly stillborn children that had taken place elsewhere in Spain, and of the macabre finds made inside some of them — bags of sand, bricks, animal bones — together with details of all the main charities campaigning for victims of the scandal.

Leticia Encona's extended family had obviously become of interest to Vladi recently, too. A new-looking piece of paper held a rough family tree, showing Leticia's father, Amancio Encona (1916-1997), and her son, Santiago, born in 1964. Amancio had a living sister, too, named Herminia, born 1928.

85

She had one son, Ramón Encona, born in 1962. A big black question mark had been written beside Ramón's name.

Danny unpinned all the newspaper articles and the family tree and put them into his shoulder bag. When he headed towards the front door, the neighbour paused and said, 'Do you want to take anything else as a memento? I've no idea when his Russian relatives will be coming, and it seems a shame to throw all this stuff away.'

Danny thought for a moment. 'I'd like his sword-stick,' he said. 'After all, what better memento is there? He never went anywhere without it.'

'I'm afraid I'll have to disappoint you,' she said, shaking her head sadly. 'My husband wanted that for himself. But do you know, we've searched the whole place from top to bottom, and that sword-stick is nowhere to be found.'

11

Outside, Danny phoned the police press liaison and asked him to check if Vladi's body had been autopsied. Yes, the officer said, there had been an autopsy and there was no doubt that Señor Lopez had died of a massive heart attack. In fact, the old man had quite literally fallen down dead: the pathologist had found a contusion on the side of Vladi's head which was consistent with his having collapsed forward without using his hands to break the fall. The body had been discovered on the morning of Thursday, October 6th and the post-mortem examination had determined that by that date the old man had been dead somewhere between 24 and 36 hours.

Even so, Danny still thought it a strange coincidence that Teresa and Vladi should have worked together, and that both should have died within days of each other. And it didn't explain how Vladi's sword-stick had gone missing.

Whatever the truth of how Vladi had come by his limp, there was no doubt the injury to his leg was genuine. The old man could not walk without a cane, and he had always used that sword-stick, just as he had always worn the same ratty old cardigan, baggy trousers and black beret. He couldn't have walked outside to where he died without the cane, which meant it should have been lying beside him when the neighbour found him — that is, unless someone had been to Vladi's house in the interim period.

Danny had been considering various hypotheses. If Vladi had taken documents from the archive, it was possible someone had wanted to get them back. What if Teresa del Hoyo had given Vladi a lift home on the Tuesday night she had disappeared, and they had surprised one or more burglars? After all, Vladi was supposed to have been out all evening on the Tuesday, but instead had returned home early.

And if they had surprised burglars, there was no question as to what Vladi would have done, especially if he was drunk: he would have unsheathed that sword-stick and attacked them without a second thought. The stress and excitement of the situation could have caused the old man's heart attack.

Danny drove back to the *Izquierda Unida* office in Almería city. When he went upstairs, he found about a dozen youngsters sitting around. Some were printing badges, while others were working on a poster that bore an image of Teresa del Hoyo's face beneath the slogan NOT ONE FEMICIDE MORE!

First, Danny had coffee with Pepe Juarez and explained everything he knew about Vladi's death. Then Juarez went outside, stood atop a table, and made the announcement to the younger party members. The news was greeted with disbelief and tears. When Juarez came back into his office, he was accompanied by a young woman he introduced as Lidia, the girl that had shared an office with Teresa del Hoyo.

Lidia was a Lisbeth Salander lookalike: short and petite, with lots of piercings, dark-eyeliner and lipstick. She nodded when Danny asked her if she remembered Gordon Pavey coming to the *Izquierda Unida* office.

'Yes, there was an *inglés* who came here.'

'Do you remember when?'

'He came a couple of weeks ago. On a Thursday.'

'So, September the 29th?'

'If you say so.'

'Do you remember what he and Teresa talked about?'

'They spoke about the municipal archive in El Cerrón and how to get access to it. The *inglés* said he wanted to speak to Vladi.'

'Why did Pavey want to access the archive in El Cerrón?'

'I don't know. But Teresa and Vladi seemed very excited about something he had told them. That first day the *inglés* came, they were here until gone midnight, and they were thick as thieves after that. And on the Friday evening, the *inglés* was in here with Vladi and Teresa for hours making scans of some old books. Don't ask me what they were, though. I think it was something they had taken from the archive. I didn't see the *inglés* again after that. I got the impression he had disagreed with Teresa and Vladi about something.'

'Would the scans be on Teresa's computer?'

'On that crapped out old thing? No, she did most of her work on a laptop. Plus, the scanner broke while they were using it on the Friday.'

'And where is her laptop?'

'I've no idea. With her family, I suppose. But there was something Teresa had on her office computer. It was an MP3 file: the *inglés* was helping them to translate it into Spanish.'

They crossed the room to the other office. Lidia booted up Teresa's pc and found the MP3 file.

The speakers crackled into life. Danny recognised the interviewer's voice straight away: it was Leonard Wexby, asking questions in English of Frank Dale.

'Where did Teresa get this?' Danny said. 'And why?'

'The *inglés*, Pavey, brought it with him.'

Danny asked to make a copy on his pen drive. Then he drove home.

Pavey had probably seen Wexby's article on the internet, noticed the mention of Santa Cristina and asked him for the file of the whole interview. That was what Leonard had meant about the name cropping up.

Not for the first time in his life, Danny cursed the name of Leonard Wexby. The old weasel obviously knew something. The trouble was, getting information out of Leonard would inevitably involve drinking, and Danny knew from bitter experience that Wexby-inspired hangovers could last for days and were immune to the effects of paracetamol.

When Danny got home, he went into his office and finished the *Gente de Hoy* article on Teresa del Hoyo's murder and sent it through to Paco Pino. He stuck to the basic facts presented in a chronological order, as he knew from experience that the sub-editors at the magazine would hack his text around anyhow. He sent it through to Paco accompanied by a reminder not to put his name on the resultant article.

Then Danny made a fried egg sandwich and began listening to the MP3 file. The relevant information started around the fourteen minute mark. Frank Dale's London accent filled the room, interspersed by Wexby's questions.

'*...the building had been abandoned about a year when we went there,*' Dale's voice said.

'*When was that?*'

'*It would have been in the autumn of 1970. The director fell in love with the place as soon as he saw it. It was perfect for a mad scientist's lair: that creepy-looking tower, the mountains behind it.*'

'*And yet you mentioned you did not enjoy working there.*'

Dale could be heard to shuffle in his seat.

'*Yeah, well, I had a nasty experience there.*'

'*One that you could tell me about?*'

A lighter clicked, smoke was exhaled.

'*All right,*' Dale said, '*I'll tell you, but you won't believe me.*

'*It started when we were trying to find extras for the shoot. I mean, normally you couldn't keep the local Spanish people away from the set. You'd be shooting in the middle of nowhere and you'd still get dozens of the buggers wandering into shot or trying to pinch things. But when we advertised locally for people to do a crowd scene up at Santa Cristina, do you know how many we got? None. Not one person came forward.*'

'*Why not?*'

'*It turns out the locals consider the place to be cursed. There's a local legend about a ghost, The Pallid Woman, who sneaks into people's houses at night and smothers their children. The Spanish claimed this evil spirit had possessed a local woman, driven her mad and made her burn the clinic to the ground.*

'*Anyway, late one night at the end of the shoot, I'd been drinking with two of the grips, and we decided to go and investigate the cellars up at Santa Cristina. You know how it is with young blokes and ghost stories, we were daring each other and we were drunk enough to not worry about bringing the whole lot down on our heads. Damn stupid, when you think about it.*

'*We found one room in the cellar that wasn't too badly affected. Half of it was full of rubble from the rooms above. It looked like an office had collapsed down into it. There was a burnt desk and filing cabinets full of papers. Of course, most of the papers were ruined by damp and mildew and the few that weren't we couldn't understand. Eddie said they looked like medical files.*

'*And there was a fridge, too. One of the big metal ones like you find in hotel kitchens. It was all dented and burnt to buggery but we dragged the rubble away enough so that we could open it.*'

Dale cleared his throat and when he began to speak again, there was a slight quaver to his voice.

'*Inside, there were a load of towels and surgical instruments. At least, that's what Eddie said they were — they looked like bloody fireplace tongs to me. Christ knows why, but I decided to lift these towels out. I*

91

didn't realise what it was they were wrapped around until Eddie shone the torch on it.'

'What was it?'

'It was a dead kid. A baby, I mean. All shrivelled up, like the water had been sucked out of him.'

'No!'

'As God's my witness. I held the bloody thing in my hands. At least, I did until I realised what it was and scarpered. Honestly, I've never been so scared in my entire life. You want to see how scared I was?' There came the sound of fumbling. *'There. That's how bloody shat up I was. Must have caught my arm on a nail on the way out or something. It was pissing blood but I didn't even notice until we'd been in the car ten minutes. Twenty-six stitches I needed in that. I was damn lucky not to get septicaemia.'*

Ten seconds of silence followed, before Dale said, *'Do you want another drink? I know I damned well do.'*

The rest of the interview meandered. Danny realised he'd become so engrossed in listening that he'd let his food go cold, but when he started eating again, he found he'd lost his appetite.

Danny lit a cigarette. Dale's story had given him goosebumps. Of course, the most likely explanation was that the man had either invented the story or had found a child's doll — darkness and drink could make a man see almost anything in the right circumstances — but it was still an intriguing twist to the story, especially given Gordon Pavey's interest in the illegal adoptions.

He was still pondering the interview when his mobile pinged with an SMS from Marsha: *Turn your Skype on*

When Marsha's face appeared on Danny's computer screen, he saw that she looked worried. Her hair was tousled, her eyes were red and her voice held none of its usual ebullience.

'Is something the matter, girl?' Danny said.

'No. Well, yes.' She ran her fingers through her hair. 'The simple truth is that I've done something stupid and I think you're going to be angry with me. But I did it with the very best intentions.'

Danny lit a cigarette and regarded the mournful face on the computer screen.

'OK,' he said, 'you'd better tell me what it is, hadn't you?'

12

Ramón Encona placed the plastic shopping bags on the step to his mother's house and fumbled the key into the heavy door. Across the street a group of old women were talking in quick, quiet voices. Ramón knew they were talking about him and he could guess what they were saying: Have you seen? He's back, Herminia's boy.

Ramón made a point of pausing to consult the time so they got a good look at the 4,000 Euro Tag Heuer strapped to his wrist. Apart from some clothing and his collection of eau de cologne, it was the only thing of value he'd managed to grab before fleeing the police raid that had closed down the Seville brothels where he'd been working. Then he turned and stared at the women until they looked away. Ramón's thin, bloodless lips twisted into a smile. After eighteen years away from El Cerrón, it was good to see that being a member of the Encona family still mattered.

The whole *get-the-shopping-for-Mother* routine had been Manolo Acosta's idea. 'We need a look at those documents, Ramón,' the lawyer had said a month earlier, folding his hands on his gut, 'so you're going to have to swallow your pride and get back into your mother's good books. I know she pays a young girl to collect her shopping every Tuesday. There's your in. Go round to her house, tell her you're a changed man and offer to help out.'

Ramón hadn't thought Mother would go for it. He'd not spoken to her once in the eighteen years he'd been away from El Cerrón, and they hadn't parted on amicable terms. But when the front door had finally creaked inwards, Mother had not reacted with surprise at seeing her son. Instead, she had looked at him down that long, bony nose of hers, and a sparkle of triumph had shown in her rheumy eyes.

'Look who's finally come crawling home to Mother,' she had said. 'I suppose you're in some kind of trouble, aren't you? I won't forgive you, if that's what you've come to beg for. You're a wicked, wicked little boy who never prayed enough.' Then she had turned and shuffled away, leaving the door unclosed, and Ramón had simply followed her inside.

Naturally, the old bitch wouldn't let him do her shopping at a supermarket like a normal person. Instead, she insisted Ramón buy her groceries from six different shops, all of which were located in narrow pedestrian streets, which meant Ramón couldn't use his car. But then Mother knew that, didn't she? Back in the early '80s, when Ramón had done his national service, he'd been forced to see an army shrink, and the shrink had asked Ramón once whether he thought his mother had loved him as a child. The question had made Ramón laugh. 'Love me? Man, she didn't even *like* me.'

The high-ceilinged hallway of Mother's house reeked of bleach, polish and disinfectant. As he did every Tuesday, Ramón paused by the mirror that hung inside the front door and checked that the shopping bags hadn't rumpled the trousers of his sharkskin suit too badly. He licked the tip of his little finger and smoothed his eyebrows down as he gazed at his reflection, daydreaming of the moment when the huge house would finally be his. Mother was 83 and in ill-health. Manolo Acosta had paid a private investigator to pull her medical records, and Mother's list of ailments was satisfyingly long. Acosta's medical source reckoned she had 12 months to live, tops.

Ramón had done his homework. The housing market in Spain might have gone to shit, but there were always buyers for prime, centrally located real estate like Mother's house. A similar property further down the road had sold last year for more than 950,000 Euros. The purchaser had demolished the place and was building flats. Ramón smiled as he thought of that: there would be plenty of people in El Cerrón who would take an especial pleasure in knocking down Herminia Encona's house.

But the main problem was going to be the inheritance tax: the more you inherited, the higher the percentage you had to pay, and on amounts greater than 800,000 Euros, the tax was 34%. That was why Ramón had contacted Manolo Acosta in the first place: the crooked bastard knew all sorts of legal wrangles to get around the tax.

First off, there was a 150,000 Euro exemption for benefactors with a 65% or greater disability. Acosta claimed he had a tame doctor who, for 15,000 Euros, would draw up the necessary paperwork to have Ramón declared a cripple. And there was another 120K allowance for direct descendants who inherited properties in which they habitually resided.

When Ramón told the lawyer that Mother had thrown him out thirty years ago, Acosta had waved his hand disparagingly. 'Don't worry about that. All that matters is what's down on the electoral roll. And I know just the right person in the town hall to massage certain documents,' he'd said, waggling his fingers the way a magician does before a trick. Then his face had become serious. 'But first things first. We really need to determine whether or not your mother is the actual owner of the house.'

'Why the hell wouldn't she be?'

'Your parents married in 1960 and you were born in 1962, right? But your mother had already been living in the house two or three years before that, hadn't she? Which means that the house was likely gifted to her by your Uncle Amancio — which, in turn, means that she took up residence in the middle of the dictatorship. Do you know what the law was like for women back then? They couldn't even *travel* alone without written permission from a male relative.

'Of course, I imagine it would have been different for your mother due to her links with the regime, but even so, it's something we need to pin down. It's possible that the house actually belonged to your Uncle Amancio, and your mother is only in possession of the usufruct. If that's the case, you won't be able to sell the house. Or it might even go to Amancio's descendants.'

The words had left Ramón sick with worry. With his brothel-income gone, his inheritance was the bedrock of his future. And now it might turn out that the damned house would go to Cousin Leticia. Or worse, to that little shit, Santiago. It was entirely possible that the house had belonged to Uncle Amancio. After all, it was he who had held the real power back then, with his seat on the Falangist provincial council and doctor's payroll. And hadn't Amancio snatched the house from a family of Reds? What if he had simply given Mother this usufruct thing and nothing more?

Ramón needed to find out.

At the top of the stairs a glass door opened onto the living room. As he did every Tuesday, Ramón opened the door silently and laid the shopping bags on the floor. Old age might have dulled some of Mother's faculties, but she was still as sharp as broken glass when it came to watching Ramón.

The décor in the living room was exactly as it had been in Ramón's childhood: the gilt-edged bible atop its ornate lectern, the framed portrait of Franco with its motto, *España, una, grande y libre* — Spain, one, great and free. Ramón crossed the room on tiptoes and opened the door to Mother's study. He had checked all the other rooms in the house on previous visits. The documents relating to the house had to be in there somewhere.

During Ramón's childhood, the study had always been filled with paperwork relating to Mother's work with the Falange's *Sección Feminina*; now, it was filled with all sorts of junk and clutter: piles of cardboard boxes and files, tables, chairs, racks of clothing. Ramón stepped between two of Mother's fur coats and started work on one of the piles of cardboard boxes at the back of the room.

The deeper he dug, the older the artefacts he unearthed. Mother seemed not to have thrown a single thing away. There were even dozens of empty cigar boxes from the brand that Uncle Amancio had smoked. The smell of them brought back a sudden sharp memory of the fat prick. He was the only person Ramón hated more than Mother: one of the first things Ramón had done on returning to El Cerrón was go to the cemetery and take a good long piss on the huge marble cross that marked Uncle Amancio's grave.

There was a big flat box at the bottom of the pile that was different from all the others. When Ramón retrieved it, he saw that the box lid had silver stripes set across it diagonally and that the name and address of a tailor was written in gilt lettering in one corner.

Inside was Mother's wedding dress, carefully wrapped in folded sheets of tissue paper and muslin. Ramón lifted the dress out and laid it on the floor. He wanted to check the bottom of the box.

The deeds to the house weren't there. There was, however, an old envelope addressed to Mother. It held a letter dated January, 1959, and an invoice addressed to Herminia Encona for the sum of 20,695 pesetas. The letter read:

Dear Señorita Encona,

I am afraid that given the complexity of the design and the cost of the materials used — not to mention the numerous alterations you required me to make — that a refund is out of the question. As you will know, my designs are all bespoke and made to fit the specifics of a single woman, therefore your suggestion that I try to sell the dress to someone else is impossible. All I can offer you are my condolences and hope that God grants you the strength to overcome the bitter blow you have been dealt.

The letter was signed by the same tailor whose name was on the box.

What the hell did the letter mean? Ramón's parents had not met until April 1960, at a Falange event held to celebrate the war victory. God knows, Ramón had heard the story enough times as a child. Why had Mother been trying to return a wedding dress a year before that?

He was about to look through the photo albums for 1959 when he heard a faint creak from upstairs. He stood, slipped through the study door and crossed the room to the shopping bags.

The faint shuffle of slippers sounded on the tiled floor, and Mother appeared. She walked with a stick now, her crooked back bent so that her head jutted forward from her shoulders parallel to the floor, like the neck of vulture. She wore a long nightshirt and brought with her the smell of stale bed sheets and airless rooms.

'Ramón! What are you doing sneaking around inside my house? Didn't I teach you to knock, you wretched child?'

'It's Tuesday. I brought your shopping.'

'I know what day of the week it is.' She paused and steadied herself against the wall, the better to fix her dark eyes on Ramón. 'Where's my change?' she said, extending a wrinkled paw. 'And I hope you've remembered to bring the receipts this time. What did you buy with the last lot of money you stole from me? Cigarettes and whores I'll bet. Don't roll your eyes at me, boy. You let that little pig's tail of yours do all your thinking for you. Always have. I used to listen to you pleasuring yourself when you were a youngster,' she said, shuffling after Ramón as he took the shopping bags through to the kitchen. 'I should have snipped it off then and saved us all a lot of trouble.'

Ramón felt the muscles in his jaw tense. It was the same bullshit every Tuesday. First, she demanded the change from her shopping. Second, she accused him of stealing from her and berated him for his wickedness. Then she wept at memory of her husband, a man whom she had always hated in life — so much so that Ramón's father had spent most of his life away from the family in Cordoba. Finally, Mother would watch him unpack the shopping, firing instructions as he did so: 'Not there. Tins go in the cupboard. Don't put fruit in the fridge.'

'There you are,' Ramón said when he had finally packed the food away to Mother's satisfaction.

She sneered at him.

'Don't look so damned pleased with yourself. I always said you would never amount to anything, and now here you are, a whisper from fifty, traipsing the streets like a servant with your mother's shopping.' She gave a short, mirthless laugh. 'The men of your generation have no pride, no virility. Small wonder the country is awash with sodomites and Mohammedans.' She clasped her hands together. 'Ay! Spain of my heart, what have they done to you?' Then she turned back towards Ramón. 'There, you've done what you came for. Now get out of my house.'

He went downstairs, opened the front door and slammed it closed without having stepped through. He looked at himself again in the mirror. His face was flushed, his hands shook and his right eyelid fluttered as he fought to control his tic.

That fucking laugh of hers: he couldn't stand it. Every Tuesday he steeled himself because he knew it was coming — but today he'd been *that* close to grabbing the old bitch by the hair and tossing her down the fucking stairs. As a younger man he would probably have done it, but age had taught him the value of pragmatism.

He took deep breaths and calmed himself. One day he would show Mother what he really thought of her. But not yet.

He stood in the hallway and waited until he heard the faint sound of military music coming from Mother's bedroom. Then he crept back upstairs, back towards the study and its boxes.

13

Adriana Sanchez looked at Danny over her wine glass.

'What is it with all these maudlin questions about my parents and the civil war tonight? Are you drunk? You've hardly eaten a thing.'

It was the second time Danny had tried to bring the subject round to his grandparents. Danny reached into his pocket and fingered the folded print-out of the letter Marsha had emailed him. He was desperate to discuss its contents with his mother, but he knew that if he was to stand any hope of getting a sensible answer, he would have to broach the subject carefully.

The problem was, his mother was right: Danny *was* drunk. What he'd read in the letter had upset him so much that he'd knocked back an entire bottle of red while he waited for his mother to arrive, and they'd polished off another two during dinner.

He rubbed his forehead, trying to focus. Part of him thought he should leave the letter-conversation for another night: he and his mother had a tempestuous relationship at the best of times, and alcohol did nothing to improve the situation. And Danny was seriously pissed off with Marsha. But that train of thought was for another time. First, this situation had to be dealt with.

They were sitting on the patio outside Danny's house with the remains of chorizo sausage, roasted peppers, and bread and cheese on the table between them. His mother was casually dressed in loose-fitting clothes, her long hair swept backwards and held with a wooden hair pin. She was 60 now, and growing old well. She'd no right to — not with the amount she smoked, drank and ate — but then the whys and wherefores of entitlement had never been of much interest to Adriana Sanchez.

Danny pulled the cork from another bottle of Campo Viejo. His mother watched him as he refilled their glasses.

'So?' she said. 'Are you going to explain? First of all you phone out of the blue and demand that I come round for dinner. Then you do nothing but talk about ancient family history.'

'You know that I've been thinking of writing a book on the *abuelos'* experiences, don't you? How they escaped the civil war, how they ended up in England, how they lived out their—'

Adriana Sanchez scoffed.

'Who on earth would want to read that, darling? I really cannot understand why you're so fascinated by the civil war. It was a shabby, cruel little conflict, and it brought out the worst in Spain and in the Spaniards.

'My mother let it poison her entire life. God, you've no idea of the lugubrious evenings she used to make me endure as a young girl, listing all of her friends and relatives that the Reds had murdered. Sure, she mellowed when she had you to look after, but she was tethered to that war the way a goat is to pole: all she ever did afterwards was to walk in circles around it.'

She lit a cigarette and sipped her wine. Then she frowned.

'I say, this book idea isn't anything to do with that woman of yours, is it? I know she was pushing all sorts of half-baked ideas at you. I don't know what you seen in her, I really don't.'

'That woman has a name.

Adriana Sanchez gave a sigh of exasperation when she saw Danny's expression. 'I just think you could do so much better, Danny. I'm your mother. I only want what's best for you.'

'Marsha *is* what's best for me.'

'Oh, come off it. I mean, her dress sense alone is reason to dump her. Did you see that ridiculous kaftan she was wearing?'

'It was a dress.'

'Oh, what's the difference when it's bigger than a size 10?'

'Maybe you get confused because you're old enough to remember kaftans being in fashion.'

Her cigarette paused on its way to her mouth. 'You *are* drunk, aren't you? You wouldn't speak to me this way if you weren't. God, I wish you were this quick to leap to my defence.'

Danny drew a deep breath.

'All I'm saying is that whom I choose to pursue a relationship with is nobody's business but my own.'

'So you're "pursuing a relationship" with her, now, are you?' Adriana Sanchez said, watching Danny as she allowed smoke to drift upwards from her mouth. 'Well, I doubt you've ever had to "pursue" her very far, Danny: she was all over you at that restaurant last month.'

'Right, that's enough about, Marsha,' Danny said, slamming into the table as he stood.

'And now you're going to shut yourself in your office and sulk. Do you want me to leave? I mean, I have been persona non grata at this house ever since you met that wretched woman.'

'Is that what all this is about?' Danny said from the doorway. 'Because when I met Marsha, I asked you to move out?'

'Of course not,' she said, but her sudden inability to meet Danny's gaze told him all he needed to know.

'So that's why you've always had it in for her,' Danny said. 'It all makes sense now.'

Irritation showed on his mother's face.

'Well, what did you expect? When you told me I had to move out because you'd met an English girl, I was expecting some winsome little rose. Instead, it transpired you'd thrown me out in favour of some heffa—'

'Don't say it. I don't want to hear it.'

'I'm your mother, Danny. The only family you've got.'

'Actually, that's not true.'

She was sharp, despite the amount of red wine she'd drunk. The implications of what Danny had said registered immediately.

'What do you mean?' she said, her eyes narrowing as she scrutinised him. 'What have you done?'

Here it was. Anger had forced the words from Danny's lips before he really knew what he was saying, but there was no getting away from it now.

Danny took a deep breath and then he showed her the printout of the letter and began to explain how he had been trying to compile information on the *abuelito's* family in Málaga and the brother that had stayed behind in Spain and taken control of the family's olive oil export company and that one person had sent him an address in Málaga and that he had written to the person and—

'You mean that letter is from Eusebio Sanchez?' his mother hissed. 'Are you telling me you knowingly contacted that prick? Because, you know who he is, don't you? That's the son of your grandfather's brother. You remember him, don't you, Danny? The one that stole the *abuelito's* business?'

'Yes, I know all that. But that's not the point. It's what he wrote back that concerns me. Look at the second-to-last paragraph.'

Danny tried to hand her the print out, but she shook her head.

105

'I don't want to touch the bloody thing. You read it out.'

Danny skipped the letter's opening and went straight to the part that worried him.

'*I have to say that, while I am intrigued to discover I have relations in England, I do not much care for the tone of your previous correspondence, especially those parts that intimate that members of my immediate family somehow stole or illicitly took possession of property that did not belong to them.*

'*Given that you have contacted me seeking information on the man José Daniel Sanchez Fernandez , I am forced to say that it was common knowledge in my family that this man actively collaborated with the Reds during their misrule of the city, and purchased his eventual release from prison by denouncing and revealing the hiding places of other members of the right. It was also common knowledge that his failure to return to Spain after the war was prompted by the shame he felt at having saved his own neck by handing others over to the Marxist execution squads. If you feel the need to have proof of this, I will gladly—*'

'Enough!' Adriana Sanchez cried, slapping the table so hard that the plates leapt into the air and the wine glasses tumbled. 'I cannot *believe* you have done this, Danny.'

'Don't worry, there's a historian I know in Málaga who has written books on the civil war. I'm going to ask him to look into the matter. I'm sure he'll be able to—'

'You mean you've actually stooped to believe this utter bullshit, Danny? How could you? How *could* you?' she said, standing suddenly. Her face was red and she was trembling. Danny had never seen her so angry.

'And for your information, it was *that* bastard's father—' she pointed at the letter — 'who was the family's turncoat. He did nothing to help your grandfather when he was in prison in Málaga — in fact, he would barely acknowledge that his brother existed — because he was too worried about keeping in good graces with the Reds.

'But when the other lot invaded the city, not only did dear Eusebio's father manage to avoid execution himself, he got to keep the family home *and* steal your grandfather's business. Now, how the hell do you think he managed that, Danny? Go on, you're the hotshot investigative reporter. Let's see if you can link A to B on this one. It was because Eusebio's fucking father was there, pointing the finger at everyone who had had anything to do with the left.

'God, do you think just because you've read a few Paul Preston paperbacks that you can hope to understand what happened to people back then? You do realise there were three sides in that war, don't you? That's what your *abuelito* used to say. There were the left and the right — and in between there were the poor bastards from every political persuasion who only wanted to keep their children and parents safe from all the madness and murder. Newspapers might print everything in nice, neat black and white, Danny, but life is rarely as clear cut. I'd have thought you'd have learnt that by now.'

As she spoke, Danny had stood up and walked towards her. But when he tried to put his hand on her shoulder, she slapped it away.

'Don't touch me! I won't forget this, Danny,' she said, sniffing away tears. She picked up her bag from the table. She looked deep into Danny's eyes.

'Just tell me this: why? Why have you done this? Why have you contacted this bastard? Didn't I always tell you never to go poking around in our family's history?'

Danny could always read his mother's mood. The reverse was equally true. When Danny looked down, sudden

107

realisation dawned on her face, and eyes which had been aflame with anger became cold and hard.

'My God, it wasn't you that contacted him, was it? It was *her*, wasn't it?'

There was no point lying. 'Marsha was only trying to help get my book project off the ground,' Danny said, but Adriana Sanchez spoke over him.

'Her trying to poison you against me, I can understand. But to sink so low as to bring my parents into it...' She snatched her handbag from the table. 'I won't forget this. You have betrayed me and you have betrayed your grandparents. Now get out of my way,' she said, kicking over a chair as she pushed past Danny.

Part II — El Desentierro

1

'You see, Ramón?' Manolo Acosta said, leafing through the documents on the desk. 'As I suspected, your mother only had the usufruct back when she lived in the house alone. But your uncle ceded that to your father when he married your mother, which means she inherited the property when he died.' He tucked the documents inside a cardboard folder. 'Where did you find the stuff in the end?'

'In a box at the back of her study,' Ramón said. 'Behind that wedding dress I told you about.'

Acosta stubbed out his cigarette. 'I can see this wedding dress business is worrying you. What does it matter if your mother tried to return a dress? Brides get cold feet. It happens all the time.'

'But why did she even have a wedding dress in 1959? My parents met in 1960.'

'Perhaps you've got your dates wrong.'

'No, I checked her photo albums. There's a picture of my parents when they first met, and it's dated April 3rd, 1960.'

'Listen, inheritance-wise there's nothing your mother can do. Spanish law dictates 2/3rds of the parents' estate passes directly to the children, no ifs, no buts. The wedding dress is nothing to worry about.'

'It's a loose end. I don't like them,' Ramón said, staring at the wall.

Nothing in Acosta's office had changed in the time Ramón had been away from El Cerrón. There was the same imitation leather sofa, the same framed photo of Real Sevilla football team. And there was Acosta himself. He was in his early sixties now, but he was still leaking out of the same cheap polystyrene suit, his sweaty face beaming insincerely beneath that same grotty rug of a hairpiece.

'What if my father had other children?' Ramón said. 'Could they have any right to a share in my inheritance?'

'But you don't have any siblings, do you?'

'Not that I know of. But what if my father had more children? In Cordoba, I mean.'

Acosta's chair creaked as he leant back to consider the matter.

'What makes you think that he did?'

'Do you know how fanatical my mother was about that church abstinence bullshit? Fasting, hair shirts, cords tied around her thigh. She still sleeps without a pillow now and she's 83. I can say with a pretty high degree of certainty that the night I was conceived was one of the *very* few times my parents ever had sex. Small wonder they used to call my mother *La Inmaculada* behind her back.'

'You knew about the nickname then?' Acosta said. It meant The Immaculate. He rubbed his sweaty forehead. 'Well, if there were any bastard brothers or sisters knocking around, it could complicate things, especially if they had decent legal representation. But I don't think they would stand much chance of getting a share of the inheritance. The worst they could do is tie you up in the courts. I've seen cases of contested wills last more than a decade.'

'I want to know. Find out everything you can on my father.'

'Give me his details, then. What was his date of birth?'

Ramón thought for a moment and said, 'No idea.'

'You don't know your own father's date of birth?' Acosta said with a chuckle, but his smile quickly faded when he saw Ramón's expression.

Nobody laughed at Ramón Encona.

'The prick was hardly ever around,' Ramón said. 'And when he did come back to town, he spent most of his time drinking with Uncle Amancio and reminiscing about the damned war. Besides, my mother wasn't real big on celebrations. Her idea of a birthday party was praying for twice as long as she usually did.'

Acosta gave him a please-yourself shrug.

'I can find the details,' he said, 'although I remind you I charge by the quarter hour and that the bill is already in four figures.'

'Don't worry, I'm good for it,' Ramón said as he got up.

Acosta's office was on El Cerrón's central street. The wind outside was sharp with the clear, penetrating chill of the high mountains. Ramón crossed the road, thinking about what Acosta had said about the bill. Ramón needed to find a way to earn some money while he waited for Mother to die because, sooner or later, the lawyer was going to realise that Ramón wasn't feeding from the same trough as the rest of the Encona family.

As he walked, his thoughts turned to murdering Mother. He'd spent many long nights lying awake considering various subtle ways of hurrying her demise, but he knew he would never get away with it. Acosta had been keeping tabs on Mother, and she had held a long interview with her own lawyer a few days after Ramón returned to the town. She was up to something, and Ramón was damned if he would go to prison because of her.

She'd caused him enough misery already.

Ramón's earliest childhood memory was of the dog, a newborn mongrel runt abandoned in the bushes that Ramón had stumbled across when he was perhaps five or six years old.

Ramón had thought it dead, but when he knelt and touched the back of his knuckles to its soft, pink, furless tummy, the dog's paws had fluttered and its lidded eyes had turned towards him.

He had tucked the animal under his arm, and kept it hidden in his room while he nursed it with milk and scraps of food.

Three days later, Mother found it. She had taken it straight downstairs, stuffed it into a hessian sack and drowned it in a bucket of water while Ramón screamed and threw himself at her. Then she had beaten him with a leather belt.

But then she used to beat him for everything and anything: for scuffing his shoes, for reading comic books, for coming home late, for fidgeting in church. And for talking to girls. That was the big one. She was obsessed with that, his little pig's tail and what he did with it. And Mother had enjoyed punishing him. They were the only times Ramón could remember her smiling.

But the more she had tried to beat the sin from him, the deeper it had taken root. By the time he was eight or nine, Ramón had begun to find freedom in defiance. He spat, he swore, he stole, he smashed street lights and windows, scratched people's cars. And he learned that he didn't need Mother to buy him toys. He could simply take them from other children. After all, who was going to complain? He was an Encona.

By the time he was ten, he could take whatever Mother could give him with barely a murmur. He would kneel down, grit his teeth and let her beat him until she was bent double from the exertion of the blows. Then he would calmly stand and ask her if she'd finished. And the experience with the dog had taught him an important lesson: affection was weakness. Ramón had never allowed himself to become emotionally fettered to anyone or anything ever again…

He was nearing the centre of town now. He hadn't meant to walk so far. He was about to turn back, when his nephew, Santiago, appeared at the end of the road, talking into a mobile phone.

Ramón's nose wrinkled: other than Mother, it was the first time since he'd been back that he'd seen any of his relations. Santiago was wearing a 3/4 length Cashmere coat and a scarf worn in a slip knot. He looked good in a well-fed, middle-aged way. He had obviously done well for himself. But then how could he not? He was the mayoress's son.

Thoughts of Cousin Leticia reminded Ramón of the typed letter that had been slipped under the door of his rented flat a few days after he returned to El Cerrón: *What the hell are you doing back here? The conditions of the agreement still apply. Don't forget that. And don't try phoning. Leave my son alone.*

Ramón hadn't forgotten the agreement, and he knew why Cousin Leticia wanted to keep him away from Santiago: for all his money and arrogance, Little Santi was weak and stupid and lacked sufficient smarts to realise quite how deeply his defects ran. Ramón had always been able to manipulate him.

He pretended to gaze into a shop window until Santiago drew level with him on the opposite pavement. Then he began to follow him.

Wherever Santiago was going, he was in a hurry to get there. He walked so quickly that Ramón practically had to jog to keep up. Santiago walked for two hundred metres, away from the centre of town, and then turned into a narrow street and stopped in the shadows by the service door of a supermarket.

He was clearly waiting for someone. Ramón watched from a doorway down the road and wondered who it could be. The most likely explanation was a lover. The ladies had always loved little Santi, and he had always been ready and willing to unbuckle for any rancid skank. But if it was a woman, the relationship wasn't going well, Ramón thought as he watched his nephew pacing back and forth, biting his lip.

But it wasn't a woman he was waiting for, Ramón realised when he saw Álvaro Iglesias hobbling up the road, red-faced from the effort of walking uphill.

Ramón chuckled to himself. Here was another person he'd not seen since he'd been back. God, Iglesias looked terrible. Álvaro had always been a porker as a kid, but he must weigh more than 20 stone now and was limping on his right leg. Perhaps the fat bastard had gout.

Santiago did not greet the newcomer. When he saw Iglesias, he steered him into the doorway and the two men began to talk.

Ramón watched them with interest. He recognised what was going on between the two men: they shared some secret. That much was obvious from the furtive way they were talking.

Santiago began the conversation hissing at the other man, his expression one of barely restrained fury as he punctuated everything he said with small, sharp hand gestures. Álvaro appeared to be pleading with him, shaking his head.

Ramón watched them talk for upwards of a minute. Then Santiago put his hands to his head, as if in disbelief, and launched a kick at the nearest rubbish bin. There was a final terse exchange and Santiago turned and swept out of the car park, heading back towards the centre of town at a brisk pace.

Álvaro remained behind for a long while. He seemed to be crying. Then he waddled off in the opposite direction.

This time, Ramón followed the fat man. There was something going on, and Ramón was going to find out what.

Álvaro walked back through the town to the DVD rental shop he owned. When Ramón opened the shop door, Álvaro was busy counting jellies and boiled sweets into freezer bags.

'Getting your lunch ready?' Ramón said.

It took a moment for the fat fuck to realise who it was. Then Álvaro's eyes went wide and his face paled. He started to stammer something about what a surprise it was to see Ramón and when did he get back and hadn't it been a long time and didn't he look good and why hadn't he phoned and where had he been, but when Ramón turned the open sign around so that it showed closed and locked the shop door, Iglesias fell silent. Ramón walked towards him with slow deliberation, leant his fists on the counter and gave Álvaro the hard, threatening look he'd used earlier to silence Acosta.

'I want to know what's going on between you and my nephew. And I'm not leaving until you've told me *everything*.'

'What do you mean? I haven't seen Santi for—'

Ramón struck him an open-handed slap to the face, the way he would have struck a woman. 'Tell me the truth, you fat prick. What's going on? You just saw him.'

Álvaro began to speak, his double chins wobbling as his panic increased, spit flying from his mouth as he babbled.

More lies.

Ramón hit him again, enough to really hurt this time, but still not enough to show him any respect. Álvaro was shaking, but he was still lying, pleading with his hands together.

Ramón hit him again.

Álvaro burst into tears.

'It wasn't me, Ramón,' he said suddenly, the words tumbling over themselves in his desperation to convince, snot pouring from his nose. 'I never touched a hair on her head. You have to believe me. It was *El Porquero*. He was the one that did it. I

116

only got rid of her afterwards. That was the deal. And the business with the landfill: I never meant for it to happen. I didn't think they'd ever find her in among all that rubbish. It was all just a big mistake.'

It took Ramón a moment to realise what he was talking about.

'¡*Joder*! Do you mean the murdered girl? The one that's been all over the papers?'

Álvaro's tears dried as self-interest took over.

'You can't tell anyone, Ramón. It wasn't meant to happen that way.'

Ramón changed tack. He patted the fat man's shoulder and made soft consoling noises.

'Hey, it's me, Álvaro. I wouldn't do anything to hurt you, would I? Not after all the shit we've been through back in the old days.'

Then Ramón pulled up a chair, sat down opposite the counter and said, 'I think you'd better start at the beginning, Álvaro...'

2

Danny awoke late. After his mother had stormed out, he'd remained on the patio, strumming flamenco chords on his guitar while he brooded and drank. Now, he was hungover and worried, as it occurred to him that Adriana Sanchez had driven home with at least a bottle of red wine inside her. He'd so far sent six separate text messages asking his mother to confirm that she had got home safely. She was yet to reply.

He swallowed four Nurofen Express tablets with a pint of water and brewed coffee. He was used to arguing with his mother, but he'd made a real mess of the whole business the night before. He couldn't really imagine having presented the letter in more inauspicious circumstances.

But it was the implications of the letter that really worried Danny.

His grandfather, the *abuelito*, had died when Danny was seven, but he was the closest thing Danny had had to a father. He remembered the man clearly: the homely smell of pipe tobacco that infused his clothing, the conspiratorial wink he always gave as he secretly poured himself a second glass of anis in the mornings — just for the cold, Danny — and the good-natured way he would deflect the *abuela's* nagging.

José Daniel Sanchez had been a hard-working man, but his every spare moment had been dedicated to Danny: paper aeroplanes, skimming stones, climbing trees, jumping streams. It would break Danny's heart if it turned out that Eusebio Sanchez's claims were true.

He had to know, and so the first thing he did was to send a long email to the historian contact he had mentioned to his mother. If the historian did not come up with the goods, then Danny would drive over to Málaga and search through the records himself until he discovered the truth about what had happened with the *abuelito* at the prison.

He thought about Marsha as he typed.

The Skype conversation the day before had ended with Marsha in tears as she explained how, with the help of Lourdes, she had begun contacting olive oil companies in the Málaga area, asking for information on the Sanchez family business and Danny's grandfather, and had ended up with Eusebio Sanchez's name and contact details.

'I just think it's such a fascinating story,' Marsha had said as she sniffed and wiped smeared mascara from her cheeks. 'How the anarchists locked your grandfather up, how your grandmother got him out, how they escaped to Gibraltar and came to England. And then all that stuff about them being ostracised by the Republican exiles in England afterwards. I was sure there was a book in it and I only wanted to help get you started. I know I've taken a terrible liberty, but I did it with for all the right reasons.'

Danny had merely nodded at that. She was right, she had taken a monstrous liberty going poking around in his family history like that. But Danny could not really be angry with Marsha. There was no doubt she had done it with the best of intentions. Marsha was a very get-up-and-go type of person, and when she got the bit between her teeth there was no stopping her.

When Danny finished the email, he made more coffee, and sat down at the table in the corner of the living room that held his magnifying lamp and paintbrushes and pots of paint.

Marsha had given him the 1:72 scale Airfix model set for Christmas, which contained everything needed to recreate a part of the Sword Beach D-Day landings: gun emplacements, landing craft, British and German soldiers. Danny had been genuinely speechless when he unwrapped it.

'I saw the way you were looking at Kevin Spacey's diorama when we were watching *House of Cards*,' she'd said as she snuggled in next to him in bed. 'Then I remembered how your fingernails were always grotty with paint back when we were at school, so I figured you might appreciate a model.'

She'd been right: it was the first time since his childhood anyone had surprised him with a present that he genuinely wanted. Of course, Adriana Sanchez had showered him with gifts as a kid, but there was always the sense that she was trying to make up for not having been there — she had forgotten more of Danny's birthdays than she had remembered, and she'd rarely been there for Christmas.

Danny spent half-an-hour dry-brushing highlights onto the uniforms of his British infantry. Modelling always helped him to feel calmer. He was cleaning his brushes with white spirit when his mobile pinged with an SMS from his mother: *Why would you care if I made it home safely or not?*

Danny put the mobile back in his pocket, feeling better. The petulant tone of the message was a good sign, as it meant his mother's anger was cooling. He would leave it a few days and then ring and sort things out. Hopefully, by then he would have an answer from the historian.

Danny washed his hands, sat outside and browsed the headlines of the Spanish press on his laptop.

Teresa del Hoyo's murder was still front page news in the local press. Most of the articles covered the secrecy surrounding the police investigation, with one article claiming police were close to making an arrest thanks to DNA samples taken from Teresa's body. Danny checked the coverage in all of the newspapers and made sure that nobody had leads on anything he didn't. Then he looked at the rest of the day's news in the local papers. When he saw the headline, EL CERRÓN GRAVE DEFILED, he knew where his day's first port of call would be.

According to the article, a child's burial niche from the 1960s had been smashed open and the rotted remains of the coffin dragged out onto the ground. Worse, the body of the dead child, Manuel Garcia Hernández, had allegedly been stolen. The newspaper had interviewed the now-septuagenarian mother of the dead child. She was quoted as saying, '*It's like losing him a second time...*'

There was a great deal of speculation on the newspaper's internet forums as to why anyone would want to steal the skeletal remains of a baby. A number of theories were posited, from the likely to the ludicrous: sick joke, drunken dare, family feud, Satanic rite. But there was one option nobody had mentioned: what if the body had not been there in the first place?

Danny knew the Spanish journalist who had written the article, so he phoned her.

'Hello, Inma. How'd you get onto this story about the desecrated grave in El Cerrón?'

'I know the family. Apparently, they go there every year to place flowers around the anniversary of the child's death, but when they turned up yesterday morning, they saw the grave had been smashed and that the cemetery workers were trying to hush the whole thing up, so they phoned me.'

'So the grave had been smashed open to coincide with the anniversary of the death? That's interesting.'

'Yeah, it is, but the family has no idea why. The poor thing has been dead more than fifty years. I spoke to the mother, but she wasn't the easiest person to talk to. I think she's starting to lose her marbles. Anyway, the council is going to be holding a press conference at midday if you want to come along.'

Danny asked her for the mother's contact details. When Inma gave him the address of a town close to Almería city, Danny said, 'Do you mean to say the family isn't from El Cerrón?'

'No, the child was stillborn at a clinic that used to be there.'

Danny said nothing. There was the link.

But when Danny thanked Inma, she said, 'Hold on a second. You haven't told me why you're so interested in this. And it's strange that you haven't asked me the clinic's name,' she said slowly. 'It makes me wonder if you don't already know something about this.'

'You'll find out at midday, won't you?' Danny said.

Danny got to the cemetery at 11:30.

El Cerrón's cemetery was surrounded by a high, white wall and would once have been situated far from the urban nucleus, but El Cerrón had expanded so much that the cemetery now faced buildings on the town's outskirts.

Danny smiled to himself as he thought of the *abuela*. The presence of graveyards within English towns had always scandalised the old woman. 'How can these people bear to build their houses next to a place where the dead sleep?' she used to say. 'Perhaps it explains why they are all so pale: the spirits come and scare them witless in the night.'

Burials in Spain usually take place above ground, the bodies interred in long blocks of ossuary niches. The cemetery at El Cerrón was divided into rows of concrete blocks, four inches high, perhaps fifty or sixty long, the blocks situated parallel to each other like bookshelves in a library. Lapidary stones with oval photographs and religious motifs covered the rectangular niches.

Manuel Garcia Hernández's grave was located in a far corner of the cemetery. It was one of the older niches, situated at about chest height. A fluttering X of Guardia Civil incident tape covered the entrance of the niche. The lapidary stone seemed to have been smashed in the centre with a mallet blow: jagged triangular shards of marble were still stuck to each of the four corners. The area below the grave had been swept, but chunks of brick and marble were still visible on the ground. As he looked at it, Danny remembered Guillermo Belasco and his claims that other graves had been desecrated. Danny had forgotten to ask the man about it.

A groundsman was sweeping bay leaves into a dust pan on the cemetery's central walkway. When he saw Danny approach, he threw his cigarette to the ground and screwed it beneath his boot.

'I heard some other graves had been desecrated,' Danny said. 'Can you show me where they are?'

The man's eyes went wide. 'I don't know nothing about that,' he said.

'Do you mean to say it didn't happen? Or that it did happen, but you don't know anything about it? I had it on good authority from someone linked to the council that graves had been desecrated.'

Mention of the council increased the groundsman's agitation. He started sweeping again then realised there was nothing left to sweep. 'I don't know nothing,' he said, spilling dry leaves from the dustpan as he hurried away.

What a curious reaction, Danny thought. Perhaps there was some truth to the story after all.

123

When Danny got to the gates, he found Inma and a few other journalists arguing with a young female representative of the town hall.

'How the hell can this be?' Inma was saying. 'You told me this morning the press conference would be held *here* at the cemetery gates at midday. And now we find that our midday press conference was actually held an hour earlier at the town hall? You expect me to believe that nonsense? Tell me, did anyone actually get this supposed email?'

Danny smiled — a last minute change to a press conference schedule was an old trick when people wanted to avoid commenting on contentious issues — but it worked to his advantage. While Inma and the others continued to argue, Danny slipped away and headed back to his car.

El Cerrón's town hall is a three storey building constructed in the 19th century Spanish style, with high, wide windows. It occupies one end of the town's central plaza; the other three sides are formed by lines of buildings whose first storeys jut forward to form a shaded arcade filled with shops and cafés. As Danny entered the plaza from the far end, the white walls of the buildings shone in the sharp sunlight that had finally broken through the clouds.

Inside the town hall's foyer was a glass case that contained a model of the proposed layout of the Arroyo Springs golf course, with the urbanisation fully realised on the plateau above. Brochures were stuffed into plastic sleeves on one side of the case. They were similar to the brochures Danny had seen at the portacabin, but these were an updated version which drew attention to the "unique investment opportunity" the golf course offered now that a court battle with ecologists had been won. At the bottom of the brochure was a logo Danny recognised: *Grupo Halcón Developments S.L.*

He smiled. So the construction company responsible for the golf course had also planned to build the urbanisation right next door. What a surprise.

Danny was trying to determine which department of the council could give him information on the cemetery when he heard a commotion in the hall behind him: a council session had ended, and the councillors were emerging into the foyer. And there at the centre of a group of suited men was a woman that Danny recognised.

'Señora Encona,' he said in a voice that rose above the hubbub, 'could I ask a quick question?'

3

Carmen del Hoyo stared at the flickering computer screen as the laptop booted up. It felt like she'd been there for hours already.

The problem was, Carmen was no good with computers, and Teresa's laptop used some strange customised version of Windows, which meant nothing was where it was supposed to be. She'd got nowhere the night before. In the end she'd been forced to phone a friend from her church up in Barcelona and ask for advice. The friend asked what it was she was looking for on the laptop.

'That's the problem. I don't know.'

The friend had suggested Carmen check that the documents in each file were arranged according to the last date they had been modified on. That way, she could see what Teresa had last looked at.

The desktop wallpaper was a screenshot of *La Pasionaria*, one arm raised as she declaimed into a microphone. That was no surprise. The wretched woman had been a hero to the whole family, to everyone except Carmen. She had found the church early in life, had always voted for the conservative *Partido Popular* and had never made a secret of it. It had always irritated Carmen that, despite going against everything her family stood for, it was Teresa who had always been seen as the rebel and individualist.

Most of the recent documents on Teresa's laptop related to El Cerrón and the attempts to locate the mass grave where the Republicans had been buried. There were lists of the names of the fourteen victims and details of the victims descendants.

Other Word files detailed all sorts of wild conspiracy theories: that the mayoress of El Cerrón was withholding or had destroyed documents that revealed the whereabouts of the grave, and that her father had been involved in the murders.

From the Word documents on there, it seemed Teresa had made much of the fact that she was related to one of the victims. Of course, there was no mention that the man's brother, Great Uncle Pepe, had had his head smashed open with a spade by anarchists at the beginning of the war. Teresa had conveniently forgotten to mention that. But then this whole business with the civil war graves wasn't about justice, was it? If it had been a simple case of finding the remains of these people and giving them a decent, Christian burial, Carmen would have been behind it. But it wasn't. The search for the bodies was a political act, pure and simple, and Teresa had been too naïve to see it. Also, in the case of El Cerrón, it was highly debatable how innocent the fourteen executed men and women had been. It was almost certain that some of them had taken part in that terrible business at the beginning of the war with the nuns and the well.

The computer's desktop also contained a recently created folder entitled Archive — Scans.

Inside were three PDFs. The first was entitled Santa Cristina — *Legajo de Abortos*. Carmen frowned. It meant Ledger of Stillbirths.

She opened the file and took her reading glasses from their case in her handbag. The file consisted of scans of handwritten pages from a ledger. The handwriting was the same in each case, a smooth, sloping script written with a fountain pen.

As Carmen read through the PDF, she realised the file's name was entirely accurate: it contained scans of pages from a medical ledger for somewhere called the Santa Cristina clinic which recorded incidents of stillbirth. In each case the name of the mother, the child's name, the date of birth and the suspected cause of death was listed. In more than three-quarters of the cases, the cause of death was listed as otitis media.

Carmen's frown deepened. Wasn't that some ear infection? How had so many children died from such a minor ailment? She looked through the PDF file. The dates ran from 1946 until 1969 and there had been dozens deaths from it over the years. In each case, the doctor signed his name only as A.E.

The second PDF contained scans of the admissions book for Santa Cristina. The third held scans of a medical ledger detailing the births that had taken place at Santa Cristina, although this was incomplete — it looked like the scanner had conked out halfway through, as the scans became increasingly blurry towards the end of the PDF.

Was this what Monsignor Melendez had been referring to? Carmen should phone him. But first she wanted to check Teresa's email. The problem was, it was password protected, but Carmen saw there was a button she could click that gave her a clue as to the password: *Russian that resisted.*

That was no bloody use to anyone. What connection did Teresa have to Russia or to Russians? Then she thought of what Monsignor Melendez had said about Vladimir Lopez.

She tried various combinations of the man's name, but it was hopeless. There was nothing to tell her whether the password was in lower or uppercase.

After that, she began to look through Teresa's picture files. There were hundreds of photos from Teresa's childhood. It looked like she had taken all of the old photo albums and made digital scans of them all. The family's entire history was here, black and white photos of her grandparents, blurry old Polaroids from the '80s.

The most recently modified file was one marked *Teresa & Sami (hot stuff!!)*

Carmen clicked the file open.

4

Leticia Encona paused on the stairs that led to the first floor offices and turned to face Danny.

Encona was a short, stocky woman in her late sixties, her hair and clothing obviously chosen to enhance a femininity that she'd failed to conjure up: despite the softly coiffured lines of her fringe and the pastel hues of her skirt suit, there was something unattractive about the aggressive jut of her jaw and the faint sneer on her thick lips.

'I remember you,' she said, fixing her eyes on Danny. 'The English journalist. What do you want?'

'I have a question about the recent desecration of graves at the local cemetery. Have you got any information on it? Because the groundsman at the cemetery obviously knew something, but seemed scared to speak about it.'

Sudden silence descended on the room. The mayoress smiled the way all politicians do when a question has thrown them, while a portly, well-dressed man with dark, curly hair stepped forward and whispered something in her ear. She listened and nodded.

'I can confirm that another grave was damaged, but it was nothing serious. We speculate that it was adolescents in both cases.'

'Why wasn't it reported?'

'If we were to issue a press release every time teenagers broke something, newspapers would be the size of telephone directories.'

Her flunkies laughed and directed their laughter towards Danny.

'So it wasn't left-wing extremists that desecrated the grave then?'

That shut the whole room up again. The suited man behind Encona did more whispering, but this time she shoved his hand away and stared Danny down.

'Who told you that it was?'

'I can't reveal my source.'

She sneered. 'Then I suggest you go and speak to this source if he knows so much.'

'What about the Arroyo Springs project? Is it still going ahead, or is it now officially a dead duck?'

'As I've explained to the press on a number of occasions, the Arroyo Springs project encountered a minor setback thanks to the actions of a group of known troublemakers, but the council's policy has now been completely vindicated by the courts. Leave your name with my press officer and we'll email you as much information on the project as you need. And now if you'll permit me, I have work to attend to.'

Danny was heading towards the door when he felt a tap on his shoulder. The curly-haired man from the staircase was standing behind him, his hand extended.

'Hello,' he said. 'My name is Santiago Encona. I'm the mayoress's press officer. Can I buy you a coffee, Señor Sanchez?'

Danny accepted the man's soft, moist handshake. 'Any relation to the mayoress?'

'I'm her son,' he said.

Yes, Danny could see the resemblance now: they had the same broad face and heavy features.

They walked to one of the cafés in the plaza outside. Danny ordered iced coffee, Encona 'his usual'. Danny noticed the waiter hurried to bring them the order and ignored other customers in the process.

'So, you work for *Sureste News*,' Santiago Encona said, beaming like it was the most exciting thing he'd ever heard.

'I do some freelance work for them.'

'That's quite fortuitous. The council has been thinking of advertising in the British press.'

Danny said nothing. Encona continued to beam at him as Danny lit a cigarette.

With his expensive suit, 300 Euro shoes and masses of cologne, Encona had the pro-politician look down perfectly, but there was something about him that made Danny think he wasn't quite as competent and controlled as he looked. He had missed a patch shaving, his eyes were bloodshot and bagged, and there was a spot of blood on his white collar. He looked stressed. It was a look Danny was unused to seeing in Spanish politicians, especially ones who had been appointed to positions by their mothers.

'Was it Señor Belasco that told you about the other grave?' Encona said.

'As I told your mother, I don't reveal my sources. But why is it the groundsman at the cemetery was so jumpy when I asked about the desecrated graves? I mean, I'm guessing he's on the council payroll.'

'I've no idea. It's not really my remit. Perhaps it might help if you told me why you're so interested in what happened at the cemetery?' Encona said.

'It's part of something else I'm looking into.'

'Which is?'

'You know that building up on the plateau above the golf course? Santa Cristina. I've been told at the municipal archive that certain documents relating to the building were recently

132

stolen. And the man that likely took them is now dead. It could be the two are connected. And I'm curious as to why the council decided not to publicise the theft.'

The edges of Encona's smile sagged.

'I don't know anything about that,' he said.

'Really? Because if the council had decided not to issue a press release, surely that decision would have come from you, wouldn't it?'

'Listen,' Encona said, straightening his tie. 'This is precisely the reason I wanted to speak to you. There are certain business deals currently being finalised that might be negatively affected by bad publicity centred on El Cerrón. The last thing we need now are wild allegations of desecrated graves and medical files going missing.'

'So you *did* decide to hush up the theft from the archive?'

'No.'

'So how did you know they were medical files that had gone missing?'

Encona was getting really flustered now. 'I didn't say... I mean, perhaps someone might have mentioned something. But I wouldn't have known personally. I'd have to—'

'I hope you don't play cards, Señor Encona — not with a poker face like that. So what's this business deal you mentioned? Do you mean the golf course?'

Encona did — that much was obvious from his sudden inability to meet Danny's eyes — but he said, 'I'm not at liberty to say. But I can assure you this business at the cemetery is absolutely nothing of consequence. That is why the council is only interested in seeing hard facts go into print.'

'Hard facts? Doesn't that normally mean "your version", or am I being cynical?'

'Listen,' Encona said, leaning forward in his chair and lowering his voice, 'the council will happily work with you on any stories you want to do. All I'm saying is that we'd want to read what you wrote before it went into print. Because, as I mentioned before, we *are* considering advertising and I'm sure we could make it go your newspaper's way. And, naturally, if it did, I'd be sure to mention your name...'

Danny nodded as he considered this. Then he looked Encona full in the face. 'Have you been the council's press secretary long?'

'Why do you ask?'

'Because I've been a journalist 20 years, and I don't think I've ever heard a more ham-fisted attempt at offering me a kickback.'

Encona's chair scraped as he stood up. Without the 100-watt smile, his face had a shrewish quality to it.

'I've tried to be reasonable, Señor Sanchez, but I can see you are not a professional. Print anything defamatory, and I'll see you in court.'

He left without shaking Danny's hand. And without paying, Danny realised when the man had gone.

Danny was hungry, so he stayed at the table and ordered a Coca Cola and some food. When he was done eating, he phoned Julio, a radio reporter whose family was from the south of Almería province.

'What can you tell me about the council in El Cerrón?' Danny said when Julio answered. 'How corrupt is it?'

'About usual for Andalusia.'

'That bad, eh?'

Julio laughed. 'Think Tammany Hall with sunshine and mountains and you've more or less got it. Mayoress Encona has had the entire town sewn up for the last God-knows-how-many years. Her brother-in-law is the chief of police and the council offices are filled with her cousins, nephews and nieces; every business, shop and trader has to go through her. Clientalism doesn't even begin to describe what she's set up there — it's almost feudal.'

'Why do people keep voting for her, then?'

'Money. Businessmen love her, because she's ridden roughshod over every legal and ethical premise in order to expand the town. It has more than tripled in size since she got hold of the reins. That meant a hell of a lot of business at the beginning.

'Also, her father was a prominent Falangist during the dictatorship and the town's first elected mayor when Spain became a democracy. Leticia took over directly from him, so the town has been Encona-run since 1978.'

'What was the father's name?'

'Amancio Encona. But he was before my time, so I didn't really have much to do with him. He died in the late nineties.'

'What about Santiago Encona?'

Julio scoffed. 'He's been riding *mamá's* coattails since he was a teenager. He's had all the money and business connections anyone could hope for handed to him on a plate, but everything he touches turns to shit. He used to have quite an appetite for the sordid side of life back in the day — drugs, booze, hookers, that sort of thing — but I think *mamá* laid down the law and he's cleaned up his act.'

'So when did he start as his mother's press secretary?'

'As I said, when it came to honest toil, Santiago was hindered by a lack of both appetite and aptitude, so it was a given he was going to end up in politics sooner or later. But he's only really the press secretary in name. I very much doubt he's allowed to draft any press releases. He's not the sharpest tool in the box.'

'What about the name Santa Cristina? Does that ring any bells?'

'Vaguely. Wasn't it a health clinic that burned down? Why do you ask?'

'Santiago didn't seem to appreciate my asking about it in connection to that golf course they want to build up there.'

'Ah, well he wouldn't. You see, he's part of the consortium that bought the land.'

'Santiago Encona is a part of *Grupo Halcón Developments*?'

'Yes. But that's common knowledge around town, and all the paperwork is in order. I know, as I've checked. They bought the land from the church back in the early noughties. Besides, the Arroyo Springs project died a death a long time ago.'

'Not according to Santiago Encona.'

'Well, that just shows how dumb he really is. The whole country is falling apart because of the construction bubble, there are more than a million unsold new homes, and yet Santiago Encona is *still* convinced he can refloat a project that involves building hundreds of time share apartments. I think part of the problem is that he sank so much of his own money into it, he has to try and make it work.

'But if you're looking for dirt on the Encona family, there's an interesting titbit I picked up the other day: Ramón Encona is back from wherever the hell he's been for the last eighteen years.'

'And who's he?'

'Ramón is the family's dirty little secret. Herminia Encona is the mayoress's aunt, Amancio's sister. Ramón is her boy.'

'So he's Santiago's uncle?'

'Technically, yes. But there's only a few years' difference between them, so they're more like cousins.'

'And I take it this Ramón Encona is a wrongun?'

'Oh, yes, absolutely venomous. I remember him from school. He had a cruel streak a mile wide. I remember one time, Ramón smeared an entire tube of superglue over the palm of a leather glove and stuck it to an older boy's face. It was a miracle the kid didn't suffocate. Being an Encona, though, nothing ever came of it.

'But unlike Santiago, he's not dumb. They used to run around together as young men. That was when Ramón was dealing drugs. Santiago used to trail around after him, stuffing cocaine up his nose. Then there was some scandal and Ramón disappeared. Rumour has it, Leticia paid him to go away and stay away. That was, up until last month.'

'Any idea why he's back?'

'Rumour has it the mother is on the way out, so he might have been lured back by the thought of his inheritance. But who knows with a guy like that? Perhaps he outstayed his welcome wherever the hell it is he's been. I'll tell you one thing, though: unless age has mellowed the guy, it won't be long before he starts causing trouble.'

5

When Ramón had milked Álvaro Iglesias for every last detail on the girl's murder, he went to one of the bars in the town's central plaza and began to watch the town hall. Screw the agreement he had made with Cousin Leticia. He was going to speak to Santiago. And then he was going to break the bastard, the way he'd used to break the girls back in Seville. He just had to find the right moment to approach him.

Ramón's mind was racing. What Iglesias had told him was barely credible — but that was why it had the unmistakable ring of truth. And it was typical of Santiago to have orchestrated such a monstrous cluster-fuck.

According to Iglesias, it had all started the week before when Santi had offered to pay Álvaro to go burgle some old man's house in Enix. Álvaro had been vague on the precise details of why Santi had wanted him to do it, but fatso had been certain about one thing: someone was trying to blackmail Santiago.

'Something had happened at the cemetery,' Álvaro had said, 'and then Santi found out the Reds had stolen a box of medical files from the municipal archive and were using it to try and screw him over. So he paid me and *El Porquero* to go break into this house, but we didn't find the files he wanted. All we got were three old ledgers from some health clinic.'

Ramón had nearly broken into laughter at that point. What a couple of burglars to choose: Álvaro, the morbidly obese blubber-butt, and *El Porquero*, a congenital idiot. But that was all to the good: if Ramón played his cards right, his financial problems were sorted. Because if anyone was going to be screwing Little Santi over for money, it was going to be Ramón. They were family, after all.

A little after midday, Ramón saw Santiago exit the town hall with a blonde, curly-haired man who wore jeans and a denim jacket and carried a camera and shoulder bag. Ramón watched them take a table on the patio of a bar on the opposite side of the plaza. The man looked foreign, but there was no doubt they were speaking in Spanish: despite his expensive schooling, Santiago's grasp of foreign languages was non-existent.

Ramón supposed the man must be a journalist. After all, little Santi was mummy's press secretary now, wasn't he? Ramón wondered how many of the press releases Cousin Leticia actually allowed the dumb bastard to write. Not many, if she had any sense.

After five minutes, Santiago Encona rose suddenly and walked away from the table. He and the journalist had not parted on good terms — Ramón recognised the pissy look on Santiago's face from when they were children, that look spoiled kids have when they fail to get their own way.

Ramón followed Santiago across town and watched him climb into his Jaguar, perform an illegal U-turn and race away towards the old bullring. Ramón watched the car until it was out of sight. If Santiago had taken the road east out of town, he must be going to Uncle Amancio's old house. Mother had said something about Santiago inheriting the place. That was good. It meant Ramón could get to speak to him alone.

Although Ramón was technically a cousin to Santiago's mother, he was only two years older than Santi. As the elder child, Ramón had delighted in getting his nephew in trouble. It had been the one thing that made any sense in Ramón's childhood. They could lavish all the gifts and attention they wanted on Santiago, but nothing would change the fact that the foundations of his whole being were built on sand.

As adults, Ramón had watched with glee as Santiago stumbled from one disaster to the next. He'd been handed endless business opportunities, and every one had gone belly-up thanks to Santiago's combination of poor judgement and arrogance. And then there had been the scandals: drunken car crashes, fights, affairs. Only Santiago's surname and his mother's influence had seen him through.

Well, mummy wasn't going to get little Santi out of this one.

The country house was a huge three-storey place halfway up a mountain, surrounded by fields of olive trees that stretched away to the horizon, more than fifty acres of the damned things. Ramón parked in the road outside. The trees were heavy with olives and the air had an oily tang to it. The property's driveway was a hundred yards long and shaded by trellised grape vines. The afternoon sun shone through the green canopy as Ramón walked towards the house.

Santiago was outside, giving orders to the workers who maintained the property's grounds. Astonishment showed on his nephew's face when he saw Ramón sauntering towards the house. They made momentary eye contact, then Santiago turned away and walked inside. The property's head groundsman came towards Ramón, shaking his head and indicating that he come no closer.

'You can't come in here, Ramón,' he said. 'You know the rules. If you don't—'

'Tell Santiago I know about the girl. I'll wait here while you deliver the message,' Ramón said, sitting down on a stone bench.

A minute passed, then Santiago reappeared.

'What do you mean?' he said. He was trying to bluff, but he had already dropped his voice and begun to steer Ramón away from the workers. 'I've no idea what you're talking about. What girl? If my mother finds out—'

'I've just spoken with Álvaro Iglesias. The fat bastard has ratted you out, *primo*.'

Ramón watched with satisfaction as Santiago's face paled and he looked back over his shoulder. The workers were all staring at them.

'Meet me at La Piltra,' he said.

La Piltra was a small house on the far side of the property, a kilometre from the main house. It was where they had used to go as young men to party. Ramón drove there at a leisurely pace. Ten minutes later, Santiago's car skidded to a halt on the gravel outside.

'Listen, Ramón, I don't know what that fat idiot has told you, but I can assure you it's all—'

'I'll tell you exactly what he told me: he says it was all your fault.'

'My fault? How the hell does he work that one out?'

'As far as he's concerned, he went to the old man's house on your orders to steal some medical ledgers or something. And as for the girl, well, that was all down to *El Porquero*.'

'That's bullshit,' Santiago hissed. The look on his face pleaded for understanding. 'I never meant for them to hurt anyone. The old man was supposed to be out all night speaking at a political demonstration. But he came back early and caught them at the house. Then he set about them with some ruddy sword stick he had on him. He stabbed Álvaro in the leg. When *El Porquero* tried to restrain him, the old bastard collapsed and died.'

'I know,' Ramón said. 'And the girl saw everything. So they panicked and bundled her into the boot of Álvaro's car.'

Santiago was shaking his head, speaking faster now as indignation overcame caution.

'The dumb bastards hadn't even had the sense to wear masks. I was in Madrid when it happened. I didn't find out they had the girl captive until I came back on the Thursday night. Álvaro phoned me on my home number to ask what he should do with her.'

Ramón could guess how that conversation had gone. Santiago wouldn't have come right out and told him to kill her — he was just about smart enough to have figured that bit out — but he would have known her captivity could have come back to bite him on the arse. Self-preservation had always been Santi's default setting. The girl had seen everything and she could identify her kidnappers. That meant definite prison time for everyone involved. So Santi would have thrown money at the problem and then washed his hands of it.

'Do you know how *El Porquero* killed her?' Ramón said.

'Jesus, of course not. And I don't want to either.'

Ramón examined his fingernails. He was enjoying himself now. 'Álvaro told me all about it. You know why they call him *El Porquero*, don't you?'

'His father was a swineherd.'

'That's right. So the only thing he'd ever killed before were pigs...'

He let the implications of that sink in. Santiago gave a low moan as his head sank between his hands.

Ramón said, 'It's one of the reasons poor Álvaro is so shaken up: she was still dangling there when he went to collect the body.

'Of course, you and I know why *El Porquero* did it that way,' he said, keeping his tone conversational. He really wanted to make the bastard suffer now. 'But what do you think the police will make of it? Cruel and unusual, that's what they'll think. Sadistic. Stuff like that really gets them lathered up. They'll pull out all the stops to find the bastard who did it.'

'But they won't find him, will they? I mean, there's absolutely nothing to link them to the girl. It was all so random, anyway.'

'True enough. And Álvaro had the sense to drive the girl's car away from the house and dump it somewhere else, so the police probably won't make the link between the burglary and her death. But I guess it all depends on whether *El Porquero* got horny while he had the girl up there at the old slaughterhouse.'

Santiago's eyes went wide.

'Do you think he raped her?'

'She was there for two whole days before he killed her. Do you seriously think that dumb animal managed to keep his hands off such a pretty young thing for all that time? Bearing in mind he used to boast about fucking his father's pigs.'

'Oh, Jesus. But how does that affect us?'

Us. Ramón smiled inwardly. He'd forgotten how easy it was to play Santi.

'It only matters if *El Porquero* has done prison time.'

'He has.'

'What for?'

'Statutory rape. With one of his nieces.'

Ramón pretended he didn't already know this and drew his breath sharply.

'If he's got prior for a sexual offence, the police might have taken a DNA sample from him. And if he didn't have the good sense to wear a mask to a burglary, do you seriously think he would have ensured the girl's body was DNA clean? They can get it from anything nowadays: semen, pubes, a flake of skin under a fingernail.

'And if they do come up with *El Porquero's* name, it's going to be bad news. You can never tell what a halfwit like that is going to say, can you? The police will dance rings around him.'

Understanding finally dawned on Santiago's face. He moaned and put his head in his hands.

'But don't worry, *primo*. I can help you.'

'How?'

Ramón patted him reassuringly on the back. 'Let's just say, if you're in the market for a permanent solution to the problem *El Porquero* poses, I'm your man. But I warn you: it's not going to be easy. Or cheap.'

6

Josefina Hernández lived in a small hamlet, one of dozens like it in the province of Almería where the line between rural and urban was unclear. Danny parked outside a cafeteria filled with glass and shining chrome, but had to pick his way across a street littered with goat droppings.

Josefina Hernández was typical of her generation. She had the crook-backed, bow-legged stance of someone who had spent a life stooping in fields and spoke the thick, lisping Spanish of the Andalusian pueblos.

When Danny arrived, she was in the yard beside her house throwing cornmeal to a group of scrawny chickens. He took some photos of her among the hens, then they went inside to the living room.

First communion photos of grandchildren in sailor suits and lacy dresses fought for space with gaudy gilt-edged images and statuettes of the *Virgen del Mar*, the patron saint of Almería. The television was tuned to a local channel running a phone-in tarot card reading service. Piety and superstition together in the same room: that too was typical of people like Josefina Hernández, a reminder that a different Spain existed beneath the patina of money and modernity democracy had brought. *La España profunda* it was called, Deep Spain, a country of superstition and ignorance, of secrets and spite, a place where the edges of Spain's First World status began to fray.

A thick-armed man in builder's clothing came in as Josefina poured coffee and was introduced as José, her youngest son. 'A fine looking boy,' Danny said when he went into the kitchen to fetch milk.

Boy. Not man: a subtle way of reminding Josefina why he was there.

That was rule number one when dealing with delicate interviews: let the interviewee choose their moment to approach the subject. Not only was it common human decency, it was the only way to get all the information. With a story like this, facts were like a flock of birds at rest: rush at them and they would simply flutter away.

'I suppose you want to know about this business with Manuel and the grave?' she said eventually as she settled on the sofa. Her son sat next to her, his thick arm wrapped protectively around her shoulders.

'If you feel up to it.'

She nodded.

'When was Manuel born?' Danny asked.

'October 13th, 1961.'

'Where?'

'In a hospital. Or rather a clinic. The doctors said it would be a difficult birth as it was my first so I was taken to a private clinic.'

'That must have been expensive.'

'It was an act of charity. A priest organised it. They came for me in an ambulance.' She sounded rather proud of the fact. 'But my other children were born at home.'

'Do you remember the name of the clinic?'

'Of course: Santa Cristina. I remember it as that was my sister's name.'

'How many children do you have?'

'Four. That lived. Manuel died of complications soon after I gave birth.'

'What do you think happened to Manuel's grave?'

Her head dropped. When she spoke again, the words were a whisper. 'That? It was destiny.'

'Destiny?'

'It was God's punishment. His wrath.'

'I'm sorry. I don't understand.'

She stood and opened a drawer in an old sideboard.

'I did not show this photo to the other reporters. They were children themselves. They were too young to see such things.'

She walked toward Danny but paused in the middle of the room, stroking the surface of the photo with her index finger. '*Mi sol, mi vida, mi alma,*' she said: my sun, my life, my soul.

They were whispered words Danny recognised from his own childhood, the tender words Spaniards use to address their children and grandchildren. A single tear rolled across the pitted surface of her face as she handed Danny the photo. José put his arm around his mother's shoulder again.

It took a moment for Danny to realise the woman in the black and white photo was Josefina: not only was she fifty years younger, the expression on her face was twisted by exhaustion and grief as she stood in a nightshirt holding a swaddled child. The baby's eyes were closed. It took a moment for the implications of what Danny was looking at to sink in.

'They photographed you holding your dead child?' Danny said.

'Yes!' The old woman's voice was fraught with emotion. 'And that is how I know the poor thing was cursed.'

'Cursed? How?'

She sank into a chair, staring at the trembling hands in her lap. 'Manuel was my first child. I married on April 12th, 1961. He was born in October.'

April to October.

Six months.

'That's right,' she said, seeing realisation dawn on Danny's face. 'We cursed that poor child with our sin. Two years we were engaged and not once did my sweet husband ever pressure me, may he rest in peace.' She made the sign of the cross. 'But one night I thought "well we are to marry anyway" and...'

Her head bowed in shame.

'And you think that cursed the child?'

'I know it for a fact. That photo was taken twenty minutes after I gave birth, and when I held the child he was cold. Do you hear me? Cold like a tombstone. So that is what I think happened at the graveyard.' She waved a forefinger towards the ceiling. 'God's wrath. He does not forget. They used to say that about the bodies of the Reds they executed after the war, that the earth would spit the bones up as it did not want them. This is the same. The child was conceived out of wedlock and now he has been taken from sacred ground. The police said there was nothing left of him. Not a single bone. He has paid the price for our sin. For my sin.'

Tears rolled along the wrinkled seams of her face. José patted his mother's arm.

'I think she's had enough questions,' he said. 'But I'll walk you out, Señor Sanchez.'

On the pavement outside, José lit a cigarette and offered one to Danny.

'You must understand, my mother is from a different generation,' he said. 'She grew up after the war. Spain was another country back then. Women received little or no education, and what they did receive came from the church. And my mother was from a family of Reds. The children of those families were always singled out for special treatment by the priests and nuns, to make sure they grew up with a really healthy fear of damnation.' He sneered. 'I've never set foot in a fucking church since I became a man. But the real reason I wanted to speak to you is to ask what *you* think really happened at Manuel's grave.'

José watched Danny's face carefully.

'I don't think Manuel's body was ever in the grave,' Danny said.

José nodded, as if that was what he'd been expecting to hear.

'Ever since this business about the illegal adoptions began to hit the news, I feared something terrible had happened. But please understand, my mother would not survive knowing the truth. She is old and frail and even the suspicion that her first born was stolen would finish her. That's why my brothers and sisters and I have decided that we will look for our brother once mother has passed and not before.

'I don't know what you plan on writing, but I implore you not to mention anything that might lead my mother to suspecting the truth.'

'I understand that completely,' Danny said. 'You have my word that I won't mention anything that could upset your mother.'

They shook hands.

José said, 'In that case, I can tell you that my mother did not tell you the whole story.'

'Should I be getting my notebook and pen out again?'

He nodded. 'My brother, Manuel, was supposedly stillborn, which meant he died without being baptised. And one of the nuns at that Santa Cristina place was on at my mother from the second Manuel died, telling her that his soul was doomed to eternity in purgatory. Imagine that: minutes after giving birth, not only do they tell you your child is dead, they start banging on about his fucking place in heaven.

'Anyway, this nun said that she could take care of the body and ensure it was buried on holy ground — as long as my mother let the clinic take care of the burial.

'She said the nuns could pray for an intercession for Manuel and that God, in his infinite mercy, would allow him entrance into heaven — but that if my mother insisted on trying to claim the body for herself, this nun would ensure the child was taken away and buried among the heretics at the English Cemetery and that the child would be doubly damned. The cynical bitch.'

'Do you know the nun's name?' Danny asked.

'Yes. I made a point of finding it out: Sister María Pilar Arriola.'

7

Back in the mid-nineties, there had been a time when Ramón Encona supplied most of the drugs that were sold in and around El Cerrón. He had been exceptionally good at dealing drugs because, unlike those around him, he'd never developed an appetite for substances he sold: dope made him listless and paranoid, pills made him sick, and cocaine gave him palpitations.

Primitivo Pozos — or *El Porquero* as he was known in the town — had been one of his best customers, and had acted as Ramón's enforcer when people were late with payments. The good thing about Pozos was that, besides being built like a draught-horse, he was remedial, which made him exceptionally easy to manipulate, and he had always accepted his payment in cocaine or pills.

Ramón hoped his appetite for drugs was still the same as it used to be.

Pozos lived at the old slaughterhouse his father had once owned. Ramón remembered the place as having been dirty but functional, the way rural places with animals always were, but when he rounded the corner in the dry riverbed that led to the property, he saw the place was now practically derelict.

A small flat-roofed house overlooked a wide yard of beaten earth surrounded by mud walls which had crumbled away to nothing in some places. A confused mass of black cables and peeling duct tape hung from the roof, connecting the house to the electricity. Beyond this was the wooden gate that led to the slaughterhouse, a building made from concrete and breeze blocks. There was no glass in the windows of the slaughterhouse and Ramón could see that part of the ceiling had collapsed inwards.

Weeds poked through the cracked surface of the concrete pathway that led to the house's door, and rusting pieces of equipment littered the yard: ladders, tool boxes, a cement mixer. The window of the house was open and Ramón could hear the tinny sound of a television from within.

Pozos's van was parked close to the slaughterhouse. Ramón crept to the driver's side door and tried it. The vehicle was not locked, so he quietly opened the door and took the paperclip from his pocket. He had unwound the thing earlier so that it formed a single length of metal, and he slipped this into the keyhole of the ignition, and waggled it back and forth, so that it went in nice and deep. Then he snapped it off and closed the vehicle's door.

From here, he could see inside the half of the slaughterhouse that was still intact. A filthy mattress lay on the floor and he could see the rusty hooks and chains that were once used for hanging slaughtered pigs while they bled out.

That was where the del Hoyo girl had been imprisoned and where she had died. Ramón shook his head in disbelief as he examined the place: fresh spatters of blood were clearly visible on the inside of the door and on the walls. Ramón bet the whole place was filled with traces of the girl's DNA. It was a wonder the police hadn't arrested the lot of them already.

A wooden coop beside the slaughterhouse held six or seven scrawny looking chickens. And there was a dog, too, a miserable bag of bones that was tied to a tree with a length of washing line barely six feet in length. Ramón's eyes narrowed as he looked at the dog, then he looked towards the house. He was going to enjoy this.

Ramón crossed the yard and knocked on the door of corrugated metal. The television went quiet, someone fumbled with the lock, and the door creaked inwards.

Time had done nothing to improve *El Porquero's* looks. His single eyebrow still rode low above his deep eye sockets, and his face was a physical embodiment of the neglect outside, an effect heightened by-his-now piebald scalp. It was a drinker's face, and the whites of the man's eyes were greyish and bloodshot. Some of his muscle had turned to fat, but he was still a big man: 6' 4" and at least eighteen stone.

'Ramón?' Pozos said slowly. 'Is that you?'

'In the flesh.'

'When'd you get back?'

'Not long ago.'

El Porquero wore a ratty old dressing gown. He stood staring stupidly at Ramón, his brow furrowed as he tried to process the information.

'What do you want?' Pozos said.

'Is that anyway to greet an old friend? Aren't you going to invite me in?'

Pozos's house was really just a box of bricks and cement. There were no rooms as such, just a single rectangular space. Plastic buckets stood beneath a sink filled with unwashed plates. Half-a-dozen plastic bin-liners lay beside it, overflowing with empty tins and crumpled cans. A small television sat atop a plastic crate, a filthy sofa placed before it. Apart from a rickety wooden chair and a pile of cushions set out as a bed, it comprised the only furniture.

The interior smelt strongly of a number of things, none of them pleasant: damp, sweat, unwashed clothes, rotten food. And alcohol — not the wholesome smell of a pub, more the stink of the bins out the back. Empty bottles and crumpled cans littered every horizontal surface.

Ramón knew that the best lies always use as much of the truth as possible, so when he'd sat down and done a bit of catching up, he began telling Pozos about when and why he had come back to town, and about his time at the whorehouses and the police raid that had broken it up.

Pozos rolled a cigarette from a plastic bag filled with butts and his big wet mouth hung open as he listened to Ramón describe the types of clothes the girls had used to wear and what they had charged for the different services. As Ramón talked, he saw the big man had put his hand in the pocket of the dressing gown and was rubbing his crotch.

Ramón pretended not to notice and began to explain that he was planning on starting up dealing drugs again.

'I figure I'll start off with coke. That never goes out of fashion, does it? I'll buy it in 100 gram batches, and cut it the way we used to: a bit of glucose and a touch of that lidocaine gel to give it a nice numb when it hits the back of the throat. Do you remember?'

Pozos remembered all right. He was licking his lips and a hungry light shone in his bloodshot eyes.

'And that's why I'll need your help,' Ramón said, leaning forward to pat Pozos on the arm. 'I'll need you to handle the distribution, the delivery and the collection of payments — all the sort of stuff you used to do for me. And of course, I'll pay you the old way. Is that of any interest to you?'

Pozos nodded his head eagerly. Then he asked the question Ramón had been hoping he would ask.

'Have you got any on you now?'

'Any what?'

'Coke.'

Ramón gave him a knowing smile.

'You mean you want an advance?'

'No, I'll pay. I've got money here.'

'OK,' Ramón said, rummaging in his pocket and withdrawing a twist of plastic. 'This is top quality draw, so it's 50 Euros for the half-gram. But you're an old friend, so I'll give you a full gram for the same price.'

Pozos rummaged for money in a plastic bag. Ramón took the filthy, wrinkled notes from him and dropped the wrap into the man's big, leathery palm. Then he stood up.

'Anyway, I've got things to do. Shall I swing past here tomorrow and collect you? We'll get things rolling.'

'Don't you wanna do a line?' Pozos said as he wiped a plate clean.

'Nah, it never really agreed with me. Still, that leaves all the more for you.'

Pozos grasped his hand.

'Thanks for this, Ramón.'

Ramón patted him on the shoulder. 'You enjoy the coke. There'll be plenty more where that comes from.'

Outside, Ramón held his breath until he was twenty yards beyond the house, then sucked in the clean air. It would take him a week to get the stink of that shithole out of his nostrils. Once his nausea had subsided, he walked a little way back along the dry riverbed and squatted in the bushes to wait.

Back in Seville, there had been a Catalan who claimed to have killed a love rival by mixing rat poison with the guy's heroin. Ramón hoped the same premise was going to work with cocaine.

Earlier that afternoon, Ramón had driven to Almería city, walked up into the La Chanca district and bought a gram of cocaine from one of the gypsy kids that sold it on the street.

Then he went back to his flat, crushed up the pellets of rat poison he'd also purchased, and mixed them with the cocaine.

Hopefully, with the dim lighting inside the house, Pozos would not notice the strange colour of the cocaine he was about to snort: the poison pellets had been grey. The man's size also worried Ramón. There was no knowing whether the dose would be high enough to kill a fucking ogre like that.

Time would tell.

Ramón leant against a tree trunk. He felt dirty all over, as if cockroaches were crawling on his skin. When he got home he would need to stand under the shower for a whole hour. There was nothing Ramón hated as much as feeling dirty...

Ramón was eleven years old the first time he hit Mother. It happened early one morning when she had decided to beat him for not making his bed properly, and Ramón's temper had snapped and he had walloped her across the face. The blow had not been hard enough to truly hurt her, but her eyes had gone wide with a fury so fierce that Ramón had fled the house.

He'd been naïve enough to think that by staying away he could escape Mother's wrath. But hours later, when he was walking the streets, Uncle Amancio's car had skidded to a halt beside him.

Uncle Amancio had beaten the shit out of him right there in the middle of the town. It had stopped traffic on the main street as his uncle kicked and punched Ramón across the road from one pavement to the other, the first real stomping of Ramón's life.

Then, once Ramón was bloodied and dazed, Uncle Amancio had bundled Ramón into the boot of the car, driven him back to Mother's house and dragged him up to the rooftop terrace.

Ramón had thought the man meant to throw him off the house and kill him — he knew the stories about what his uncle had done to the Reds after the war — but instead, Amancio had dragged Ramón by his hair towards the place where Mother had four chicken coops beneath an awning.

He had pulled one of the coops out into the centre of the roof, pushed Ramón inside and locked it. Then he pushed it on to its back, so that the wire front faced upwards, and went back downstairs.

The coop was so small that Ramón could neither stand nor lie down. He had knelt as best he could inside, his knees and hands slicked with chicken shit and feathers.

But that wasn't the punishment.

By ten in the morning, the July sun had rounded the house's chimney and begun to shine fully on the coop. They had left him there all day. By that point Ramón had been shaking and weeping in a delirium of thirst and exhaustion, his skin burnt red raw.

When Uncle Amancio finally dragged him from the coop, Mother had stood behind his shoulder, laughing. Amancio had stood over Ramón and said, 'If you ever lay a hand on anyone of my blood again, you'll get the same. Remember that.'

Ramón had remembered it. And, six months later, when Ramón had belted Mother again, he'd been ready for Uncle Amancio. The fat prick had come flying round to the house in a rage and tried to repeat the rooftop stunt, but Ramón had been ready for him and had slashed open the meat of the man's palm with a kitchen knife.

It had been one of the sweetest moments of Ramón's childhood. He could still picture the look of genuine terror in Amancio's eyes as he stumbled backwards, his hand pissing blood, and realised that the child in front of him could easily poke those seven inches of razor sharp steel into his belly or his chest or his eyes.

Ramón had waved the knife towards him and said, 'If you ever lay a hand on *me* again, I'll kill you.'

He knew that the threat had worked, because he had heard Amancio shouting downstairs afterwards: 'From now on, he's your problem, Herminia. I never want to set eyes on him again. He's all yours now...'

That event had been the first real triumph of Ramón's life, but as he grew older his memories of the experience had soured. He found himself thinking less of besting Uncle Amancio, and more of that first time when the fat prick had kicked him senseless in the middle of the street.

Ramón had initially assumed the reason no one stepped in to prevent a grown man from beating the shit out of an eleven-year-old was because they were all afraid of Amancio — after all, he had been a powerful man back then, both physically and politically — but later on, as snapshot memories of the onlookers' faces had began to appear in his dreams, he had realised the truth: no one had stopped Amancio because they were all glad he was doing it. In fact, some of the men and women had been smiling and laughing as they watched.

The realisation of that was like a red raw splinter lodged deep down in the very belly of his being. From that moment on, he had never been able to shake the feeling that people were secretly laughing at him. And it was why he'd always known that, long before things went belly up in Seville, he would one day return to El Cerrón. He had unfinished business here. One day, he was going to find some way to show the ignorant peasants here who the fuck Ramón Encona really was...

The door to Primitivo Pozos's house burst open with a bang and the big man emerged, coughing and choking and clutching at his neck, hawking and spitting like he had something stuck at the back of his throat. Halfway across the yard, he suddenly went into a spasm and fell to the ground. Ramón peered around the side of the tree and watched as the muscles and tendons in the big man's face, neck and arms bulged and contorted.

The spasm passed and Pozos staggered to his feet. But when he got to his car, Ramón heard him scream in frustration. There was no way to get the key into the ignition. Ramón had planned the whole thing well.

Pozos staggered back towards the house, but then another spasm hit him and he fell.

His death took nearly an hour. It was a fascinating process to watch. Each seizure was more severe than the last, and the interval between them became progressively shorter. A weaker man might have succumbed more quickly, but Pozos kept getting up. Even when the seizures had locked into a near continuous spasm and his back was arching upwards so far that Ramón thought his spine must break, he still managed to claw at the door of the car.

Finally, he fell silent.

Ramón waited five minutes then went over to check he was dead. Pozos was rigid as a post, his face locked into a hideous grimace, the eyes bloodied and bulging outwards like boiled eggs. Ramón toed the corpse then rocked it back and forth with his foot.

Then he went inside the house, took tins of food from the shelf, and a can opener and a knife from the drawer, and walked round to where the dog was. It whimpered and cowered when he came towards it, but Ramón made shushing noises as he opened the cans and tipped tuna and hot dog sausages onto the floor. The dog sniffed them, then began to wolf them down.

Ramón took the knife, cut the washing line that tied the dog to the tree and watched with satisfaction as it began to wander around the yard, sniffing.

'Primo,' he said when he phoned Santiago's number. 'That little problem we discussed has been taken care of. Meet me where we agreed with the money.'

8

Danny went home and Googled the nun's name.

The search returned a slew of results, many of which were from websites dedicated to the victims of illegal adoptions in Spain. The stories told on them were painted with every shade of human misery: mothers seeking children, children seeking parents, brothers and sisters seeking siblings. Some had been searching for missing relatives for more than forty years.

Nearly all of the forum threads dedicated to Sister Arriola contained the same black and white image of the nun, taken at some point in the 1970s, when she had worked at a birth clinic and orphanage in Tenerife. She had been a plump woman with a round, happy face. Despite the austere edge given to her appearance by the starched white wings of the wimple she wore, she exuded a benign, benevolent air.

The comments within the threads gave a totally different impression of the woman. There were dozens of posts detailing the sadistic punishments Arriola had imposed on the children under her care in Tenerife: beatings, humiliation, withholding of food. The comments claimed she had held an especial antipathy towards pretty young girls on the cusp of puberty, and there were posts from four different women who claimed the nun had ruined any possibility of them having a normal sex life.

According to the website, Sister Arriola had died in 1997, but a number of the threads contained links to newspaper and magazine articles.

The photo of Arriola repeatedly used on the forum was actually from a 1995 article in a Tenerife newspaper which had run with the headline, Orphanage Traded Children Like Cattle.

But it was the photo lower down the article that drew Danny's attention. It showed a metal chill cabinet. One of the heavy doors was open and inside a naked baby was clearly visible, resting atop folded blankets.

According to the article, the doctors at the birth clinic attached to the Tenerife orphanage had kept a child's corpse refrigerated, and each time a stillbirth needed to be faked, the newborn was spirited away to another room while the refrigerated corpse was swaddled and presented to the parents as evidence of the child's death.

Danny lit a cigarette. He thought about the photo of Josefina Hernandez and what she had said about her child being cold. Then he remembered Frank Dale's discovery in the depths of Santa Cristina. Danny didn't know whether to feel happy or not at the realisation.

The journalist who had written the 1995 article was named Natalia Duva. When Danny phoned the Tenerife newspaper that had originally published the article, he found that Duva was now the editor.

'Yes, I remember the article very well,' she said. 'God knows it took me long enough to get the damned thing into print.'

'Really?'

'I first wrote that article in 1984.'

'And it took you that long to get it published?'

She gave an ironic chuckle. 'Yes. At least, to get it published the way I wanted.'

'Can you tell me why?'

'It started in the winter of '84. At that time, I was working for a magazine on mainland Spain and we got a lead on a former nun who was making all sorts of outrageous claims about what had been going on at an orphanage and birth clinic in Tenerife. As I'm from Tenerife, I was chosen to interview her. What she had to say was unbelievable.

'This former nun claimed newborn children were being stolen to order for rich families and that there was a network that extended across the entire country. She claimed sometimes they were charging as much as 250,000 pesetas per child. That was the price of a flat back then in the '80s.

'The former nun claimed they chose their victims carefully: women from poor families, unmarried mothers, feminists, divorcees, the sort of women who wouldn't be listened to if they made a fuss.

'There were even cases of women being given padding to wear so that they could fake a pregnancy before receiving their stolen child. That was how cynical the nuns were. And how certain. They would identify a woman as a target during her pregnancy, gain her trust and from that moment on, her child was lost to her.

'Anyway, this former nun also claimed that they kept a dead baby on ice at the birth clinic which they used to convince mothers that their child had been stillborn, and that she had a friend who was prepared to smuggle us into the clinic to take photos as proof. So I flew down to Tenerife with her and it was just like she said. There was the birthing room and right next door, in a refrigerated cabinet, they had a dead baby wrapped in towels.'

Her voice broke with emotion.

'I've not seen anything quite as distressing as that in 30 years of journalism. And so I wrote my article as an exposé of the child trafficking that was going on.

163

'But the magazine's damned subeditor turned the whole story around. He said the editors had decided the subject of the child trafficking was way too controversial and instead they concentrated on the whole dead-baby-in-the-freezer thing. By the time they'd finished messing around with it, the article read like a cheap piece of sensationalism and the more serious issues were glossed over.'

'And this child abduction was going on in the 1980s?'

'The last recorded case of a child being stolen from its mother was in 1987, Señor Sanchez.'

'But Franco died in 1975. How did it manage to continue so long into democracy?'

'Firstly, the church still ran some of the social services: hospitals, schools, orphanages. And there were serious loopholes in Spanish law that allowed the practice to develop and flourish. Firstly, the Franco dictatorship made a law in 1941 that allowed birth certificates to be altered so that a child's adoptive parents could be declared the child's biological ones. It wasn't changed until 1987.

'And such was the shame attached to children born out of wedlock, it was also perfectly legal for a doctor to put "Mother Unknown" on the civil register in order to protect the identity of unmarried women.

'And nobody realised the extent of what had happened until the advent of the internet. That was when people started forums on the subject and it became apparent how many lives these bitches had ruined. ANADIR, the main NGO campaigning for the victims of this, think there might have been as many as 300,000 cases of child trafficking between the end of the civil war and 1987.'

'Why did you come back to the article in 1995?'

'I left the magazine in 1989, returned to Tenerife and started worked for this newspaper. But in 1995, by a complete fluke, I stumbled over Sister Arriola's trail through a mutual friend. So, without telling her why, I arranged to interview the nun.'

'What did she have to say for herself?'

'She was an old woman by then. But she admitted everything.'

'She admitted it?'

'Why wouldn't she? She didn't think she had done anything wrong. It was a classic case of noble cause corruption. As long as the intentions are good and you are convinced of your own righteousness, it doesn't matter what you do. Isn't that how real evil in the world always occurs? In fact, Arriola thought she had done the children a favour by placing them with good, solid Catholic families. And, of course, she was very proud of the fact she had made so much money for the church.'

'Why isn't she quoted in the article?'

'Because lawyers from the archdiocese got to my editor and insisted on seeing the article before it was printed. They went through everything Sister Arriola had said with a fine toothcomb, dismissed them as the ramblings of a senile old woman and threatened legal action. Meanwhile, the church's tame press went to town on me. They brought out my connections to the PSOE, dredged up the fact that some of my uncles had been prominent socialists, and made damned sure that everyone knew that I was divorced. By the time they'd finished, my impartiality was totally discredited.

'If I'd had more time, I would have nailed her, but I only got two or three minutes alone with Arriola before some of the younger nuns realised where the line of my questions was going and hurried her away.'

'Did this Sister Arriola ever mention having previously worked at a clinic in Almería? La Clinica de Santa Cristina?'

'I think she did. I know she had lived somewhere in the south of Spain up until the late sixties. But I never thought to ask. I was more concerned about the story she was telling me.'

The late sixties. That was when the Santa Cristina clinic had burned down.

Danny thanked Duva and hung up. He massaged his head. He was still hungover, but there was nothing for it: he needed to speak to Leonard Wexby.

'I'm coming round tonight at eight, Leonard,' Danny said into the phone. 'I expect to find you shaved, clean, sober and ready to talk.' He put the phone down before Leonard could answer.

Afterwards, Danny walked to a supermarket and bought two bottles of Bombay Sapphire. Then he drove to a car park beside the beach and dozed with the seat back, listening to the soft hiss of the surf as sunlight danced on the mill-pond waters of the Mediterranean.

He needed his rest: it was going to be a long night.

9

Carmen stepped out of the confessional. She felt better now.

The photos on Teresa's laptop had given her quite a turn. They had started with simple shots of Teresa in various states of undress — without a bra, sliding her knickers down — but had ended with videos that showed her actually copulating with her boyfriend in the most extreme pornographic detail. She had never believed such filth possible.

She was inside the city's cathedral. She had always thought the place a little showy, with its ribbed ceiling, marble pillars and choir of walnut, but today as she wandered its cloisters, she found the building's size and splendour comforting.

When she came to the chapel behind the main altar, she knelt and began to pray a rosary, and for the first time since the whole business with Teresa began, she felt the serene sense of clarity that marked the presence of the Lord's hand. Tears of gratitude rolled down her cheeks as she turned her face upwards and thanked Him for his grace and his benevolence.

When she rose, she found that a portly man in late middle-age wearing the vestments of a sacristan was standing quietly behind her. It took her a moment to recognise who it was.

'Antonio?' she said, smiling. 'Is that you?'

They embraced. As always, Antonio smelt of beer and recently consumed food, but in a hearty, healthy way. His red face beamed as he held Carmen's hands and looked at her.

'What on earth are you doing here?' she said.

'I am moving up in the world, Carmen. I am now one of the sacristans at the cathedral. The old church — well, it was never the same once Father Javier passed. Not that I am criticising the new priest, mind. But it seemed time for a change before I got too old to be of any use.'

'Nonsense, you look wonderful.'

'Wonderfully fat,' he said, patting his stomach. Then his face became serious. 'But here I am blathering stupidities when you must have the weight of the world upon your shoulders. How is your mother?'

'Better. The doctors think she will return home soon.'

'That is good. They paint such a bleak picture on the television news, don't they? And poor Teresa... I will always remember her smile. And let us pray that the police untangle this mess quickly so that you might know some peace.'

'I'm sure they will.'

'In the meantime, surrender your pain to the Lord. And rest assured that all of your friends from the parish are only a phone call away.'

'Don't worry. A friend of Father Javier's has been most attentive to my needs.'

'Really? Might I ask whom?'

'Monsignor Melendez.'

Antonio's thick eyebrows drew together in a faint frown.

'What's the matter?' Carmen said.

Antonio smiled again. 'It's just that the name is not familiar to me. And I thought I knew all of Father Javier's clerical friends. I served him for more than 30 years, after all. But my mind is not what it once was. Anyway, I must get back to my duties.'

They embraced once again and promised to stay in touch. But when Carmen walked through the cathedral door, she found the feeling of serenity was no longer with her.

10

Leonard Wexby lived in a beautifully restored 19th century farmhouse close to the town of Sorbas.

Danny was on his second Wexby-poured gin-and-tonic now, a 70/30 mix garnished with a single ice cube and a thick slice of lemon.

'You used to be able to pick this stuff up in junk shops,' Wexby said, motioning towards a glass cabinet in which various civil war helmets were displayed. 'But around the early nineties people started to get wise. Still, that's all the better for me. I must be sitting on a fortune.'

The top layer of the glass cabinet held three military helmets: one of the oddly shaped Spanish M26 helmets favoured by the Republican army, an Italian M16 emblazoned with the Yoke and Arrows insignia of the Falange, and a French WWI helmet that had belonged to an International Brigade volunteer; on the shelf below them were a red and black anarchist cap, a red Carlist beret and armbands and pennants from the CNT union. A Mauser rifle was bolted to the wall beside the cabinet.

'Look at this little peach I picked up recently for an absolute steal,' Wexby said, putting his drink down, opening the glass cabinet and withdrawing a book. 'William Rust's *Britons in Spain* with the original dust wrapper and,' he said with a flourish, carefully opening the book to reveal a number of signatures on the frontispiece, 'signed by all the leading British members of the International Brigade. They're all there: Tom Wintringham, Fred Copeland, Bill Alexander.'

Danny nodded and tried to look interested. A tour of Leonard's latest acquisitions was always part and parcel of a visit to the house, but the truth was, this wasn't really a social call, and Danny was concentrating more on pacing his drinking. Danny outweighed Wexby by at least three stones, but he knew from bitter experience that trying to match him drink for drink was a recipe for disaster. Leonard was one of those slender men who seemed to possess hollow legs when it came to strong spirits, and Danny knew he had to keep a clear head until he'd got the information he wanted out of Leonard.

With the tour finally completed, they went to sit in the living room, a huge open space with a tiled floor and a large fireplace.

Physically, Leonard had always reminded Danny of the actor, John Hurt, and there was a certain theatricality to the way he spoke, too, especially when delivering his anecdotes. He was dressed tonight in a white shirt and chinos and had a red paisley cravat tied loosely around his neck.

'Let's talk about Frank Dale, Leonard,' Danny said, taking a seat on the sofa.

Wexby sipped his drink, then tucked a fresh Dunhill into his cigarette holder.

'What is it you want to know?'

'Did you put any stock in the story he told you? The one about the dead child in the basement?'

'Well, Dale certainly believed it. And you should have the seen the size of the scar on his forearm. But then haunted houses have a habit of making people see things, don't they? For all I know, Dale could simply have seen a child's doll, and let his imagination do the rest.

'But it is curious that you should mention Dale and his ghost story at this particular juncture, because I had an email recently from a Spanish chap I know. He's a sort of collector of local folklore, and he investigates supernatural occurrences:

apparitions of the Virgin, ghosts, poltergeists, that sort of thing. He sent me a—'

'If you're about to chew my ear off about The *Dama Pálida* legend, I don't want hear it. I don't believe in heaven or hell, and I definitely don't believe in ghosts.'

Wexby smiled at Danny through a veil of cigarette smoke. 'What a grey, joyless world you committed atheists inhabit. And this from someone who by his own admission slept with the lights on for two days after watching *The Blair Witch Project*?'

Danny rolled his eyes. 'That was different. I live alone in a house in the middle of nowhere. The mind plays tricks. Anyway, it wasn't anything a few stiff drinks before bed didn't cure.'

'Amen to that, my boy,' Leonard said, reaching for the bottle of Bombay Sapphire. 'But just humour me for a moment and take a listen to what this chap has sent through.' Leonard rose and walked to his computer. 'As I said, he is a sort of folklorist-cum-paranormal investigator and he sometimes leaves sound-activated recording devices dotted around Santa Cristina in the hope of catching evidence of the *Dama Pálida*. A few days ago he sent me something ... curious.'

The MP3 file began with the faint sound of the wind and creaking branches.

'Is that it?' Danny said, but Leonard waved his hand for silence and said, 'Can't you hear it? Let me turn it up.'

There was nothing to the recording but the distorted sound of the wind. Danny was about to tell Leonard to turn it off, but stopped and leant his head to one side. There *was* something else there, a sound below the wind, soft and low. It sounded like a moan.

'You hear it, don't you?' Leonard said, arms folded in satisfaction.

'Yes. But it could be an animal.'

'Keep listening.'

The moan continued, so quiet it was barely distinguishable from the other sounds. Then it stopped for a moment and a new sound came, a short sound, repeated four times. Then the wind swallowed the sound and the recording stopped.

'That was a voice, wasn't it?' Leonard said.

Danny blew air. 'I'll admit, it sounded like one.'

'And did you hear what it was saying? I think it was saying "*socorro*".'

Danny laughed. '*You* might have heard that. I heard a lot of distorted crap that could really have been almost anything. Besides, why would a ghost be crying out for help?'

'Don't get me started, dear boy. If it was the woman's spirit, she could have been asking for release from her eternal torment.'

'I don't want to waste any more time on this. Tell me about Santa Cristina. You said you knew something.'

'I do. And rest assured that the real story of Santa Cristina is far darker and *far* more interesting than the Pallid Woman and her smothered babes.

'But quid pro quo, young Daniel. I know from the light in your eyes — and from the way you seem to be allowing your drink to evaporate rather than be imbibed — that you're on to something. Tell me what it is, and then I promise I'll divulge every last scrap of info.'

Danny had been expecting this moment. He examined Wexby's face. It was clear he knew something. But Leonard was quite capable of exaggerating its importance in order to get information out of Danny. And the two men were potentially rivals. Newspapers didn't care about who found what first.

Danny began his story with Teresa del Hoyo and Gordon Pavey and Vladi and the documents that had been stolen from the archive. Then he made a brief allusion to Santa Cristina and the children's graves in the English cemetery before changing subject again.

Wexby listened with interest. When Danny had finished, he said, 'Historical archives, stolen documents and Spanish babes buried among the heretics? Could it be you've stumbled across evidence of illegal adoptions here in Almería, Daniel Sanchez? Come on, out with it. Old Leonard might have been sacked a few years ago, but my mind's not so pickled yet that I can't spot a scoop when I see one.'

'Tell me what *you* have, and then we'll discuss what I have.'

'And you're planning on selling this to the nationals?'

'Naturally. If I can get the story watertight.'

'Well, what I know ties in very well with your angle on illegal adoptions. And if we could pin something to the Encona family, we'd be heroes to half the population of Almería.'

'The Enconas? What's the link between the family and Santa Cristina? I mean, I know Santiago Encona is part of the golf course consortium, but that news is old hat now.'

Wexby's sly smile returned. 'Oh, so you don't know then?'

'Know what?'

'Leticia Encona's father was the chief obstetrician at Santa Cristina.'

'What?'

'I thought that would catch your attention. Doctor Amancio Encona.'

Danny had his notebook and pen out. 'Tell all.'

'Nothing would please me more. But let's talk about my reimbursement, first.'

Danny had known something like this would be coming. Leonard was no fool, nor was he prone to sudden bouts of charity.

'Let me guess. You want to co-write the article with me?'

Leonard's grin was curiously adolescent. 'You'd think at my age I'd have developed a little more artifice, wouldn't you? But yes, Daniel Sanchez, if I must be laid bare with such sledgehammer crudity then, for my sins, I do.'

'But why? You can't need the money.'

'Certainly not. But money isn't everything, is it? All my life I've been a somebody: Leonard from England, Leonard the legal translator, Leonard the journalist. Now what am I? Chicken-legs bloody Leonard shuffling down to the clinic for his pills every Wednesday. Leonard the old duffer. Leonard the boozer. I want to be a big fish in a small pond again.'

'OK. Depending on how significant your info is, we'll write the article together. Do you want to shake on it?'

'Certainly not, I don't know where you've been,' Leonard said, reaching for the bottle of Bombay Sapphire. 'We will seal our agreement like gentlemen: with a drink.'

They chinked glasses.

Danny leant back on the sofa, pen poised.

Leonard tucked another Dunhill into his cigarette holder.

'So, where to begin,' he said slowly. 'After that 2006 interview with Frank Dale, I found the story of Santa Cristina had really piqued my interest, so I began to root around, interviewing local people, consulting newspaper archives.

'Do you know why the locals consider Santa Cristina to be cursed? It all started long before the place was burnt to the ground. Apparently, the whole *Dama Pálida* thing started because there was an unusually high incidence of infant mortality at the place...'

He went to the bookshelves, where he searched among piles of box files, then returned to the table with a blue ring-bind folder. He lay his cigarette holder on the edge of the ashtray and opened the folder. Inside was a mass of press clippings, old photographs and sheets of A4 covered with Leonard's spidery handwriting. Wexby withdrew a pile of papers and photographs. When Danny reached for them, Leonard shook his head.

'Allow an old man the indulgence of telling the story his own way.

'When Mr Dale got to talking about Santa Cristina, he got his legend mixed up with local history. Because, while the *Dama Pálida* is nothing more than a particularly detailed spook story, this—' he tapped the sheet of paper — 'is most definitely true.'

Leonard handed Danny a black and white photograph. It showed a wild-haired woman clad in torn, filthy rags. Her vacant gaze seemed to stare straight through the camera's lens and one of her hands was held upwards, as if poised to scratch at her face with ragged fingernails.

'Who is this?'

'That, Señor Sanchez, is María Topete.'

'And who is she?'

'She is the woman who in 1969 burned Santa Cristina to the ground. Apparently, she took a jerry can of petrol, doused some straw that was piled in a wooden outhouse adjacent to the main building and tossed a match in. It went up like a tinderbox. It was a miracle no one was killed.'

Danny looked at the photo with renewed interest.

'What's her story then?'

'This is the bit that's going to interest you, Danny. Let me show you another photo of poor María.'

He handed Danny a studio portrait of an attractive young woman wearing a bridal veil. Danny compared the two photos.

'It can't be the same woman.'

'It is. Look at the nose and chin. And what's more, those photos were taken only seven years apart.'

Danny shook his head as he realised Leonard was right: it *was* the same woman.

'What the hell happened to her?'

'That wedding photo was taken sometime early in 1961. The next year, Maria gave birth at the Santa Cristina clinic. Unfortunately, the child was stillborn. Now, popular legend has it that grief at the child's death drove her out of her mind and she took to wandering the hills clad in ragged scraps of clothing, weeping and telling all and sundry that the child had been stolen from her by the *Dama Pálida*.

'However, I did a bit of digging and managed to track down the Topete family. And this is where the story gets really dark. Because it wasn't the stillbirth that drove poor María out of her mind. It was this,' Wexby said, tapping the folder on his lap. He withdrew another photo.

'You see, on the first anniversary of the child's death, María received an envelope. Inside there was just one thing: a photo of a one-year-old child, sat on a wooden chair, staring into the camera. And every year, on the same date, another photo was delivered, of the same little boy, a year older.'

He handed Danny a series of black and white photos. Each one depicted a young boy, who had been posed identically in each picture, sitting rigidly on a wooden chair placed before a brick wall. There were seven photos in all, taken at various intervals in the boy's childhood: in the first, he was barely old enough to sit on the chair; in the last, he sat looking awkwardly into the camera, his hands folded in his lap, his black hair shaved high at the sides and back.

'Whoever was sending these obviously meant for Topete to think this boy was actually her child, I suppose?' Danny said after looking through them.

'Maria certainly thought so. And I'm inclined to agree. Look at the child's nose and eyes. Don't you see a family resemblance? And the photos stopped once Santa Cristina had been burned down and Maria was sectioned. She died in a psychiatric hospital in 1975.' Leonard's eyes twinkled. 'Isn't it so wonderfully Garcia Lorca? *Blood Weddings* has nothing on this.'

'But why would anyone do this?'

'Well, it was Maria Topete's nephew that had those photos. He was convinced that María's husband, a man named Gualterio Blanco, had had some falling out with Amancio Encona, although he was unsure as to how.

'The most likely explanation is the political manoeuvring that was going on in Spain at the time. Encona was a *camisa vieja*, an old shirt as they used to call those who had fought alongside Franco in the civil war, whereas this Maria Topete's husband was one of the younger upstart technocrats that had come to power in the late fifties. There was no love lost between those two camps, believe you me.'

'So, they stole her child because of a political falling out? I don't buy that.'

'Do you realise what an utter bastard this Amancio Encona was? He served with the Carlists during the civil war and supposedly murdered more than a dozen people once he got back to El Cerrón. Let me show you a photo of him.'

He handed Danny another black and white image showing a line of three men walking at the head of a religious procession.

A wooden image of the Virgin del Mar was visible behind them, a huge, gaudy thing carried on the shoulders of a multitude of people. The pavements were crowded with men and women making the stiff-armed fascist salute. The caption read "Civil Authorities Lead the Procession, El Cerrón, 1954".

'The man on the far left is Amancio Encona.'

'Yes,' Danny said. The resemblance to Leticia Garcia was marked. She had inherited the broadness of her father's face and the aggressive jut of the jaw. Amancio Encona wore the dress uniform of the Falange, a smart white military jacket with leather straps running up either breast, passing beneath the lapels of the jacket.

Danny looked more closely.

He'd seen that uniform before: the man's face, too.

When Leonard went to the toilet, Danny took out the photo he'd found at Sally Allen's house, the photo of the couple outside Santa Cristina. There was no doubt: the third man in the photo was Amancio Encona.

He didn't say anything to Wexby, though. He wanted to keep an ace up his sleeve. It was unlikely that Leonard had told him the whole story, so he needed to keep a bargaining chip for further down the line.

Wexby had more photos of Amancio Encona from the fifties. In one of them he was arm in arm with a woman.

'That is his sister, Herminia Encona,' Leonard said. 'A real bitch by all accounts. She was head of the SF, *La Sección Feminina*, the Fascist women's organisation.'

Danny examined the woman. She was dressed all in black, her face framed by a *mantilla*, a black silk veil draped over a comb which rose from the back of her head. She looked small and frail next to the bulk of Amancio Encona, but her dark eyes stared towards the camera with obvious hauteur.

By eleven, the second bottle of gin was half-empty, although by then Danny had switched to beer in the hope he could dilute the spirits in his stomach. The conversation meandered: Spanish politics, history, local gossip. This was how evenings at Leonard's normally ended, with Danny slowly nodding off to the gentle sound of Wexby's voice. By midnight, Danny had assumed a semi-horizontal position on the sofa. Ten minutes later, when Wexby asked if he was still awake, there was no answer.

'I do have a guest bedroom, you know,' Leonard said, lifting Danny's desert boots and placing a towel beneath them.

11

The phone woke Carmen, slumped in the armchair in her parents' living room. She couldn't even remember having fallen asleep. In fact, she had no memory of even really having come home after her visit to the cathedral.

She did not reach her mobile in time to answer, but when she looked at the screen she saw the Guardia officer, Nuñez, had called.

The time was 23:34. Carmen phoned him back.

'Señorita Del Hoyo? I thought you'd like to know: we've found the man we think killed your sister.'

'What? Who is he? Where is he?'

'His name is Primitivo Pozos. But I'm afraid that he's dead.'

'Dead? How?'

'We can't be sure at the moment. It looks like he suffered some sort of seizure while snorting cocaine at a derelict property in El Cerrón. But I thought you would like to know that, from first impressions, it looks like he died an extremely painful death.'

'Where are you? I want to see the place.'

'I'm afraid you can't come here.'

'Why not? I've a right to see where the bastard defiled my sister.'

'It's a crime scene. No one is allowed in there at the moment apart from the specialists who are gathering evidence.'

When Carmen put the phone down, she sat brooding on the sofa.

She knew the feelings were unworthy of her, but she was glad the bastard was dead. An eye for an eye. It was God's prompt and righteous vengeance. But it seemed an easy escape. She had wanted to see Teresa's killer put on trial and humiliated and then sent to prison.

A restless, angry sensation began to gnaw at her. Why wouldn't they let her see where her sister had died? No one had more right than her to view the place. All this last week, she'd been an impotent observer, reeling from one horrid revelation to the next.

Well, not any more. That was not the way Carmen del Hoyo had ever lived her life. She lived by the Lord's rules and no one else's.

She swept up her car keys and headed for the door.

Part III — Secretos a Voces

1

Danny awoke at 08:24 with a shaft of sunlight shining directly onto his face. He sat up on the sofa and smacked lips that were gummy with stale tobacco and sour gin.

He didn't feel too bad, but it was early days. Like everything else in middle-age, Danny's hangovers were slow-starters and required two or three hours of wakefulness to attain maximum potency. He fished in his bag for the travel toothbrush he carried everywhere.

Leonard was sitting at the breakfast bar in a silk dressing gown, cigarette holder in hand. When Danny emerged from the toilet, rubbing his temples, Wexby offered to make Danny a full English breakfast. Danny said coffee would do.

'So, where do we go from here?' Leonard said as he filled the kettle. 'You do remember the deal we struck last night?'

'Write up what you told me about María Topete, the destruction of Santa Cristina and the photos of the kid and we'll take it from there.'

Leonard handed him a cardboard file. 'I've already taken care of that. You'll find 1,200 words of my distinctively muscular prose in there together with high res print outs of all the relevant photos.'

Danny opened the folder and glanced over what Leonard had written.

'My, we are keen, aren't we?'

'Just remember to put my name on the by-line if you sell the story to a national.'

'Make me that coffee and I'll even put your name before mine.'

Danny was halfway through the drink when his mobile rang. It was Sally Allen.

'Mr Sanchez? You haven't published anything about Mr Pavey yet, have you?'

'Nope.'

'Thank the Lord. Can you come back over to my house right now? I'm afraid the situation has taken a rather unexpected turn.'

It was a thirty minute drive to San José. Danny drove back to his own house first, changed into new clothes and swallowed some Nurofen Express tablets. He put the folder of information Leonard had given him on the desk in his office. Then he drove to San José.

He parked outside Sally Allen's house and gathered up his camera, notebook and shoulder bag. The sunlight seemed exceptionally bright that morning. Or perhaps it was the after-effects of the gin humming behind his eyes. He reached into the glove box, put on his aviator sunglasses, turned towards Sally Allen's property — and all hell broke loose.

The white gate to Sally Allen's compound burst open and a small woman dressed in tweed emerged. Sally Allen followed her out onto the pavement, where the woman in tweed turned to say something, but Sally Allen began shouting her down. Her opponent retreated backwards a few steps, then stood her ground suddenly, as if something she'd heard had infuriated her, and the two women began talking at the same time. All along the street, doors and windows were opening as mystified neighbours sought to see what the rumpus was.

A Spanish neighbour helped Danny to calm the women and get them both back inside Sally Allen's garden, whereupon the big woman burst into tears. The neighbour took her to get a glass of water. Danny sat down in the garden with the woman in tweed.

The newcomer was around Sally Allen's age, but her polar opposite in practically everything else: she was small, thin and impeccably dressed, with her hair pulled back into a tight bun. She introduced herself as Miss Naseby. The name suited her, Danny thought, suited her painfully precise enunciation and stuffy English manners.

Despite this, the woman's colouring was unmistakably Mediterranean. Deep-brown eyes were framed by crow-black hair, and her skin was the type that looked tanned all year round. It was curious how her physical appearance belied the clothing and mannerisms. The effect would have been almost comical had she not looked so obviously distraught: her eyes were sunken and bloodshot and there was a nervous, gnawed-at look to her that spoke of uneaten meals and sleepless nights.

'I'll come straight to it, if you don't mind, Mr Sanchez,' she said, 'as I've far more pressing matters at hand. Ms Allen informs me that you plan to write an article based on allegations that Gordon Pavey defrauded her of money owed as rental.

'Mr Pavey and I have been members of the same church congregation for years now, so I wish to inform you that her allegations are complete nonsense — and that I will see to it legal action for libel is vigorously pursued if you print a single word defaming Mr Pavey's good character.'

Danny couldn't help but smile at the hectoring, forthright tone — Naseby spoke like a Latin Katherine Hepburn. He flicked his spiral-bound notepad open. 'First, of all, let me assure you that I have no intention of writing any such article.'

'Are you certain? Because Ms Allen seemed very sure you were going to "name and shame" Mr Pavey.'

'She's got her wires crossed there.'

Naseby relaxed a little. 'Good. Because not only can I vouch for the excellence of Mr Pavey's character, he was also here in Spain on my behalf and at *my* expense. So I'm sure you can see that the idea of Mr Pavey running away without paying is quite ludicrous.'

She unclasped her bag and withdrew a Polaroid from a cardboard file. Her expression as she handed it to Danny indicated he would need no further proof of Pavey's impeccable credentials.

The picture of Gordon Pavey showed him standing against a backdrop of cold, wet English countryside, one hiking boot placed atop a boulder as he posed for the photo, a large rucksack strapped to his back. His hair was obscured by the hood of a plastic raincoat, but his neatly trimmed beard showed him to be brown haired.

'Do you know where Mr Pavey is?' Danny said. 'I'm very keen to speak to him.'

'That is precisely the reason I am here in Spain, Mr Sanchez.' The knuckles of Naseby's thin hands showed white as she clasped her handbag. 'Poor Gordon seems to have disappeared.'

'Really?'

'As I mentioned before, Mr Pavey was here in Spain...' Miss Naseby paused, searching for the correct word — '*investigating* something of a deeply personal nature which is entirely separate to the matter at hand. We were in contact via the telephone for the first few days he was here, but since the morning of Sunday, October the 2nd, I have heard nothing from him.'

'Was the matter he was investigating something to do with a headstone at the English cemetery? And with the Santa Cristina clinic?'

It was: Naseby practically flinched when Danny said Santa Cristina.

'How do you know that?' she said.

'Mr Pavey left a receipt here from a local marble company, together with a photograph.' Danny fished in his bag and took out the receipt and the photograph of Santa Cristina.

Naseby frowned and held out her hand.

'Those articles are my property. I've no idea how they came to be in your possession, but I'll thank you to give them back.'

'That receipt is for a headstone,' Danny said as he handed them over. 'I went to see it at the cemetery. It was for a person called María del Mar Torres García. Mr Pavey also seemed to have had an interest in the illegal adoptions that occurred here in Spain. What's more,' Danny continued, 'I know who the Spanish man in that photo is.'

Naseby looked away, her lip trembling. She made an effort to compose herself.

'That's all very interesting, but I'm afraid Gordon's whereabouts is all that matters to me at the moment.'

'Perhaps I can be of some assistance. If you give me all the facts, I'm sure I can put you in contact with the right people.'

Naseby took out a small notebook and began to read.

'Gordon came here on the 28th of September. I'm afraid I don't use the internet, so telephone was the only way we had to stay in contact, and Gordon promised to phone every day.

'During the weekend he phoned to say that he was being helped by two Spaniards with whom he was going to access an historical archive which contained documents pertinent to the Santa Cristina building.

'My last communication with Mr Pavey took place thirteen days ago, on Sunday October the 2nd, when he telephoned to say he had discovered documentation of direct relevance to the matter he was investigating, but that he had had a falling out with the Spaniards. He said they wanted to use the information for political ends, and that he had told them that was of no interest to us. However, he said that he had made scans of all the relevant documents and had them on a pen drive. Then he said that he expected to remain in Spain for at least three more days. That was the last I heard from him.

'I was not initially too worried, as Gordon is a very impulsive, adventurous type of man and so I assumed he was too busy and had forgotten to phone. It was not until the Tuesday that I began to worry. When I attempted to phone Gordon's mobile, I found it returned the number unavailable signal, so I made numerous calls to the guesthouse on the Wednesday and Thursday, but received little help from that wretched Allen woman.

'I told her I feared something had happened to Gordon, but all she seemed worried about was her damned money. I continued to call all that weekend but there was never any answer.'

'Ms Allen went back to the UK.'

'That's no excuse. If anything has happened to Gordon, I will see that damned woman swing for it, even if I have to pursue the matter through the civil courts. Imagine not reporting that one of your guests had gone missing.

'Anyway, on Saturday the 8th, I contacted the UK consulate, but they were unable to make any headway due to the fact that Ms Allen was incommunicado. However, they did circulate Gordon's details to the Spanish authorities, who confirmed that no one of that description had been hospitalised or involved in an accident.

'The consulate finally managed to make contact with Ms Allen yesterday, whereupon she fed them the same nonsense about his owing her money, so I decided to fly out here and take matters into my own hands.'

Danny had been making notes while she talked, trying to keep his expression neutral. If what Naseby said was right, Pavey could have been missing for as long as 13 days. That wasn't good.

'Have you contacted Mr Pavey's bank to see if there has been any activity within his accounts?'

'I hadn't thought of that.'

'Well, the UK police can help you with that if you tell them Mr Pavey is missing.'

'But what can I do here? I'm certain that Gordon has not returned to the UK. Can you suggest a decent interpreter?'

'Don't worry,' Danny said, 'I'll translate for you. Do you know the details of Mr Pavey's hire car firm?'

'No. But I do know he hired the vehicle from the airport.'

'Let's drive to the airport now then. There are only four or five rental companies that have booths there. One of them will remember Mr Pavey.'

Sally Allen had been lurking on the edge of the conversation for a few minutes. As Danny headed for the door, she caught his arm and said, 'You will make sure she knows I did nothing wrong, won't you? It seems the situation was a little more complicated than I initially thought.'

Danny looked at her sadly. 'I've a feeling things are going to get a lot more complicated before the day is over, Ms Allen.'

2

Carmen del Hoyo turned her car onto the main autovia that led towards El Cerrón. It was the second time in as many days that she was going to the town.

The night before she had driven to El Cerrón and begun asking people on the street for directions to Primitivo Pozos's home. An old man had finally told her that Pozos didn't live in the town, that he lived at his father's slaughterhouse, so Carmen had driven out there and taken a look at the filthy place.

It had been close to 02:00 when she arrived there, but the police had set up floodlights and officers in white overalls were collecting evidence. The stark light had given the slaughterhouse's cracked and crumbled edges a ghostly appearance, and Carmen had shuddered as she thought of Teresa being chained up in such an indescribably wretched place. You could smell the stench of it a hundred yards away.

Uniformed officers came over to her vehicle as soon as she arrived. When she told them who she was, the female officer in charge of the crime scene came over to speak with her.

'You really should not be here, *señorita*. Please, go home and let us do our jobs. I will phone you as soon as I know anything at all, I promise you.' By that time, photographers and journalists had begun to arrive, so Carmen left before any of them recognised her.

She had spent that morning at the hospital with *Mamá*. Now, she was going back to El Cerrón.

The newspapers had printed a picture of Pozos, a huge grotesque troll of a man. Carmen drew satisfaction from the certainty that he was suffering in hell, but it wasn't enough. Today, she was going to find Pozos's family and she was going tell them exactly what she thought of the bastard. Then she was going to show them the photos she had put together of Teresa so that they could see what the man had destroyed. She had Pozos's name. That was enough. Everyone in these tiny Spanish towns knew each other: it wouldn't take long to find where his relations lived.

She listened to a discussion programme on COPE, the radio station run by the church, as she drove. The panel of guests were talking about the wantonness and sinful nature of modern Spanish youth, comparing their lax attitudes towards sex and relationships with those of their parents' and grandparents' generations.

Carmen found herself nodding in agreement with most of the points they were making — that was, until one of the panellists said, 'Look at the recent murder that occurred in Almería. The female victim was a drug addict, an advocate of abortion, and a well-known church-hater. I have it on good authority that she lost her virginity at an absurdly young age, and, while still a teenager, had sex toys and pornographic magazines hidden away beside her bed.'

It took Carmen a moment to realise that they were talking about Teresa.

'This being a Christian channel, I will not go into further details,' the voice on the radio continued, 'but the circumstances of her death are a damning indictment of the penalties that can be incurred by leading a sinful life. Had she spent less time on her back and more on her knees praying, there is little doubt in my mind she would still be with us today and able to—'

Carmen turned the radio off.

How the hell had these bloody journalists discovered that business about the vibrator and the magazines? No one had known outside the family. Carmen had mentioned the matter to Monsignor Melendez during one of their discussions on Teresa, but there was no way he would have told anyone.

Teresa must have told her friends about it, Carmen decided. She had always been so flippant and open about sex anyway, and had taken especial pleasure in revealing details she knew would shock or scandalise others. Still, Carmen would have expected a better standard of journalism from the COPE. But then all these damned journalists were the same.

When the ordeal of Teresa's disappearance began, Carmen had been stupid enough to believe that the media had wanted to help and her good nature had allowed them to blindside her. Well, she knew better now: Teresa and her family's pain were commodities to them and nothing more. Monsignor Melendez had been right to warn her of them. The press were jackals, the whole lot of them.

She parked on the outskirts of El Cerrón and began asking in shops about Primitivo Pozos and where his family lived. Everyone said the same thing, that Pozos had no family. 'But his friend, Álvaro, owns a DVD shop,' an old woman said. 'You might speak to him.'

Carmen walked to the shop with the folder of photographs pinned tightly beneath her arm.

The shop door opened onto rows of shelves filled with DVDs and the smell of stale air and bodies. Wall shelves contained more films, stacked floor to ceiling, the plastic covers of which were torn and frayed. Faded movie posters filled the whole expanse of the shop window, preventing daylight from entering.

At the back of the shop six grimy, outdated PCs were set up on trestle tables. A thick knot of cables ran across the table tops, which was connected to an eight way plug socket wrapped with duct tape. A group of four boys playing an online game were the only customers, bellowing insults as they shot and slashed at each other.

The glass counter in the corner opposite the door was piled high with packets of crisps and boxes of sweets. A hugely fat man sat behind it. The counter was covered in newspapers — he seemed to have purchased every single one, local and national — and they were all turned to the articles detailing the death of Primitivo Pozos and his role in the death of Teresa.

'What do you want?' he said when he noticed Carmen.

'You're Primitivo Pozos's friend, aren't you?'

The man's eyes went wide with panic as he said, 'No. I don't know him. Not well, anyway.'

'Everyone in town says you were best buddies. And I find it strange you're so interested in his death,' she said, motioning towards the newspapers.

'I didn't know him,' the fat man said, his voice becoming shrill.

He was lying. Carmen opened the folder and began slapping the photos down onto the counter, one by one.

'There,' she said, pointing towards the first photo, 'that's my sister when she was four. In that one she's eight. Ten. Fourteen. Don't look away, you cowardly bastard,' she said when the man sank his head into his hands. 'I want you to see what your friend destroyed. Do you know he raped her? And then he strung her up by the ankles and bled her like a—'

'No!' the fat man cried, knocking over boxes as he staggered to his feet. Carmen saw that he was crying. He ran across the room towards a room at the back, smashed the door open, fell to his knees and started to vomit.

The four children at the back of the shop had all stopped playing and were staring at Carmen in that wide-eyed, open-mouthed way children do when they witness shocking adult behaviour.

Carmen gathered up the photos and left the shop. She had got what she had come for. For the first time in days, she actually felt better. She knew the church would have told her to rise above such petty, base emotions, but it felt good to vent her anger on someone who truly deserved it.

She stood outside the shop staring up at the cloudy grey sky. Her anger faded and she became aware that she was trembling. That always happened when she lost her temper.

She crossed the road, went into a cafeteria and ordered a coffee, then sat at a window table and said a silent prayer, asking forgiveness for what she had just done. She would need to go to confession that evening.

She was finishing her drink when she saw the fat man chivvying the four boys out into the street, locking the door and pulling the shop-wide metal shutter down. His fat face was pale, his eyes red from crying, but there was something unmistakably furtive about his manner, something nervous and flighty, like an animal caught alone seeking the protection of the pack.

And then it occurred to Carmen: what if this Pozos hadn't been alone when he killed Teresa? What if others had been involved?

Carmen left money on the table and hurried from the café. She wanted to see where the fat man went.

It was a simple matter to follow him across the town. The man's obesity meant he walked at a snail's pace — it was as much as Carmen could do not to catch up with him. Not that she really needed to see the man to follow him: the slipstream of sweaty stench that trailed behind was noticeable at twenty metres.

After ten minutes, they began to enter the *casco antiguo*, the original part of El Cerrón. The buildings here were older, the streets narrower, the traffic one way. When they crossed the central plaza, Carmen realised the man was heading towards the town hall.

She looked at her watch. It was gone three pm: the place would be closed now.

She saw him knock on the building's main door. A policeman opened it and they spoke. Then he let the fat man inside and closed the door.

Carmen walked up the steps and banged on the door.

The same policeman opened.

'We're closed,' he said.

'Why did you just let that man in, then?'

'He's got business with a councillor.'

'Really? Which one?'

The policeman did not like Carmen's tone. 'What business is that of yours?' he said, then closed and bolted the door.

Carmen began to walk back towards her car.

Was it her imagination, or had the fat man run to the town hall looking for protection? What on earth was going on? She thought about the documents she had seen on Teresa's computer, the articles she had written about the search for the Republican dead in El Cerrón. Could that be involved?

She was on her way back to the car when she saw the newsstand. She was three or four steps past it before she realised whose face it was she had just seen on the front of one of those terrible scandal rags, *Gente de Hoy*.

Carmen walked backwards slowly, hardly able to comprehend what she was seeing. It was clearly an old photo — Teresa could barely be more than nineteen — just as it was clear from her bloodshot eyes and hazed expression that she was either drunk or stoned. She picked up the magazine.

The headline read 'A Death Foretold? We Uncover Murder Victim's Sordid Secrets. By Danny Sanchez.'

3

Danny was driving towards Almería airport. Miss Naseby was sitting on the passenger seat, her hands clasped on her handbag. They'd agreed to see if the hire car company knew anything about Pavey's whereabouts. After that, Danny would take her to see a contact he knew in the National Police.

'Of course, it would be much easier for me to help if I knew why Mr Pavey is here in Spain and what it is he is investigating,' Danny said.

Naseby sat quietly for a moment, considering this, then unclipped her bag and withdrew a cardboard file. 'I think I'd better start at the beginning,' she said, then fell silent, as if unsure how to continue.

She took out the photo of the three people standing in front of Santa Cristina.

'Those are my parents,' Miss Naseby said, indicating the couple in the centre of the photo as Danny glanced across. 'At least they were the people I grew up with.' She shuffled nervously. 'You see, I always suspected I was adopted. You can see from the photo that I bear no physical similarity to either of my parents. And one notices things: whispered conversations, awkward silences, an unwillingness to discuss certain topics during adolescence.

'But my father was not the sort of man with whom one could broach a subject of such delicacy. Or any sort of subject, really. He was a harsh man, and we did not get along. And when I decided as a young woman to become a member of the Church of England, I'm afraid that was the final straw.'

The bridge of her nose trembled slightly and she gave a deep sigh.

'Anyway, none of this was really relevant until 1994. By that time my mother was already dead and my father fell seriously ill, so it fell to me to take care of him. As a result of this, I became privy to certain medical details I had not known before.

'It transpired that, as a young man, my father had received a war wound, the nature of which left him...' She blushed as she sought for the correct words. 'Suffice to say, the wound was located in his groin and it had injured him in the most distressing and debilitating way a man can be injured.

'Given that I was born in 1949, I became curious as to precisely when this wound had occurred as it meant that Harold Naseby could not be my biological father.

'I assumed he had received the wound in World War II, but when I began to look through his personal effects, I discovered that the war wound had occurred far earlier, in March of 1938.'

'He fought in the Spanish Civil War?'

'Yes.'

'So he was a member of the International Brigades?'

'Quite the opposite. He fought for the nationalist cause.'

'Really? That's quite unusual.'

'My father was a devoted Catholic and he hated communism. According to correspondence of his that I later found, Franco's Nationalist Agency in London arranged for my adoptive father to travel to Burgos posing as a journalist. He left England with nothing but his father's .44 revolver and a Spanish phrasebook. It seems rather rash when one considers it, but people were very different back then, weren't they?

'He ended up fighting for the Carlist troops, the *Requetés*, before he was wounded in the groin by a hand grenade and sent home. The whole experience left him a very bitter man.

'Anyway, he died in 1995 and I gave no further thought to the matter. However, a few months ago I discovered that I had misplaced my birth certificate.' Miss Naseby moistened dry lips. 'Now we come to the strangest part.' She opened the file again and withdrew a birth certificate. The cardboard smelt fresh and new. 'I contacted Somerset House and requested a new copy. As you'll see, not only am I listed as being born in Almería, Spain, but Harold and Elisabeth Naseby are clearly listed as my biological parents — *not* my adoptive ones.'

Danny slowed the car as he glanced at the document.

'Naturally, I began to search through my parents' effects,' Naseby continued, 'and discovered that my father had maintained correspondence with a former comrade from the civil war named Amancio Encona. In 1948 this man wrote to him. I have the letter here. The original was written in Spanish, but I had it translated, she said, unfolding a sheet of paper. She began to read aloud:

'*Dear Harold,*

'*I received your last letter. It gladdens my heart to know that you have married and I agree with the sentiments you expressed in your letter as regards the continued success of the Bolshevik/Jew conspiracy to rule the world. War with Soviet Russia will not be long in coming and then the British will rue the day that they decided to take up arms against the Germans. Rest assured, we still know how to handle the Reds in Spain.*

'*You have been much in my thoughts recently. I well remember your bravery under fire and the terrible price that you were forced to pay in order to cleanse Spain of the Marxist filth. Developments in my own life may well render me able to help repay the debt that Spain owes you and resolve*

*the problems posed by your inability to produce an heir. Why don't we
discuss the matter further via telephone?*

'Your friend

'Doctor Amancio Encona.'

'The Spanish man with your parents in that photo is
Amancio Encona,' Danny said.

Naseby nodded. 'I had imagined that would be the case.'

'How did Mr Pavey become involved?'

'Gordon speaks good Spanish. When I found the letter, I
showed it to him and he translated it. And then we found the
receipt from the marble company, and my mind went back to
how my father had been at the end of his life. In the final
months of his illness, he became very concerned with the
expiation of his life's sins. He wanted, in his own words, "to
die with a clean sheet".

'The placing of that headstone and statue in the cemetery
here in Spain would have been one of the last things he did
while he was lucid. It clearly meant a lot to him.

'Mr Pavey phoned the marble company and enquired as to
what this work my father had ordered was. Then we found out
about that peculiar inscription on the headstone, about the
"absent little one" and the girl's name. But the truly worrying
thing was the date of birth. You see, the day she was stillborn
is the same day that *I* was born, Mr Sanchez.

'And then Gordon told me about this terrible business of the
illegal adoptions and the stolen children and the matter began
to play deeply on my mind. What if I had been one of them?
So Gordon offered to come out here to Spain to investigate
the matter for me. Literally, the next day he was off out here.
He is like that: kind-hearted but very impulsive and daring.'

She gave a deep sigh.

'So here I am: 62 years old and a spinster with no relatives and few friends. And now it seems that I have no past, either. At least not the one I thought I did. The whole thing feels like some wicked joke. What if I have a sister somewhere? Or nephews? And now it seems that Gordon has disappeared and that it might be my fault...'

She began to cry suddenly, burying her face in a handkerchief to muffle the sobs. Danny patted her shoulder as he drove. He offered to pull over, but she composed herself.

'Let's get to the airport and find Gordon,' she said.

Almería airport is fifteen minutes outside the provincial capital, close enough to the coast that the sea is visible from the departure lounge. It is a small airport, handling around twenty-five flights a day off season, most of which run between Spanish and UK destinations.

When Danny arrived, Spanish businesspeople and British tourists were gathered outside the main building, braving the fierce wind as they sipped coffee and smoked. Groups of cleaners in sky blue uniforms mopped muddy footprints from the floors.

There were five car rental companies.

Danny began asking at each of them whether they remembered a customer named Gordon Pavey and explained that the man might be missing. He struck lucky on the third try, a company named AlquilAlmería.

'Yes, here it is,' the bearded man at the booth said. 'He hired a blue Ford Focus from us on Wednesday, September 28th.'

'And when did he bring it back?'

'He didn't. In fact he dumped the damned thing in the middle of nowhere. It was two days overdue before we had to go and retrieve it ourselves.'

'Did you contact the police?'

The man became defensive. 'Do you think this is the first time someone has dumped a hire car on us? Besides, we found a contact number for a guest house inside the car and when we contacted the place, we got some English woman ranting at us about how Señor Pavey had cheated her out of money and that he was no good. So we simply charged the extra days to the customer's credit card.'

'How did you know where to find the car?'

'All of our vehicles are equipped with GPS. Once the system flagged it up as being overdue, we got a fix on its position and sent people out to collect it.'

'Can you find out where it was that Mr Pavey left the car?'

The man turned the monitor so that Danny could see the GPS map. It took Danny a moment to realise what he was seeing: Pavey's car had been left on the road that led up past the golf course and ended at the gates to Santa Cristina.

The car hire man asked him if that was all he wanted, but Danny wasn't listening. He was flicking through the notes he'd made at Leonard's house, thinking now of the recording that had been made at Santa Cristina, the recording of a soft voice crying for help and a missing man no one had been looking for.

He was right: the recording had been made on October the 4th.

'And Mr Pavey left that car there on October the 2nd?'

'That's correct.'

'I wouldn't close that screen down, mate,' Danny said to the car hire man, dialling a number into his mobile. 'The police are going to want to see that.'

4

Ramón Encona was sitting on the edge of his bed, staring at the pile of 50 Euro notes before him, his teeth clenched. He'd charged Santiago 10,000 Euros for what he'd done to *El Porquero*. It wasn't bad for a night's work. So why did he feel so gloomy? Perhaps it was because history was repeating itself.

Back in the day, Ramón had spent a large percentage of his time digging Santiago out of one problem or another: people the stupid bastard had insulted, cars he'd pranged, girlfriends and wives he'd poked.

Ramón had done it from a sense of pragmatism, because he knew that while he had Santi in his pocket he was relatively safe from local police interest in his drug dealing — after all, most of them owed their positions to Cousin Leticia, so they weren't going to risk having to arrest her son.

But in the end, it had been Santi's damned fault that Ramón had had to leave El Cerrón. There had been a business rival, a twenty-something wannabe gangster with ties to the gypsy community, who had been badmouthing Ramón all over town.

One night, Ramón tricked the kid into meeting him at a lonely place and taught the little prick a lesson with a length of bicycle chain while *El Porquero* pinned his arms behind his back. Santi's involvement had been limited to shouting encouragement as the guy spat bloodied teeth to the floor and begged Ramón to stop.

It was meant to have been a short, sharp lesson to teach the guy his place. But afterwards, Santi had gone all over town boasting how it had all been him and how he had sorted out the upstart. Somehow, the national police had got wind of it. They arrested Santi the following day.

Luckily, Ramón had learnt of Santi's arrest almost as soon as it happened. He'd known straight away that it would take the national police minutes — if not seconds — to sweat the real story out of a cowardly bastard like Santi, so when they came for Ramón, his flat and car were spotlessly clean of any trace of criminal wrongdoing.

That had been sweet, seeing the police poring over the horizontal surfaces in his flat, expecting to find traces of drugs, and seeing their growing frustration. Then the kid Ramón had chain-whipped had refused to identify him, and Cousin Leticia's lawyers got Santiago to recant his testimony, which left Ramón in the clear.

But the next day Cousin Leticia's brother-in-law, the chief of police, had come to Ramón with an envelope containing two million pesetas and the offer of a deal. 'It's yours if you leave town tonight and never speak to Santiago Encona again. If not, we'll have Santiago go forward with his testimony and make sure you go to prison.'

What choice had Ramón had? Everyone knew he was moving large quantities of drugs. It would be a cinch for them to catch him the next time he bought in supplies. Failing that, they could frame him.

He'd taken the money. He'd not said goodbye to anyone, but one of the last things he'd seen as he drove out of town was Santi on the terrace of some bar, surrounded by girls, laughing and drinking beer.

But then it had always been that way. Santiago had always been the family's favourite, the eldest male grandchild. Mother had delighted in rubbing Ramón's nose in it. One autumn, when Ramón was ten or eleven, the whole Encona family had gathered at Uncle Amancio's house to celebrate Santiago's first communion. The entire Encona clan had been there — all the cousins and uncles and aunts and nephews and nieces — more than 100 people in all, and it had taken nearly an hour to gather everyone together for a photo and get them correctly posed on the steps of the house. And just when the photographer was getting ready, Mother had said, 'Go and get me a glass of water from inside, boy.'

When Ramón returned, the photo had already been taken. Santiago had laughed at him when Ramón had become upset.

'Why would we want a photo with you in it, you dirty little runt?'

The adults had rushed to over to hush him, but Ramón could still picture the lingering look of triumph in Santiago's eyes as he was dragged away...

'It seems like your family is a source of great frustration and bitterness for you,' the army shrink had asked Ramón once. Ramón had said that was nonsense, but the shrink had insisted they do a word association exercise. The shrink had read out words like childhood, cherish, uncle, cousin and asked Ramón to say the first word that came into his head.

Ramón had seen the exercise done in films, so he knew how to fuck with it and answered with benign sounding words: bunny-rabbit, candy floss, clouds.

The shrink had removed his glasses and pinched the bridge of his nose. Ramón had taken it for a gesture of resignation, but then the shrink had suddenly looked up and fixed his eyes on Ramón's.

'What about "mother" Ramón?' he asked, 'What words do you associate with your mother?' and suddenly Ramón had found his smile became brittle and forced — because an image that had been hovering below the surface of his mind the whole test had come swiftly and sharply into focus: a wild white expanse of nothing across which stretched a long spindly shadow made of sticks and barbed wire.

The shrink had sensed something was wrong.

'What about women, Ramón?'

'What about them?'

'You mentioned in a previous session you hadn't had many girlfriends.'

'Only because I didn't have time for them.'

'Do you think it had anything to do with your mother?'

'Of course not.'

'I sense some reticence to discuss her. Is that a fair comment?'

'No.'

'Do you feel scared when you're with a woman?'

'What? No!'

'Have you ever suffered from erectile problems?'

'What the fuck? What's that supposed to mean. I've fucked more women than ... what the fuck are you implying?'

That had been when the shrink had leant forward in his chair and said in a low, stern tone: 'Private Encona, you've got exactly five seconds to sit back down again and to unball your fists, or I'll have the MPs in here...'

Ramón started. He'd been so lost in memory, he hadn't realised someone was hammering on the door to his flat. Who the hell could that be?

He took a knife from the kitchen and crept towards the door, then yanked it open.

It was Santiago. He looked flustered and angry. He pushed straight past Ramón, hands rammed deep in the pockets of his cashmere coat.

'What's the problem?' Ramón said.

Santiago shook his head, his expression part-anger, part-self-pity.

'It's that blubbering idiot, Álvaro. He's going to blow the whole thing.'

'How?'

'The girl's sister came to his shop and started screaming at him. He panicked and came straight to my office at the town hall and burst into tears in front of everyone. He's convinced the police are going to arrest him, and if he carries on like this, they are almost certain to. The way he's panicking, he might as well have a big guilty sign hung around his neck.'

'Are you saying that he's become a problem?'

Santiago rummaged inside his coat and withdrew a thick envelope, which he offered to Ramón.

'The fat prick has a big mouth. Get rid of him, Ramón.'

Ramón stared at the envelope. He realised now why he'd been feeling so gloomy earlier. The way Santiago was treating him, it was as if Ramón was just another of Santi's fucking employees.

Ramón nodded towards the envelope. 'How much is in there?'

'Ten thousand. Like last time.'

Ramón shook his head slowly. 'Not enough. Not for this. *El Porquero* was easy as he was so goddamned dumb. But Álvaro is cautious. He won't trust me. This will cost you thirty.'

Santiago's eyes went wide. 'But that's three times more.'

'What can I say, *primo*? You're not in a buyer's market.'

Encona's voice dropped to a solicitous whisper. He put his hand on Ramón's forearm.

'I simply can't afford that much, Ramón. And remember: we're in this together now.'

Ramón met the other man's gaze, contempt written large upon his gaunt features.

'And what the hell is that supposed to mean?'

'You killed *El Porquero*. You're in this just as deep as I—'

Ramón shoved his nephew back against the wall and poked the tip of the kitchen knife into his throat.

'Are you threatening me? Is that what you're doing?' He dropped his voice to a whisper. 'You're damned straight I killed *El Porquero*. And he wasn't my first, either,' he said, pressing harder on the knife.

Santiago began babbling apologies. 'OK,' he said. 'I'll get you the money. But you've got to do it now. Before the police get to Alvaro and he breaks.'

5

Vice consul Brian Smith was the last of the men to sit down.

'Danny,' he said, speaking Spanish, 'this is *Inspector Jefe* Bosquet. He's in charge of the mountain rescue team that is setting up in El Cerrón. He wants to ask you a few questions.'

Bosquet was tall and in his late-forties, his dark hair and beard peppered with grey. His thick eyebrows slanted down towards his nose, adding to the severity of his expression.

Bosquet said, 'The ground around this Santa Cristina property is exceptionally dangerous. Before I give my team the green light, I want to hear why you're so certain that Señor Pavey is up there.'

Danny opened his laptop and turned it to face the policeman. A digitalised image of the GPS data from the car rental firm filled the screen.

'According to the GPS fix on the car Pavey hired, he drove to a location on the road that leads to the Santa Cristina property on Sunday, October the 2nd. That was the last time anyone saw him.

'Two days later, when the rental firm realised the vehicle had not been returned and checked where to find it, the car was still there. It hadn't been moved in two days. That means Mr Pavey either drove into the middle of nowhere, dumped his hire car and walked back to town, or that something happened to him there.'

'And why do you think he might have gone up to the ruined building?'

'Señor Pavey was investigating a health clinic that once operated at the Santa Cristina property. He'd visited the local historical archive and knew all of the documents there had been taken from the cellars of Santa Cristina. I think he went back hoping to find more information.'

Then Danny played the policemen the recording Leonard Wexby had given him.

'This was recorded close to the Santa Cristina property on October 4th.'

Bosquet listened in grim silence.

'Yes, you're right,' he said. 'There's a voice there calling for help. I agree, the evidence is compelling. I'll tell my team to go ahead and begin searching the area. And I'll need a contact number for this ghost hunter chap. I want to know where he made that recording. It should help narrow the area we have to search.'

The British Consulate in Almería is situated close to the ferry port that links Spain with North Africa in a part of the city called *Parque Viejo*. The consulate usually closes at midday, but Danny's phone call had prompted special measures to be taken, and most of the staff were still there. Danny could see shapes moving through the frosted glass of the interview room: consular officers and secretaries who were caring for Miss Naseby.

Sally Allen had been called in earlier, but had since been taken away by the Spanish police to make an official statement.

'She'll be lucky if the police don't press charges,' one of the consular staff had said. 'Stupid cow.'

Danny hadn't responded, but he shared the sentiment: Allen didn't seem a bad person, but if Pavey had fallen into one of the holes outside Santa Cristina, her inaction had consigned the man to a long, slow and painful death. Exposure was not a pleasant way to go.

Miss Naseby was sitting in a corner of the main room with her eyes closed and her hands clasped together on her lap as if in prayer.

Danny phoned Paco Pino. 'Get over to the address I'm going to text you now. Police are searching for the body of a British man up there. I'll get 300 words together now. If you can get the photos this afternoon, we can put it out on the wire in time for tomorrow's editions.'

There was nothing to do then but wait.

Danny was working on the article when Gregorio, his friend from the church-run media organisation, COPE, rang.

'Danny, sorry, I was supposed to call you sooner,' Gregorio said. 'I forgot all about it.'

'Does that mean you know who this Monsignor Melendez is?'

'Yes, I do. And it's very strange that you should mention him, because he was at the radio station yesterday morning, and he had a long conversation with my boss.'

'Do you know what they talked about?'

'No. But ever since his visit, there's been a definite slant towards the way we're reporting on the Teresa del Hoyo murder: they've been absolutely ripping into her on some of the panel programmes and our news teams have been told to stress the fact that her killer died of a drug overdose. If I didn't know better, I'd think someone was deliberately trying to discredit Teresa.'

'So who is Melendez?'

'He's a former missionary and has done a lot of work in some absolute hellholes. But as of the late nineties, he has worked exclusively as a special envoy to the ruling council of an institution called the Legionaries of Our Lady of Sorrows.

It's a militant Catholic organisation and very secretive. Some regard it as a sect within the Catholic church.'

'And what sort of work does he do for them?'

'Well, his unofficial name is *El Apagafuegos*, The Troubleshooter.'

'So he hushes up scandals?' Danny said, opening his notebook.

Gregorio laughed. 'So they say. I've heard rumours that he's been sent in to situations where there was the possibility of problems for the church and Melendez has kept them from reaching the media. But then the whole point of his job is that nobody ever knows.'

'Why do you think he's in Almería?'

'That's the real question, isn't it? But something big must be going down for a man as important as Melendez to have spent so much time here. He has a reputation as being an absolutely ruthless bastard.'

'It doesn't sound as if you like him very much.'

'I love the Catholic church very deeply, Danny, but I loathe some of the humans that run it. Melendez represents a profoundly negative strand of the church, a strand that wishes to keep everything secret. I don't agree with him and I certainly don't agree with his methods.'

At six pm, Bosquet's phone rang. He answered and listened, then began to speak in a whisper to the vice-consul, who motioned for Danny to join them.

'They've found a male body in one of the pits and there's a wallet beside it containing Pavey's passport and credit cards,' Vice-consul Smith said. 'It looks like he's been dead for at least a week. He has compound fractures in both shins and likely bled out. The police want to know if Miss Naseby can come and identify the body. Do you think she's up to it, Danny?

Bearing in mind the corpse is quite badly deteriorated and there has been some animal damage.'

Danny looked at Miss Naseby.

'She's a lot tougher than she looks. And she speaks her mind. If she doesn't want to do it, I'll think she'll tell you.'

The consular staff had a short conversation with Naseby. She opened her eyes and rose slowly, looking calm and composed. Danny heard her say, 'Gordon has no children and I won't drag his sister all the way out here if I can spare her the inconvenience.'

The consular staff took Miss Naseby to the *Instituto de Medicina Legal* for the formal ID. Danny tried to inveigle an invitation inside but was firmly rebuffed, so Danny went to the bar opposite the place and, for the second time in a week, waited beneath the awning watching the rain.

Danny finished the news article on Gordon Pavey's death while he waited. Paco sent through the pictures and they sent it out to all the Spanish and UK nationals.

Thirty minutes later, the consular staff emerged with Naseby. They held a short conversation on the pavement. Naseby shook hands with them then looked around for Danny. When he waved, she walked towards him, holding a brown envelope. Inside were Pavey's passport, his credit card and a set of keys.

'They think it took Gordon days to die,' she said, staring up at the rain. 'I am going to find a hotel in which to stay. Then I am going to begin discussing how to bring legal action against Ms Allen. However, the pen drive that Gordon mentioned is not among his belongings. I can only surmise that it must still be in the pit where he met his death.

'I want you to help me find the information that Gordon scanned, Mr Sanchez. If he thought it worth risking his life for, I want to see it. If you get me that, I will give you all the details you need to tell my entire sorry story. I mean, I am presuming that is why you have been so uncommonly charitable towards me all this time.'

Danny listened and said, 'Only partly. But in that case, I need to speak to Teresa's sister.'

6

Carmen del Hoyo was seething. The article on her sister was a scandal.

She recognised the name of the journalist who had written the piece: Danny Sanchez. He was the bastard that had phoned her on her mobile phone, the private number she had made a point of not releasing to the press. She walked along the street, re-reading the *Gente de Hoy* article. It was spread over four pages, illustrated with photographs that either depicted Teresa in skimpy, tight clothing or utterly intoxicated. It was all in there: Teresa's drug problems, her sexual partners.

But it was the third paragraph that had broken Carmen's heart.

Teresa had had an abortion.

At first, Carmen had not believed it, but there was a long explanation from some ex-lover of Teresa's detailing where they had gone to get it done and how much it had cost.

When Carmen got into her car, she burst into tears, and for the first time in more than a week, she made no effort to stop herself. She sat with her head against the steering wheel, sobbing as the pain and fear and heartbreak flowed out of her. Carmen had never thought her sister could have been so selfish and stupid as to murder her own child.

But she needed to take steps. The business with the abortion was a new and unpleasant twist to the whole sorry business, but it needed to be dealt with. She dried her tears and phoned Monsignor Melendez.

'Carmen, my child,' he said. 'It is good to hear from you. Have you found something of import? Because I'm terribly busy at the moment and must—'

'Monsignor, I know this is a terrible imposition to ask from a man of your importance, but could we possibly meet up? I've just discovered something terrible about my sister and I fear it could seriously affect everything and I can't speak about it on the phone.

'And you were absolutely right about Teresa. I have found her laptop and there is all sorts of nonsense scanned onto the computer related to some place called the Santa Cristina health clinic.'

Melendez had been making polite excuses, but now he paused and said, 'Actually, I think might be able to clear some space in my diary. But I would have to come now. Is that convenient for you?'

Carmen said of course and drove back to her parents' flat. Once there, she made sure there were plenty of the biscuits that Monsignor Melendez liked, but when she looked in the fridge, she found the milk was sour. She looked at her watch. She had time to pop out and get more.

Carmen went to the supermarket on the corner. In the queue, people stared at her. She'd become used to that in the last week, but she realised the way they were looking at her now was different: they were no longer looks of commiseration. Women were whispering.

It was that damned magazine article.

She stared the women down, paid for the milk and then hurried out onto the street again. As she neared her parents' flat, a neighbour stopped her.

'I thought I should tell you, there's a man waiting outside your house. I think he's a journalist.'

Carmen walked to the corner. The neighbour was right: a middle-aged man with curly blonde hair and a denim jacket was standing beneath the bay tree outside the entrance to her parents' building. He had to be a journalist. He had a shoulder bag and a camera and had that cocky look to him they all had.

Carmen felt her jaw tighten. She'd had about as much as she could take from these people. She was going to give him a piece of her mind. And then she realised who it was: it was that Sanchez fellow. She remembered him from one of the press conferences, as he had been the only foreign journalist there.

When Sanchez saw Carmen storming towards him, he threw the cigarette he'd been smoking to the ground and walked towards her, hand outstretched.

'Hello, Señorita del Hoyo,' he said in Spanish, 'my name is Danny Sanchez. If you've got a moment, I'd like to—'

That was as far as he got, because at that moment Carmen took a step forward, swung her handbag and hit him as hard as she could in the centre of his face.

The blow sent him flying backwards, so that he stumbled and fell. Blood began pouring from his nose.

'How dare you?' Carmen said. 'How *dare* you come here to my parents' home after what you wrote? You have no shame. No shame at all.'

Carmen stood motionless above him, fighting the impulse to hit him again. To think that this Sanchez bastard would have the nerve to come to her house. Time seemed to go in slow motion. A group of women had stopped on the opposite pavement and were staring at Carmen, while an elderly man in a jog suit was asking her what the hell she thought she was doing.

Carmen pulled away from the man and ran inside.

As always when she lost her temper, realisation of what she had done took a few minutes to fully register. The blow had cut the man's nose badly and he had fallen heavily. What if he was truly hurt? The fact that he had written all that spiteful nonsense about Teresa would be no defence if he decided to press charges with the police.

She took a roll of kitchen paper from the cupboard, wrapped ice cubes in a tea towel and went back outside, but the journalist was already gone. A pool of cherry red blood was drying on the pathway. Groups of people were still on the pavement talking and pointing.

When Carmen went back inside she saw that the journalist had left a bloodstained scrap of paper taped to the front door of the building.

Dear Señorita Del Hoyo,

I'm not sure why you have just broken my nose, but my name is Danny Sanchez and I am a journalist. I think I may have important information as to why your sister was killed and it centres on scans made of documents relating to a health clinic named Santa Cristina. If you want to know more, please contact me before you speak to anyone else.

Below it was written the journalist's telephone number.

Carmen went upstairs and sat in the kitchen. She reread the note. Damn these bloody journalists and their games. How could he know something about Teresa's death? Surely the police would have said something?

The doorbell rang.

It was Monsignor Melendez. He came in to the flat, his expression more than usually grave. He refused the offer of coffee and biscuits.

'Show me these documents,' he said.

'I will,' Carmen said. 'But first, there is something I must discuss with you.'

'What?'

'There is a magazine article that was printed today. It claims that Teresa had an abortion.'

'Yes, I know. I saw it.'

The man's matter-of-fact tone threw Carmen for a moment. 'But if it's true, it means Teresa has sinned against natural moral law and the infallible teachings and that she died without making any form of contrition. She has knowingly destroyed life. And the church teaches—'

'I'm well aware of what the church teaches.'

'I'm sorry, monsignor. I did not mean to show disrespect. But I must know what this will mean for my sister's soul,' Carmen said when Melendez said nothing.

But he was not listening. Instead, he was looking at the note the journalist had left her.

'What is that child?' he said. 'May I?' he said, leaning over and turning the note around before Carmen had answered. His eyes flickered over the note. When he looked up, his expression was angry.

'This is from a journalist, Carmen. Did we not discuss this? Did I not tell you that journalists are not to be trusted?' He gripped her arm. 'Did you speak to him? Did you tell him anything?'

'No, of course not. In fact, I hit him in the face. I think I might have broken his nose.'

Melendez's grip on her arm relaxed. 'That is good. And as for your sister, I cannot emphasise enough the threat to the girl's soul posed by her intrigues against the church. The sin of abortion pales into insignificance beside that. Now, I believe you mentioned your having located your sister's laptop. Show it to me.'

Carmen went into the bedroom and got Teresa's laptop. She opened it out on the kitchen table and showed Melendez the PDF files.

'Are you sure this is it?' he said as he looked through the files.

'I think so.'

'Have you seen any private medical files? Details of mothers and their children?'

'No.'

'Are you absolutely certain?'

'Yes.'

Melendez closed the laptop and tucked it under his arm as he stood and made to leave.

'Where are you taking that?' Carmen said.

'I'm afraid the laptop must come with me. It contains scans of private medical records which were stolen from an historical archive. The whole laptop must be destroyed. It is the only way to ensure this information will not be used to harm the church. Naturally, I will ensure that your family is fully reimbursed for the cost of the machine, if that is what concerns you.'

'Of course it is not the cost of the machine,' Carmen said, matching the snippy tone of Melendez's words. 'But that laptop has hundreds of Teresa's photos on it. It's full of memories. And besides, this information about Santa Cristina should be shown to the police. The journalist said it had something to do with why Teresa was killed.'

'Did I not tell you to disregard anything the press told you?' Melendez thundered. 'And the media pay the police to tip them off about stories. If this laptop is shown to the police, the information on it will end up being printed.

'The church has enemies, Carmen. They seek constantly to denigrate us, to turn people away from the true path of holiness. It pains me to say this, child, but you must face up to the fact that your sister was one of these people, wild with wickedness and hatred for the church. She stole important documents, documents that could be used to fabricate lies. Now step aside and let me get on with the church's work.'

Carmen tried to reason with him, but Melendez began to push past her, so she took hold of the laptop and prised it from his grasp.

'You're not destroying the photos of Teresa. Not until I have copied them for my parents.'

'The fate of your sister's soul hangs in the balance, and you talk to me of photos? Remember, that Hell is a bleak and selfish place, and its heat comes from the bitterness and hatred of the souls that are consigned there, each soul dwelling in utter isolation. Your sister was struck down because she went against the church. I would have thought you would have learned that from the miserable way in which she was killed, butchered like so much meat. Do you mean to consign your sister to eternal damnation?'

It was as if a mask had dropped from the man's face. All the concern and benevolence that he had previously shown towards Carmen had gone, leaving only an ugly, greedy impatience. When he met her eyes, she saw that he realised his mistake and the easy, bland smile returned.

'Are you telling me that my sister's salvation depends on my giving you this computer?'

'I am saying that now is the moment for you to be a good Catholic, Carmen, and to trust in the hierarchy of the church.'

'I *am* a good Catholic. But I'm nobody's fool, either. Because I think now the only reason you were ever interested in me is because of this computer. Tell me something, monsignor. Did you actually know Father Javier or was that a lie, too?'

Any pretence of civility disappeared from the man's face again.

'Give me the computer,' he said in a cold low voice.

'No,' Carmen said. 'Once I have taken all the personal data from the computer, you are welcome to come here and watch me delete these wretched files. Now, I'd rather you left my house, Monsignor Melendez. As you said yourself, you are a very busy man and I'm sure you must have other business to attend to.'

7

Santiago Encona phoned Álvaro from a payphone and told him he needed to meet up at the *mirador*, the flat plateau halfway up the mountain slope above El Cerrón. 'He'll be there in 20 minutes,' Santiago said when he put the phone down.

Ramón drove up there in his own car, fingering the handcuffs in his pocket as he went. First, he was going to try the same trick of the poisoned cocaine. But if Álvaro didn't go for it, he would cuff the fat bastard to the steering wheel and beat him unconscious. Then he would remove the cuffs and tip the car over the side of the road, into one of the deep valleys.

When Ramón reached the *mirador*, he parked in the darkness on the far side and got out of his car.

Álvaro was on time. Ramón waited for Álvaro to park and turn the engine off before he ambled up from the car's blindside, opened the passenger door and jumped inside.

'Hello, Álvaro,' he said.

'*¡Joder!*' the fat man said. 'You scared me. Where's Santi?'

'On his way.'

'How long's he going to be?'

'Don't worry about that,' Ramón said, opening the glove compartment and resting a small mirror on it. 'I've got something here that will make the waiting go quicker.'

He took a wrap of adulterated cocaine from his pocket and began to rack out two big lines.

Álvaro shook his head.

'Don't do one for me, Ramon. I don't do that anymore. It's my blood pressure.'

223

'Come on,' Ramón said, waving the mirror under his nose.

'I can't.'

'Well hold the mirror while I snort mine,' Ramón said, handing the mirror to Álvaro.

The fat man glanced around him nervously. Ramón pretended to rummage in his pocket for a banknote, but when his hand emerged it held the cuffs. He slapped one end around Álvaro's wrist — but the fat bastard had obviously been expecting something because he threw the mirror at Ramón's face.

Ramón heard the car door open, but he was too busy trying to wipe away the dusting of poisoned cocaine that now covered his face. He coughed and spat and wiped his face with his hands. There was a bottle of water in the glove compartment so he washed his face with it until he was certain that none of the substance had got into his eyes or mouth or nose.

Then he ran to his own car and pulled out onto the road.

Then Ramón started laughing as he caught sight of Álvaro trying to run away down the road, the full beams revealing that huge great butt of his joggling.

Ramón got out of the car and retrieved the tyre iron from the boot. Then he set off at a gentle jog after Álvaro.

Álvaro kept looking over this shoulder as he ran, and began emitting high pitched squeals of terror as Ramón closed on him. The womanly sounds, combined with the asthmatic wheezes coming from ahead, set Ramón to laughing again. He was within striking distance for at least twenty seconds before he actually felled the man with a solid crack across the back of his head. Blood spurted out in a spray. Álvaro fell to the ground without putting his hands out and his face took the full force of the fall.

Ramón dragged the man off into the darkness at the side of the road. His nose wrinkled. Álvaro had pissed himself.

After that, he sat on Álvaro's chest and played around with him for a while, holding his nostrils shut and watching blood and spit bubble on his lips. Álvaro was still only half-conscious, so Ramón stuffed his mouth full of dirt and wet pines leaves until he felt the fat man began to gag and choke. Then Ramón leant forward, so that his knees pinned Álvaro's arms to the ground and closed off his nostrils.

Álvaro came properly alive. He thrashed and bucked and his eyes opened and began to spin about in panic. Ramón rode the fat man until he was totally silent. Two thick streams of dirt had poured from his nostrils.

Álvaro seemed to be trying to say something so Ramón allowed him some air.

The fat man spat out the dirt and pine leaves.

'Don't kill me, Ramón. I know stuff. About Santi. Stuff I didn't tell you before.'

'What?'

'There's a secret he doesn't want anyone to know about. He's desperate. It's something to do with your Uncle Amancio and the Santa Cristina clinic. He was stealing children. Selling them. They've been sending him videos. Smashing open graves.'

'Why would Santi give a shit about anything Uncle Amancio did? The prick's been dead for years.'

'Because Santi thinks he's got a buyer for the golf course. He stands to make millions. The deal's going through later this year. But he can't afford bad publicity.'

'How do you know all this?'

'My cousin works in the town hall. Santi's been boasting about it to everyone who will listen. At least he was until all this business started. And there's a journalist. He knows everything. Santiago made me find his details. His phone number and address are in the car, Ramón. Let me go and I'll tell you where to find—'

Ramón punched him hard in the gut and said he would tell him now.

'The glove compartment. On a card.'

Ramón thanked him, then said, 'Look up at the sky and tell me what you see.'

It was a game Ramón had not played for what seemed like an age.

Every time the fat bastard said the obvious answers — the moon, stars, clouds — Ramón cracked him on the forehead with the tyre iron.

But finally he got it.

'I see darkness, Ramón,' Alvaro sputtered through the bloody mucus mess on his face. 'I see darkness.'

'Well done,' Ramón said, patting him gently on the cheek. 'That's all there is up there, no? Nothing but darkness. And that's where I'm going to send you now, you fat fuck.'

8

Danny drove himself to the hospital. It was only ten minutes up the road, but it seemed to take him an age to get there as he was forced to drive one-handed with his head tilted back while his other hand tried to staunch the flow of blood from his nose with tissues. What the hell had the woman had in her handbag? It felt as he'd been hit with a horseshoe.

The triage nurse at the A&E department asked him what had happened. When Danny said that someone had hit him, the man looked at Danny over the top of his glasses. 'You're a little old for fisticuffs, aren't you?'

'It was a woman.'

'Oh, well, that explains it then,' the nurse said with a dismissive shake of his head.

It wasn't until Danny was sitting down, waiting to be attended, that he spotted the magazine rack and saw the cover of *Gente de Hoy* — with his name splashed all over the front. He bought the magazine and retook his seat.

The article was about as bad as it could possibly have been: cheap, trashy and poorly written. He read it through, then ripped the magazine in half and stuffed it into a bin. Suddenly, his nose didn't hurt quite as much.

He phoned Paco Pino.

'I know what you're going to say,' Paco said when he answered.

'But I'm going to say it anyway, Paco. What the fuck did I tell you? I said I didn't want my name going on it. And half of the bullshit in that article had nothing to do with me, anyway. I never mentioned her abortion.'

'Danny, what can I say? I sent them your text with my photos and I made a point of telling them not to use your name. One of the sub-editors must have screwed up somewhere. Anyway, no harm done. We got the sale. By the way, have you got a cold? You sound kind of bunged up.'

When Danny explained what had happened and where he was, Paco dropped his phone. He was still laughing when he picked it up again.

'Didn't I tell you Carmen del Hoyo was crazy?' he chuckled.

'I think you're right. But you've got to go round to her house now and speak to her.'

That stopped Paco's laughter.

'What? Me? Why?'

'I need to speak to her, but I'm stuck at the hospital. Besides, even if I could go, I'm scared she'd take another swing at me. Let's face it, she's got every right to be angry.'

'And you want me to go? No way, José.'

'Paco, this could be a major story. There's a whole other side to this thing that nobody has covered. And it looks like the church might be involved. There's a monsignor who's taken charge of the whole thing and has already been applying pressure to the journalists at COPE.'

'If that's the case, you'll never get Carmen del Hoyo to play ball. She's a fully paid up member of the God Squad. I wouldn't be surprised if she was Opus Dei.'

'Just go there and talk to her. I left her a note. Tell her I think I can help explain why her sister was killed. And most importantly, explain to her what happened with that fucking *Gente de Hoy* article.'

'So she can take a swing at me, too? I think not.'

'Paco, it's important. This could help us break a major story.'

'How major?'

'European nationals major.'

Danny could hear the photographer considering the matter. 'OK. But if she busts my face up, you're picking up the plastic surgery bills. I'm ugly enough as it is without a crooked nose.'

An hour later, a nurse called Danny's name and he was shown through to a doctor.

She said, 'Rumour has it a woman did this to you. Is she your wife?'

'No. I'd never actually met her before.'

'Hell of a first date,' she said. 'I'm going to have to reset the cartilage in your nose and it's going to smart some. I hope she was worth it.'

Thirty minutes later Danny left the hospital with a strip of Elastoplast over the bridge of his nose. He lit a cigarette and paused to examine his reflection in a window. His nose was swollen and misshapen and bruises were starting to appear around both eyes. When he turned his phone back on, he saw that Paco had phoned. Danny phoned him back.

'I've no idea why, but she's agreed to speak to you,' Paco said. 'She certainly didn't seem too happy about the prospect. She wants us to go to her parents' flat.'

They met outside the building. When Paco saw Danny, he did what any good photographer friend would do: first he pissed himself laughing, then he whipped out his camera and took some shots of Danny's injured face.

'Quit dicking about,' Danny said as he rang the intercom buzzer to the flat.

'I'm not. The kids will love these photos. Uncle Danny looks just like Kung Fu Panda.'

Carmen del Hoyo was obviously not a woman accustomed to apologising. She greeted Danny and Paco with a silent nod of her head, arms crossed, and offered them coffee. When she had made it and set out a plate full of biscuits, she said, 'I'm sorry about your nose,' in about as recalcitrant a tone as Danny had ever heard.

Danny gave a half-smile. 'I would say "no harm done" but as that's patently untrue, I suggest we just forget about it and get down to business. And for what it's worth, I'm truly sorry for the things that were printed about your sister in the magazine. It wasn't my intention for such personal and hurtful information to be made public. But I've got to ask: what the hell do you carry around in your handbag that weighs so much?'

Carmen looked awkward then said, 'I think it must have been my bible.'

'I'll never doubt the power of the Lord's word again.'

Danny said it with as much of a grin as he could muster, but realised it was the wrong tack to have taken. She looked at him coldly and said, 'What a terribly clever thing to have said.' She crossed her arms again. 'In your note, you said you have information regarding my sister's death. I hope for your sake that is true, because if this is just some cheap trick to gain—'

'It's true.'

'Then you'd better start convincing me.'

Danny told her the whole story. He began with Miss Naseby's father and the headstone; then he recounted Gordon Pavey's trip to Spain and his suspicions that Naseby might have been illegally adopted; then he explained how Pavey had contacted Teresa, and together with Vladi had gone to the archive in El Cerrón.

It was the first time Paco Pino had heard the story, too, and both he and Carmen del Hoyo listened to Danny's monologue in rapt silence.

Danny said, 'I think Vladi and Pavey went into the archive and took documents that prove illegal adoptions occurred at Santa Cristina. That would implicate both the Encona family and the church.'

'Are you suggesting the Catholic Church had my sister killed?'

'Of course not. In fact, I don't think anyone meant for your sister to be killed.'

'Primitivo Pozos hung her upside down from her ankles and bled her like a pig. I doubt that happened by accident.'

Danny said nothing. The woman's face showed a range of expressions: fury, frustration, hatred, heartbreak. He sipped his coffee while he chose his next words carefully.

'There's no doubt that Pozos was a sick and evil man and that he treated your sister in a despicable way. But what I meant to say is that I don't think your sister's path would have crossed with his had it not been for the information that was taken from the archive in El Cerrón.'

'Why not?'

'I think someone paid Pozos to go to the house to try to steal back the documents. Your sister happened to be there when he was burgling the property.'

'And you have proof of this?'

'No. If I did, I would have taken it to the police. But I think your sister made scans of the information that was taken and that they might be on her computer. And if I can see them, I think this whole thing might start to make more sense.'

Carmen del Hoyo considered this in silence. Danny recognised the expression on her face: she was trying to decide what to do, and one of the options went against her natural way of thinking.

'I take it you're not a Catholic,' she said finally.

'No, I'm not,' Danny said without any hesitation. 'In fact, I'm an atheist.'

'Then you are an enemy of the church?'

He thought about that. 'I suppose you might say I'm an enemy of some of the people within the church, people who would rather sweep inconvenient truths under the carpet rather than deal with them openly and make the church a better institution.'

That seemed to be the right answer. She sipped her coffee and said, 'If this information were on Teresa's computer, tell me why I shouldn't take it straight to the police.'

'I think you should take it to the police. Just not yet. Because as soon as you mention it to the authorities, they will take the computer from you as evidence. If you do have it, let's at least work on it ourselves and see how it fits in with the information I have already discovered. I think there is compelling evidence to suggest that illegal adoptions occurred at Santa Cristina.'

'What will you do with this information?'

'Use it.'

'To make money?'

'Yes. And to tell the truth.'

She looked at him carefully as she considered these words, staring deeply into his eyes.

'My family and I have been through hell recently, Mr Sanchez. But I want to know the truth. You are correct in the assumption that they took records from the Santa Cristina clinic. My sister has scans of them on her computer.'

9

Carmen went to retrieve the laptop from the bedroom. When she entered the room, she crossed herself and knelt in prayer. It was not the most appropriate place to pray, but she could not do it in front of the journalist and the photographer and she needed to ask the Lord's forgiveness for what she was about to do.

She stood up and returned to the living room with the laptop, which she placed on the coffee table.

The computer screen flickered into life.

'Here are the files of the scans that I mentioned,' Carmen said, indicating a folder icon on the desktop screen. 'But I have no idea what they mean.'

The blonde journalist went to work, his eyes glued to the screen as he looked through the PDF files one by one: the Santa Cristina admissions book, the birth records and the ledger recording stillbirths. The big, bald photographer contented himself with stuffing biscuits.

Carmen watched the journalist as he worked, this Danny Sanchez person. He was unshaven, his rumpled clothes stank of cigarette smoke, and there was something innately ridiculous about middle-aged men who wore earrings and denim and t-shirts. And yet she believed him. When he spoke, he did so in a quiet, calm voice, his brows furrowed in concentration, and when he'd apologised to her for the magazine article there had been no mistaking the sincerity in his eyes.

'Does this information mean anything to you?' Carmen said.

Danny nodded.

'I think what we have here confirms my suspicions. These must be the documents that Lopez and Pavey took from the archive on their first visit. And there must be something significant about them, as they returned to the archive on the Saturday morning. I think we can use this to work out which of these children were stolen from their mothers.'

'How?'

'Because I know the precise details of one case where it actually happened.'

Danny began searching through the PDF scans looking for the birth details of someone called Miss Naseby, the one case he said he knew for certain was an illegal adoption, looking for anomalies. He quickly found what he needed to look for. Naseby's mother, Elisabeth Naseby, had been admitted to Santa Cristina as a "mother in labour" on January 13th, but her name did not appear in the obstetrician's records — which was logical, as there had been no birth; she was only there to collect someone else's child.

Then Danny looked for the name of María del Mar Torres García in the records of stillbirths. She was recorded as having died on January 12th, 1949 of otitis media.

Afterwards, they began searching for the names of all the women in supposed labour admitted to the clinic that did not appear in the birth records. They then cross-referenced this with the ledger that recorded stillbirths. In every case, the fake mothers were admitted to hospital the day after a child had supposedly been stillborn.

They sat in silence as Danny sat counting the total number of cases they had identified, knowing it was dozens, hoping it would not reach the hundred mark.

'According to this, between 1947 and 1959 which is all we can really do with the records being incomplete—'

'How many is it?' Carmen said.

'Seventy-one. But then the third PDF is incomplete. It must be more.'

Paco blew air and asked if he could smoke.

'Certainly not,' Carmen said.

The two journalists disappeared downstairs.

Carmen sat looking at the list of names and dates of the supposedly stolen children. That bastard Melendez. He had played her for such a fool with his fake sympathy. Of course he would have wanted to keep this quiet.

Earlier on, after she had thrown Melendez out, she had phoned Antonio, the sacristan, and asked him if he'd had a chance to enquire about Melendez.

Antonio's response had been nervous. 'The only Monsignor Melendez we know is a member of the Legionaries of Our Lady of Sorrows and works directly for high ranking members of the church here in Spain.

'Whether it is the same man, I cannot say. But I can assure you of something, Carmen: I served Father Javier for 30 years, and saw him nearly every day and to my knowledge he never met with or even mentioned any Monsignor Melendez. And if it is the same man, I fear it would have been impossible for them to have been friends: Father Javier was an open, progressive man. He did not hold with the beliefs espoused by the Legionaries.'

Carmen had been sitting in the kitchen brooding on the betrayal when Paco, the photographer, had knocked on the door of the flat. It was the only reason she had listened to him.

The journalists returned. They had obviously been talking outside because when they returned to the living room, Danny said, 'Can we have a look at Teresa's email?'

'No. It's password protected.'

Danny gestured towards the photographer. 'Paco's pretty good with computers. He can probably get around the password as long as the email session is still logged in on the browser page.'

'But let's try the obvious route first,' Paco said. 'Is there any way of getting a prompt or clue as to the password?'

Carmen nodded.

Danny gave a slow smile when he saw it: Russian that resisted.

'I don't think we're going to need your skills, Paco. I think I can guess this.'

It took him 30 minutes with a Wikipedia page open on something called Pavlov's House to find the right combination: YakovPavlov42.

'We're in,' Danny said.

'How on earth did you know that?' Carmen said.

'It was the name of Vladimir's Lopez's house. It seems he'd made quite an impression on your sister.'

Danny opened the web browser. It took him straight into the email account's inbox. There were more than a hundred unanswered emails, all of which dated back to the days around Teresa's disappearance. Those which weren't spam were messages enquiring whether she was OK and where she was.

Danny went to the messages sent section of the email account.

The last message Teresa sent was to someone called capitanpicaro@yahoo.es.

It read:

I've sent the video. Let's hope this shows them that we mean business. If we don't get any response from this one, we will do the second grave as discussed. If that fails to get a response, I think we should take what we have to the press.

The message had been sent at 10:43 on Sunday, October 2nd.

Another email had been sent four minutes before it to prensa@elcerronayto.es.

'That's the email address for the press department at El Cerrón's town hall,' Danny said.

That second email had an attachment, an MP3 file. Danny downloaded it.

It was a video file, shot on a mobile phone. The images had been shot at night. Carmen could make out a female figure, dressed in tight black clothing, her face covered by a ski mask. She seemed to be inside a warehouse or some such place as someone walked behind her, filming. Then the clouds parted, the moon appeared, and Carmen saw the woman was actually walking through a cemetery. What she'd taken for shelves were actually the burial niches, stacked four high on either side and decorated with urns and floral tributes.

A torchlight shone on a lapidary stone. The child's name could not be made out but the date of death was clearly visible: October 2nd, 1953. The camera remained focused on the lapidary stone for a number of seconds. Then a woman's voice said, 'It is 02:12 on Sunday, October 2nd. I'm now going to open this grave and show the world what is inside.'

Carmen's jaw tightened as she heard the voice: it was Teresa's.

Teresa then took a mallet and smashed the lapidary stone into pieces. It took her a few minutes to break through the marble and the bricks behind it. She reached into the hole and pulled out a small wooden coffin, which came apart in her hands as she did so.

'Look at this,' Teresa said. 'There is nothing inside this coffin but bags of sand.'

She turned towards the camera and began to speak.

'I am sending this to you because I want you to know that the secret of Santa Cristina and its stolen children has been discovered. We will continue to break open these graves until you give to us the location of the resting place of the true martyrs of El Cerrón, the 14 Republicans who have lain buried like dogs for more than 70 years. Send the details to this email address.'

Danny looked at the date.

'This makes sense. The message was sent on Sunday, October 2nd. Santiago Encona would have received it on the Monday morning and gone racing down to the archive. That was how they discovered that documents had gone missing.'

'And who is Santiago Encona?' Carmen asked.

'He is the mayoress's son. I think he is the person that was so desperate to keep this business quiet. And the obstetrician that was responsible for stealing all those children was his grandfather.'

'So he's responsible for killing my sister?'

'It's possible,' Danny said, looking through a timeline in his notebook, 'in a roundabout way. If Encona went to speak to Belasco at the archive on Monday the 3rd, he would have found out it was Vladi and Pavey who had stolen the material. And he might have discovered that Vladi was supposed to be speaking at the meeting on the 4th. It would have been the perfect opportunity to burgle his house. But Vladi came home early, and I think your sister gave him a lift. That was when she was kidnapped.'

'Then you need to publish this right now,' Carmen said. 'Phone the press. Phone *El Mundo*. Phone the police.'

'It's not enough.'

'What the hell do you mean it's not enough? My sister has been raped and murdered. To say nothing of all these poor children.'

The journalist noted the anger in her voice. He leant backwards as he said, 'Hey, calm down. I mean the evidence is not enough: it's all circumstantial. We think we know what's happened, but we can't prove it. Not yet. If we present this half-cocked, there's a chance the people involved will be able to wriggle off the hook.'

'What do you propose?'

'For starters, someone else is clearly involved. Someone who was holding the camera in that video. And it was likely the same person that smashed another grave open recently, the one that made it into the papers.'

'So how do we find this person?'

'I think there's a good chance the person behind this capitan picaro email address knows something, so let's send a message to see what he or she says. What do you think, Paco?'

But Paco wasn't listening. He was staring intently at the list of names Danny had made of the faked stillbirths.

'Those graves that were smashed open,' the photographer said slowly. 'You said they were being smashed open on the same date as the children supposedly died.'

'Yes. Why?'

'Because there's a child here who died October 16th, 1956. Doesn't that mean that whoever's smashing these graves will do another one tonight?'

10

Ramón wiped the blood, snot and spit from his hands, then looked behind him at the fat body that lay amid the undergrowth. Álvaro's top had ridden up while he struggled and moonlight shone upon the pale, hairy skin of his gut.

He hadn't planned on killing him this way. Now he was left with the problem of what to do with the body. He couldn't leave it where it was: the buzzards and vultures would find a huge mound of blubber like that as soon as the sun began to warm it. But there was no way of burying him. The earth up there in the mountains was only about five or ten centimetres deep. Beneath that it was solid rock or slate. Ramón toyed with the idea of taking the body elsewhere and burying it, but he didn't much fancy driving with a dead body in the boot. No, he would have to make it look like a car crash. It was the only way. It wouldn't fool the police for long, but it would give Ramón time to get a nice, tight alibi worked out.

Ramón got back into his car and drove up to Alvaro's vehicle. First he rummaged in the glove compartment until he found the card with the journalist's name and address on it: Danny Sanchez. He wondered if it was the same man he'd seen Santiago talking to in the town square.

He pocketed the name and address, then drove Álvaro's car back down the road and dragged his body into the driver's seat. There was a tube in the boot, so he siphoned some petrol from the car into a water bottle. He doused the back seat with it, then lit it. He waited for the flames to really take inside the car, then he released the handbrake and gave it a shove. The car trundled for a bit, the flames dancing crazily through the rear windscreen, then began to gather pace as it rolled downhill towards a sharp bend in the road. The flames disappeared as the car pitched forward into the valley, its rear end rising up high, wheels spinning. Then came a series of crashes and bumps and it was gone. Ramón smiled, thinking how well Álvaro's blubber would burn.

Plenty of tallow in that candle.

Then Ramón drove back to town and headed for the autovia. If this journalist had found something, Ramón wanted to know what it was.

11

Danny and Paco decided it was a three-man job: two people needed to follow whoever was breaking open the graves into the cemetery so that they could get photos of the vandalism actually taking place. The third would stay with the vandal's car and get ready to follow it should the other two lose sight of the vandal.

'And I suppose you'll be expecting me to stay with the car?' Carmen said.

Danny and Paco exchanged looks.

'I hadn't been expecting you to come along at all,' Danny said.

Carmen del Hoyo's expression became combative. 'Why? Don't you think I can handle myself?'

Danny pointed at his broken, bruised face.

'I think you can handle yourself just fine. What I'm worried about is your temper.'

'What about my damned temper?'

'A job like this needs a cool head. We need to follow whoever is doing this back to their base, which means we can't risk being seen.'

'I can assure you I won't do anything to jeopardise discovering who this person is. That is, unless you try to prevent me from coming with you.'

Danny looked at Paco. The photographer gave an imperceptible shake of his head, but Danny could see there would be no arguing with the woman.

'OK,' Danny said, 'You can come. But you're right, you'll be staying with the car.'

Carmen made more coffee as Danny and Paco discussed how they would handle things. Danny pulled up a Google Earth image of the cemetery on Teresa's laptop. The cemetery could only be approached from one direction but the road looped all the way around the walls.

They set off at 10:30 and arrived at the cemetery at eleven. The cemetery was roughly rectangular in shape. After driving around the perimeter, Danny located two places where they could more or less watch all four sides. They parked off the road and hid among the trees. Paco waited on his own, while Danny waited with Carmen.

He tried to make small talk with her as the long minutes ticked by, but she didn't seem in the mood to chat.

It was cold. Danny stamped his feet. Around midnight a car arrived, full beams blazing. Danny knew straight away it wasn't the vandal: music pounded within the vehicle and he heard laughter and doors slamming. Then came the sound of bottles chinking as a group of young men and women began to drink from plastic glasses and pass spliffs between them.

They were still there at one am and Danny was becoming worried they might stay the whole night: their slurred words still had a good few hours of party left in them and one of the girls was babbling about how beautiful the sunrise was from the top of a nearby hill to which they could walk.

It was time for action.

'Hello, *policía local*?' Danny said, trying to speak into his phone without sounding like he was whispering. 'I live near the cemetery and there's a terrible racket going on.'

Ten minutes later a patrol car appeared. The youths turned the music down and made hurried attempts to hide spliff butts. Five minutes of drunken arguing followed as the police told them to move on and the youths said they weren't doing anything wrong.

Eventually the youths left. The patrol car slowed as it reached Danny's cars. A torch beam played over the interior, then the car moved off, its headlights disappearing around a corner.

Danny settled down to wait again. When he lit a cigarette, Carmen del Hoyo stared at him disapprovingly.

'Hey, I made a point of standing downwind of you so the smoke wouldn't go in your face,' Danny said.

'I don't care about the smoke. But what if someone sees the light of the cigarette between the trees? I thought we were supposed to be doing this surreptitiously.'

Danny took one long, last, deep draw on the cigarette then stubbed it out.

The car appeared at two am. It parked on the far side of the cemetery, at a point roughly equidistant between Danny and Paco's cars. A man in black clothing and a ski mask emerged, carrying a bag of tools. After taking a quick look around, he hurried towards one of the trees that grew beside the cemetery wall and began to climb up.

'OK, I'm going into the cemetery with Paco,' Danny said.

He handed Carmen a roll of tape.

'Take this and put two strips on the bumper of the bloke's car.'

'What is it?'

'It's a trick I learned from a Paparazzi photographer years ago. Retro-reflective tape stuck to a car's bumper makes it easier to follow at night. When he drives off, we'll follow him back to wherever he goes, then Paco and I will confront him.'

Carmen didn't look particularly convinced, but Danny didn't have time to argue. He met with Paco and they climbed up into the tree and over the cemetery wall.

The wind blew, rustling the dried flowers that hung from the lapidary stones. Clouds covered the moon, but occasionally it shone forth, casting pools of silver light and swift shadows on the white marble all around them.

Danny heard the sounds of talking up ahead. He crept to the end of one of the rows of burial niches and peered around the corner. The man was filming himself in front of the grave.

They waited until they heard the sound of tools clinking and dull thuds. A sudden crack rang out, followed by more muffled sounds. Danny and Paco photographed and filmed the man as he smashed the lapidary stone, reached inside and pulled out the rotted remains of a coffin.

'Let's head back to the cars and get ready to follow him when he leaves,' Danny whispered.

They hurried back to the wall. Paco gave Danny a foot up, then Danny helped pull Paco up onto the cemetery wall, making surprisingly little noise while they did so, considering they were both middle-aged, overweight and loaded with cameras.

Danny swore as he dropped to the ground on the other side. The fall seemed far further than he had anticipated.

'You drive out onto the main road and park there,' Danny said. 'As soon as he passes you, start up the motor and follow him. I'll watch for him to leave and follow him from here. Let's stay in contact via mobile.'

Danny scurried back to his car.

Carmen del Hoyo wasn't there.

Where the hell has the woman got to? Danny thought, peering into the undergrowth. The moon cast ghostly shadows amid the trees, but Danny could see no sign of her. He hissed her name a couple of times.

There was no response.

He heard Paco's car start up and watched it trundle down the road towards him with the headlights off. When he drew level with Danny's car, Paco wound the window down.

'What's the problem?'

'Carmen's not here.'

'Didn't I tell you she would blow it?'

'I can't leave her out here. You'll have to follow him on your own now, and I'll catch you up. Turn the engine off.'

They waited in silence. Danny looked back towards the wall. A few moments later, the figure in black appeared atop it. He dropped his bag of tools, then dropped nimbly to the floor behind them and scurried towards his car.

'OK, Paco, wait until he pulls out onto the main road then get after him. We'll be able to see which way he turns when he gets to the end of the road. I'll stay here and look for Carmen.'

Paco wasn't listening. He was looking towards the vandal's car.

'You won't have to look for her very far,' he said, pointing.

The man in black had reached his car now and had the boot open. And Carmen del Hoyo had emerged from the bushes beside it and was striding towards him.

'What the fuck is she doing?' Danny said as she tapped the man on the shoulder. When he spun around, she held something up towards his face, her arm fully extended, and there was a faint hiss, like an aerosol.

The man cried out, in surprise and irritation at first. Then his voice rose in pitch and became a scream, punctuated by swearing. He stumbled backwards, clawing at his face, then fell to his knees.

Paco got there first and jumped out of his car.

'She pepper-sprayed him! The crazy bitch has pepper-sprayed him.'

Carmen del Hoyo was shouting at the man.

'Who are you? Tell me who you are or I'll spray you again, you bastard.'

Danny ran up behind her and grabbed the aerosol from her hand.

'That's enough, Carmen.'

'Give that to me,' she said.

Danny took two steps back and put the aerosol in his bag.

'The guy's in agony, Carmen. I'm not going to let you spray him again.'

The man was writhing on the ground now and moaning, 'I'm blind. I'm fucking blind.'

Paco said, 'I told you we shouldn't have brought this crazy cow with us.'

Danny told him to be quiet, then turned towards Carmen.

'What the hell do you think you're doing?'

Carmen had her hands on her hips.

'That bastard knows something about why my sister was making those videos and to whom she was sending them. Do you seriously think I was going to trust you and your stupid strips of tape to take care of things? What if you'd lost him? And even had you managed to follow him, then you would have had to knock on his door and confront him.'

'We would have handled it.'

'Take a look in the mirror, Mr Sanchez. I'm 5 foot 4 inches tall and weigh 10 stones, and I managed to break your nose and black both eyes with a single swing of my handbag. "Handling" things does not seem to be your forte. Besides, you wanted to ask him questions.' She gestured towards the man

247

writhing on the ground. 'Ask away. I'm sure you'll find him responsive now.'

Paco was kneeling beside the man trying to help him. He pulled the ski mask from his head and poured water into his eyes.

Danny turned on his torch. The light revealed a young man with curly hair. His eyes were red raw and mucous was pouring from his nose.

Carmen blew air. 'I don't believe it,' she said. 'I thought I recognised the voice.'

'Do you know him?' Danny said.

'Yes, I damned well do. It's Teresa's boyfriend, Samuel.'

12

Ramón parked in the street. The journalist lived in a small bungalow surrounded by an acre of terrain filled with olive trees. There was no car in the driveway and the house was in darkness.

He drove back into town, stopped at a payphone and dialled the journalist's landline. There was no answer. Ramón drove back and parked on the opposite side of the property so that his car was closer to the house. In and out quick, that was the secret to a successful burglary.

He climbed the fence, scurried through the darkness and jemmied the front door open. He stepped into a living room. The office and bedroom were off to the right.

Ramón went into the office and looked among the documents on the desk. Álvaro had been right. The journalist was investigating Santa Cristina. Ramón spoke a little English, enough to piece together a rough idea of what the documents on the office desk said: children had been stolen from their mothers at the clinic, which meant Uncle Amancio had to have been involved.

Ramón laughed at the old bastard's greed. He could never get enough, could he? Still, this stuff was dynamite. With this, Ramón had something he could really use to screw little Santi. Cousin Leticia, too. They would pay anything to avoid having to face the sort of shit-storm a revelation like this would cause them. But he could think about that later. He needed to get going. The longer he stayed there, the more chance there was of his being caught.

Below the article, there was a photo of some crazy woman and a written account of how she had burnt Santa Cristina to the ground. Ramón remembered something about it from when he was a child. Beneath the sheet of paper were a number of black and white photographs of some kid on a chair.

Ramón shone his torch on them as he hurried towards the door.

13

'His name is Samuel Herrero,' Carmen said. 'He was Teresa's boyfriend.'

The young man seemed in less pain now that Paco had washed a couple of litres of water over his eyes.

'Is that you, Carmen?' Herrero said. 'What the fuck did you to me? I thought I was going blind.'

'I think we need to talk, Samuel,' Danny said. 'But I suggest we don't do it here, given that you've just desecrated a grave.'

There was no way the young man could drive — he could barely open his eyes — so they agreed to take him back to his flat. 'But I'm not going in the same car as her,' Herrero said, pointing in the vague direction of Carmen del Hoyo.

'And I've no intention of travelling in Señor Sanchez's rust bucket again,' Carmen said.

'That's that sorted then,' Danny said, patting Paco on the back. 'Enjoy the drive.'

Danny got to Herrero's flat a little after 3 am. The guy obviously came from a rich family — the flat was in a building that overlooked the prestigious *Avenida de Federico García Lorca*.

Before Danny parked he asked Herrero if his parents were home. Herrero said that he lived there alone.

'It belongs to my grandparents,' he said when Danny gave an impressed whistled. 'They let me use it.'

'How are your eyes?'

'I can more or less see now,' he said. 'But the skin around them burns.'

They waited for Paco and Carmen del Hoyo to arrive, then rode the lift up to Herrero's flat.

'We saw you at the cemetery,' Danny said when they'd all sat down in the living room. 'Why have you been smashing open graves? I'm assuming it was you that went with Teresa on that first occasion?'

'Yes.'

'Why were you doing it?'

'To put pressure on the town hall. We know the mayoress knows where the Republican bodies are buried, but she won't tell us. And it was important to Teresa. That's why I went tonight,' he said, turning now to Carmen. 'I did it for your sister.'

'And that's what got her killed, you bloody idiot,' Carmen said.

'Hey,' Danny said, motioning for her to calm herself, 'that's not true.' He leant towards her and lowered his voice. 'Perhaps it might be better if I spoke to him alone.'

'Like hell you will! She was *my* sister. Mine.'

Samuel was rubbing his eyes. He said, 'For your information, it was all Teresa's idea. All of it: smashing the graves open, filming ourselves doing it, sending the damn MP3 files to El Cerrón. I told her it was a dumb idea, that it was bound to have consequences, but she wouldn't listen. She was convinced she could force the council's hand because it was the mayoress's father who had been responsible for it all.'

'How did you know which graves to smash open?' Danny asked.

Samuel looked at the floor, as if debating a difficult decision.

'Come on,' Danny said, 'if you've got something relevant, now's the time to show it to us.'

He went into the bedroom. Danny heard the sound of a cupboard being opened and of items being removed and placed on the floor. Samuel came back with a cardboard box.

'Here,' he said, dumping it on the coffee table. 'This is how I knew.'

'What is this?' Danny said.

'Vladi and the Englishman went to the archive and got some ledgers that recorded the admissions and stillbirths at the clinic. They used them to work out a list of names of all the children that had supposedly died, the mothers from whom they'd been stolen and the mothers to whom they'd been given. So the next day they went back and they searched for the relevant medical files. These are all the ones they managed to find.'

Danny pulled the top from the box.

He had never imagined so much pain could be contained in so small a space.

The box contained dozens of cardboard folders. The cover of each folder was labelled with a name. They were names Danny recognised, names of people who were supposedly dead.

He opened one of the folders, then a second, and a third. They were all the same: each folder contained the specifics on how a child had been stolen from their rightful parents and given away to someone else. Some had photos, the pose always the same, the exhausted, heart-broken mother cradling a dead child she thought was hers. Danny realised the baby was identical in each shot despite the cases being separated by years. That must have been the child's corpse that Frank Dale had found, mummified.

He flicked through the folders, stunned by the malice of Amancio Encona. The bastard had kept tabs on who the real parents were, who the adoptive parents were, the birth names, the adoptive names.

And the prices he'd charged.

The information would finish Leticia Encona. Her father had made a fortune from the sales of the children.

This is what Santiago Encona had been so desperate to conceal. A revelation like this would draw worldwide press coverage, make El Cerrón a name like Dunblane, Hungerford, Columbine, a town forever associated with tragedy. It would kill any hopes of resurrecting the golf course project. Who would want to touch anything built within a mile of that place once the truth came out?

And it *would* come out. Danny would see to that. For poor Gordon Pavey, for Teresa del Hoyo, for Helen Naseby.

But first he would need some rest.

He told Samuel Herrero he was taking the files away with him. Herrero protested, but then Danny asked if he would rather he get the police involved. That took the wind from his sails.

'I tell you what, I'll scan all this information and bring you a CD of it,' Danny said. 'Once I've published my story, that is.'

Paco took Carmen del Hoyo home. She went without saying goodbye to Danny.

That was fine by him. He'd had enough of the woman anyway.

It was 04:30 when Danny pulled off the autovia and headed towards his house. He needed a shower, clean pyjamas and four hours' sleep.

He didn't notice anything was wrong until he was walking through the olive grove towards his house. The door to his house stood wide open: the door's lock had been smashed, and splintered wood surrounded the frame.

Danny was two steps inside the house when Ramón Encona emerged from behind the open door and hit Danny a well-placed blow on the base of the skull. Danny's legs crumpled and he fell forward, unconscious.

Part IV — Vidas Robadas

1

Ramón couldn't think straight. He was too angry and confused.

He was driving now, heading back towards El Cerrón, with the journalist handcuffed in the boot of the car. The information Ramón had taken from the man's office was on the front seat. Ramón's eyes flickered towards the cardboard file that held the photographs of the small boy sitting on a chair. The journalist had been carrying a box of files. Ramón had those, too, and the journalist's shoulder bag.

All his life he'd felt his existence had comprised of a tangled mess of loose threads. Now it was as if someone had yanked one of those threads free and everything had unravelled.

He looked at his watch: it was 04:47. He dialled Santiago's number. The phone was answered immediately.

'Ramón, where the hell have you—'

'Shut up and listen. Meet me at La Piltra.'

'Did you do it?'

'Do as I say and you'll find out, won't you?'

Santiago was still speaking as Ramón hung up.

He'd had it with Santiago. The little prick thought he could buy his way through life without ever getting his hands dirty. Well, not tonight. Tonight Ramón was going to get some answers.

And then someone was going to pay.

2

Danny came to in complete darkness. He blinked his eyes and tasted air that was damp and earthy. Where was he?

He searched for clues in the fuddled recesses of his mind but there was nothing of any use: his memories were all of physical things, impact and pain. His mind stung with them, the way flesh remembers a slap. Memory ended in mist. His right eye was sticky and wet. His back teeth were loose. When he swallowed, it tasted of blood.

He tried to move, but found he couldn't: his hands were pinioned behind him. He tried to move them, heard something rattle and realised he was handcuffed. And there was duct tape over his mouth.

Panic took hold of him. He rolled from side to side and felt stones stick into his belly and chest. Then he tried to kneel, but realised the danger of pitching forward was too great. After that, he lay in the darkness, fighting the impulse to cry.

Rather than worry about what he didn't know, he tried to concentrate on what he did. He was tied up. Someone had done that to him, left him here a captive. The realisation stirred a faint memory. He couldn't remember why, but he knew he was in terrible danger. The certainty of it bubbled up suddenly and gripped his guts.

He was still fighting panic when a door opened, a light flickered on and a slender yet well-built man entered. He had sallow cheeks and short, dark hair. He looked familiar, somehow.

He sat on a chair opposite Danny.

'Hello,' he said as he casually examining his own fingernails. 'I bet you're wondering why I'm not wearing a mask, aren't you?'

Danny did nothing.

'The reason I've let you see my face is because it doesn't matter: you're not going to leave this room alive.'

Instinct made Danny struggle. The man squatted beside him and made soft shushing noises. When Danny continued to struggle he clamped Danny's nostrils closed.

Danny stopped struggling.

'That's good,' the man said. He had curious eyes, Danny realised: they were so devoid of any sense of empathy that they seemed entirely black.

'But you've got an important choice to make,' the man said. 'You can either die quick and easy. Or you can have me open up my tool box and die the other way. It's your choice. And it will all depend on how you behave in a minute. You see, there's a man coming here, and I'm going to ask him some questions. And then I'm going to take the tape from your mouth and you're going to get a chance to speak. Nod if you understand.'

Danny nodded.

The man stroked Danny's hair. 'If you answer truthfully, I promise to end you quickly and painlessly.'

Car wheels crunched on gravel outside. The man rose and walked to the door.

'In here,' he shouted, then left the room.

Danny fought fear. Only a clear head would get him through this. Why was the man's face so damned familiar? He looked around the room. He was in some type of concrete garage. The box of Santa Cristina files was in the corner, together with his shoulder bag.

He heard voices from outside the room.

A second man was saying, '…got precious little time for your games. What is this damned surprise you're so determined to—'

When Santiago Encona stepped through the door, his eyes met Danny's. His jaw dropped. He tried to jerk back out through the door, but the other man pushed him forwards into the room.

'What the hell have you done to him, Ramón?' Santiago said as he looked at Danny's black eyes and the strip of plaster on his nose.

Ramón Encona sneered. 'That wasn't me. He was like that when I found him. Anyway, why should you care if I'd hurt him? We're in this together, aren't we, *primo*? You said so yourself. Especially now that you've told the prick my name.'

'Why the hell have you brought him here?'

'Because the three of us need to have a little chat.'

'About what?' Santiago said, his eyes suddenly wary.

Ramón walked to the box of files and lifted an orange folder from it, the folder that Leonard Wexby had given to Danny. Ramón opened the folder and withdrew a sheaf of papers from within.

'This whole business has something to do with Uncle Amancio and that Santa Cristina place, doesn't it?'

'No.'

'Don't try to lie to me, you gormless prick. I can see from your face that it does. That was why you sent *El Porquero* and Álvaro to that house. Because someone had stolen documents from the archive that prove Uncle Amancio was stealing and selling children, hadn't they?'

'I've no idea what you're saying.'

'Yes, you *do*,' Ramón said in a cold, hard voice. He pointed at Danny. 'I went to this prick's house tonight and I found that he has all the evidence. I don't know what he's done with it. It could be that all this is going to hit the papers tomorrow no matter what we do now. But all that's beside the point.'

The fire in Ramón's eyes was replaced now by a look that was cold, hard, dark and infinitely more frightening.

'What I really want to know,' Ramón Encona hissed, brandishing the sheets of paper, 'is why a journalist, whom I've never met before in my life and who is investigating dozens of cases of illegal adoptions, has got seven photographs here of me when I was a boy.' He stuffed the printouts of the photos of Maria Topete's child into Santiago's hand.

'There, take them. Have a good look. It's me. In fact, I can remember my mother taking these photos. She used to sit me on a chair by the backdoor, every year, the day before my birthday.'

Danny began to kick and struggle. Here was his chance. He needed to speak to the man, to explain the story.

'Let's see what he's got to say, shall we?' Ramón said.

When he took a step towards Danny, Santiago cried, 'No, don't!'

Santiago's eyes were wide with fear and for a moment they flickered towards Danny. And as their eyes met, Danny realised why Encona was so afraid: the bastard knew.

Ramón yanked the duct tape from Danny's mouth and Danny began to shout the story of María Topete. Santiago ran across the room and tried to kick Danny in the stomach, but Ramón pushed him away. As Danny spoke, Ramón Encona's face held the expression of a man upon whom the truth of some dark, painful secret was finally dawning. His palms were pressed to the side of his head, and his fingers gripped clumps of his hair, tugging at them.

'They stole you from your rightful mother,' Danny said, 'and then they drove her mad with those photos. It's all right there in the folder, the whole story. And most importantly, that bastard knew,' Danny said, gesturing towards Santiago with his head. 'Look at his face. He knew.'

Ramón turned towards his nephew. Santiago began to stutter words of explanation. Then he turned suddenly and ran. Ramón set off after him.

Danny rolled across the floor and used the wall to help him struggle to his knees and then to stand up. Outside, he could hear the sounds of running feet. A car engine started and then came the sound of a windscreen shattering. A voice cried out, a curiously shrill, feminine sound.

Danny could try to run, but he wouldn't get far with his hands behind his back. He dropped to the ground, rolled onto his back, bent his legs up to his chest and began trying to slide the handcuffs down below his feet, the way he'd seen people do in films.

His first few attempts came nowhere close.

From outside came the sound of fighting. Again the shrill voice rang out and then something heavy impacted on something organic with a sickening crunch and the voice was silenced mid-scream. Danny heard more blows, accompanied by grunts and a horrible cracking noise.

He managed to get his hands down below his feet but they were stuck there. It felt like his arms were being wrenched out of their sockets.

The fight outside was over. Footsteps crunched on the gravel.

He squatted and slid the handcuffs to the back of his knees. Then he tipped backwards with his knees still drawn up and managed to slide the handcuffs beneath his feet.

Danny groaned as he struggled back to his feet, the handcuffs in front of him now, and staggered across the room towards the box of files and his shoulder bag.

Ramón Encona appeared in the doorway. The man's hands, chest and face were spattered with droplets of blood. Pink-red lumps of matter dangled from the sleeves of his coat and in his right hand he carried a rounded stone, one side of which was slicked with gore.

'Now it's your turn, prick,' Ramón said, hefting the stone in his hand. He came at Danny in a loping stride, arms spread, ready for Danny to turn and run or make a break past him.

Danny did neither. Instead, he reached inside his shoulder bag, raised the aerosol can he withdrew from it and blasted Encona's face with pepper-spray.

The stone fell to the earth as Ramón Encona's hands shot to his face. Danny hit him again with the pepper-spray, being careful to stay clear of the man's thrashing limbs as he raged on the floor, clawing at his face.

Danny paused long enough to deliver a single, well-placed kick right in the bastard's bollocks.

'That's for ruining my front door, you bastard.'

Then he ran like he'd never run before.

3

Ramón screamed as he thrashed on the ground. It felt as if burning coals had been jammed into his eye sockets. Tears streamed down his face, and his snot and saliva tasted of foul chemicals. Even with his eyes screwed shut, the pain was unendurable and kept building.

But it wasn't only physical pain that made him scream. What really wrenched the animal howls from deep within him was the fact that, despite being blinded, he had never before seen things so clearly.

His entire life had been a sham. The journalist's explanation had hit him on a visceral level like nothing else he'd ever experienced. The pit of his stomach seemed filled with cold, dirty water. And they had known. That was the worst part. The family had *known*.

He had no idea how long he thrashed and screamed on the floor. Eventually, the pain began to become more bearable and he stumbled outside and managed to locate a faucet. He lay under it and let the cold water wash over his face.

The pain in his eyes subsided.

But the other pain was still there.

He'd wanted answers, and now he had them. He dragged himself to his feet. He had only one thought in his mind.

Mother.

He climbed into his car and began to drive, swerving wildly from one side of the road to the other as he struggled to focus on the road. On two occasions he smashed into the wall at the side of the road and was forced to slow, but bit by bit he made his way down towards the town. When he reached it, he abandoned his car at the side of the road. He could not see well enough to drive through the narrow streets.

It was early morning, but there were still late night revellers on the street and people heading to early mass, and he was dimly aware of people staring at him as he stumbled along the streets, his eyes still streaming. He didn't care.

He rammed the key into the front door of Mother's home and kicked it open.

One of Mother's maids was in the hallway. She stared at him in horror and it was only then that Ramón caught sight of his reflection in the mirror and realised his clothing was spattered with blood and gore from what he'd done to Santiago.

Ramón pushed past her and the maid fled the house, screaming.

Mother was in the living room. She was struggling to stand when Ramón burst through the door.

'Ramón,' she said. 'How dare you! What do you think you're doing bursting into—'

'María Topete. Who was she?'

Mother fell instantly silent, but her eyes became quick and sly.

Ramón threw the printouts of the boy on the chair towards her.

'I remember you taking those pictures. One every year, out in the yard. What did you do to her?'

Mother stared at him. And then her wrinkled lips broke into a smile.

'You want to know about María Topete?' she said and then spat. 'Topete was the slut that stole my *novio*, the man I was supposed to marry. So I repaid her in kind. She took my life from me, so I took you from her. An eye for eye. And then I drove her mad.'

'You bitch. You ruined my life.'

Contempt flared in the old woman's eyes. She laughed. 'I ruined your life? What chance did you ever have, you miserable wretch? You were only ever the son of a wanton slut. Your bloodline was tainted long before I took you from her. Small wonder you turned out to be such dull wastrel. They all knew. All of them. Did you not realise how we used to laugh at you?'

Ramón was holding his head now, moaning and clutching at his ears as if he could block out the sound. Mother laughed.

'And you can whistle for your inheritance. You are not my flesh and blood and I've arranged it all with the lawyers. You won't get a single cent. Do you seriously think I would allow you to enjoy the inheritance of a family as illustrious as the Enconas? I knew you were rooting around down here for documents. Did you really think me so old and weak? You were never an Encona. You're just like the slut of your mother. I hope you rot in hell when—'

She got no further, because Ramón took her by the throat. He lifted her, their eyes locked together. He could feel the pulse in her frail neck.

'Look,' he said, 'look at the blood on my clothing. That's all that's left of your precious little Santiago's head.'

He threw her backwards.

'But I won't kill you. You're done for anyway. But I know now what happened at Santa Cristina and what Uncle Amancio did. And do you know who told me? It was a journalist, and he's got everything he needs to prove the story. So while the cancer in your gut slowly gnaws away at you from inside, you are going to watch as the whole shitty story comes out in the press: about what you did, what Uncle Amancio did. The children he stole, the lives he ruined.

266

'You are going to watch while the entire Encona family is picked apart and swallowed whole by the press. By the time they're done with you, you won't be able to look your maid in the eye for the shame.'

For the first time in his life, Mother had no retort. Her wrinkled lips fluttered as they sought a response, but the sparkle of triumph that had been there moments before had dulled.

Ramón leant over her and laughed in her face. Such precise and calculated cruelty was intoxicating, but it wasn't that which amused him. It was the thought that he'd never before so truly felt a member of the Encona family.

4

Danny ran as far as he could, away into the fields of olive trees beyond the house, his handcuffed wrists held out in front of him. When his lungs were bursting, he fell to his knees and looked behind him. There was no sign of pursuit. When he had his breath back, he began looking around, trying to get his bearings. He could see the lights of a town away to his right. To judge by the silhouettes of the mountains all around him, he guessed the town was El Cerrón, but he couldn't be sure. It was still too dark.

He looked at his watch. There was an hour until daylight. There was no point in blundering through the darkness, so Danny leant against the trunk of an olive tree and looked back towards the house to make sure Ramón Encona was not trying to follow him.

After forty minutes, he heard the sound of someone moving outside the house and climbing into a car. Headlights cut through the pre-dawn gloom. The car left.

It was then that Danny remembered the box of medical files. It might still be inside the house. This entire nightmare would have been for nothing without that information.

He crept back towards the house as the grey light of dawn began to appear behind the mountain peaks.

Santiago Encona lay on the floor outside, his head smashed into a bloody mess. Danny winced as he saw the man's injuries, then looked away and concentrated on not stepping in any blood.

Danny found the box of medical files in the concrete garage. His shoulder bag was still there, too, and his mobile.

He needed to phone the authorities, but he knew the first on the scene would likely be the local police. The chief of police was Encona's brother-in-law. He couldn't risk the Santa Cristina files falling into that guy's hands. Danny could just about manage to lift the box with his fingertips, so he raised it and put it on a chair. Then he slid his forearms beneath it, took the box outside and followed the perimeter fence until he found a place where he could hide it.

Then he took his phone from his bag and called the emergency services.

'I need report a murder,' he said, 'but I don't really know where I am.'

5

By mid-morning, the Spanish media was aflame with stories of Santiago Encona's murder.

Photos of his broken body lying on the ground were on the websites of nearly every newspaper in the country, whether local or national, together with pictures of Ramón Encona, and the news that the police were searching for him.

By then, news of what had occurred at Herminia Encona's house had spread and TV crews were there to capture the moment ambulance crews lifted Herminia Encona from her house on a stretcher, her face ashen white as she stared up towards the grey, empty sky.

For a period of some 6 hours, the streets of the El Cerrón seemed alive with the wail of sirens, the rumble of television news trucks and the enquiries of out-of-town journalists asking how to get to Santiago Encona's country house.

At midday, police arrested Ramón Encona in Almería city as he tried to sneak aboard the ferry for North Africa. They had already raided his rented flat in El Cerrón and found bloodstained clothing and a hastily scrawled note which explained exactly what had happened to Teresa del Hoyo, and stressing Santiago Encona's role in it.

By late evening, Danny had given his statement to the national police. When it was dark and the police had finished gathering evidence of Santiago Encona's murder, Danny went back with Paco to retrieve the box of Santa Cristina medical files.

The story was sufficiently juicy that they were able to sell it as exclusives to various publications. Danny wrote three stories in the end.

Gente de Hoy printed a four-page special that concentrated on the story of María Topete, Ramón Encona and the double murder. It appeared on the magazine's website the day after the murders took place.

Once the story of how Herminia Encona had stolen Topete's child and kept him as her own had been picked up by other media outlets, older residents of the town of El Cerrón began to talk. They remembered that Herminia Encona had once been engaged to a man named Gualterio Blanco. 'She had the dress made and everything,' one old man told reporters. 'But in 1959 he fell out with her brother, Amancio, and he broke off the engagement. They say the dress cost a fortune to make and when the tailor refused to take it back, Herminia had her brother ruin the tailor's business.'

The second story was written in Spanish and detailed everything: Amancio Encona's child trafficking, Teresa del Hoyo's murder, the documents that were taken from the town's archive. That one was picked up by *El País* and was given a double-page treatment.

For a few days after its publication, there were threats of libel action from Leticia Encona, who played shamelessly on the fact that she had just lost her son. Then her world collapsed.

Revelations of her father's crimes had rocked the foundations of her hold on the town. An unnamed source in the council went to the police with evidence of just how her corrupt her rule had been: thanks to more than a decade of vastly inflated invoices being charged to the council with no-one to challenge them — 3,081 Euros for changing a cracked paving stone was the example the Press seized upon to illustrate the extent of the corruption — tens of millions of Euros had been embezzled from council coffers. A huge police raid on the council offices saw thirteen people arrested, among them Leticia Encona and the chief-of-police.

The third story was geared for the UK market and concentrated on Miss Naseby's experience, while covering all the really good bits from the *El País* article. The story was picked up by *The Sunday Times* and given an eight-page treatment in the Sunday magazine. The by-line read By Leonard Wexby and Danny Sanchez.

Leonard had 20 copies of the newspaper couriered to his house first thing Sunday morning. At ten o'clock, he had Danny drive him round to a dozen of the old expat watering holes, and Leonard deposited a crisp copy of the newspaper on the bar in each. Then it was off to lunch at the local country club, where the remaining eight copies of the newspaper were deposited at various strategic points.

'This afternoon's debauch will be my treat,' Leonard said when Danny blanched at the prices on the menu.

The country club was the type of place that attracted the moneyed, second-home class of expats, and the drinking went on all afternoon on the terrace beside the pool. Leonard was in his element as he drifted from table to table, cigarette holder in hand.

Towards evening, the lights came on beside the pool. Danny was arguing good-naturedly about Gibraltar with the Spanish barman, when he smelt perfume and felt feminine fingernails brush against his cheek. He turned and found himself looking into his mother's face.

'Hello, you,' she said.

'Hello yourself.'

She was in her heels and skirt suit, and wearing more make up than she usually did.

'I read your article,' she said. 'It was fascinating stuff.'

'Thank you.'

'You don't mind me coming down here, do you? I heard there were a couple of journalists throwing a party and figured it would be you.'

'Of course I don't mind.'

'I'm still cross with you, though,' she said, tapping her finger on his chest.

'But you're going to forgive me because you're here with all your fancy friends and you want to show me off?'

'Really, Danny,' she said, curling her arm through his and leading him through the crowd, 'what a cynical way you have of looking at the world.'

Danny laughed, and said, 'I wonder who I get that from,' but she didn't hear him — she was too busy calling for her friends to come meet her Darling Danny, the one from *The Sunday Times…*

The next day, Danny went to see Miss Naseby. She was preparing to return to the UK. 'But before I do,' she said, 'I want to see the grave of this Amancio Encona chap. He seems to be the root cause of all this.'

The grave was not difficult to find, as it was the only one like it in the whole of El Cerrón's cemetery. Amancio Encona had obviously planned every grandiose detail of his mausoleum with the same meticulous care he had employed in ruining other people's lives. It was a huge, ostentatious thing of glittering white marble, covered with angels and pious inscriptions. An image of Amancio Encona's face occupied the centre of the headstone, the lip curled in that cruel, mocking smile.

Beneath his name were three words, sprayed in black paint, each letter a foot-high: *Chorizo de mierda.*

There were other signs of the grave having been defiled. Marker pen glasses had been drawn on the faces of one of the angels and broken shards of beer bottles and cigarette butts littered the place. It looked as if someone had urinated against one part of the marble. Unlike the rest of the immaculate cemetery, nothing had been done to repair the damage or to remove the litter.

Miss Naseby asked Danny to translate the graffiti.

'*Shitty Thief* would be about the closest approximation.'

She mouthed the words as she regarded the damage. Then she nodded in a gesture of slow approval.

'You said in your article that Gordon discovered a cache of medical files that revealed who had been stolen from whom.'

Danny had been dreading the question.

'Yes.'

'Am I among them? I mean the details of my real parents?'

'No, they're not.'

Naseby looked away and her eyes misted with tears.

'I didn't think they would be. That was why Gordon went back to Santa Cristina, wasn't it? He wanted to go into the cellar and find my file.'

'I think so.'

'So, he died because of me.'

'No. I think he died because he did something incredibly stupid — despite having the best intentions.'

She stared up at the cloudy sky with moist, bloodshot eyes. Then she said, 'I think I want to go home now.'

After all the articles were published, Danny gave the entire cache of medical documents to one of the associations campaigning for justice for the victims of illegal adoptions. The association set up a special forum dedicated to the children of Santa Cristina. They ended up having to employ two permanent workers to deal with the flood of enquiries they received when the information became public.

But there was one file Danny did not give to the association. The file detailed what had occurred to Josefina Hernandez's son, Manuel.

Danny called ahead and made sure that he got to speak to the son, José.

José met Danny in a café close to the house. Danny pushed the file across the table to him. 'I made a promise that I wouldn't publish anything that could harm your mother. I'm here to honour the promise. But you might want to reconsider delaying your search for your brother, because all the information you need to find him is right there.'

Afterwards, he drove round to see Carmen del Hoyo. She was at her parents' flat. Her mother was home from the hospital now, and the family were working on rebuilding their lives.

Carmen made coffee and Danny sat with her and her parents in the living room. When he came to leave, Carmen saw him to the door.

'I read your article in *El País*,' she said.

'And?'

'You did what you said you'd do, Señor Sanchez: you told the truth. I suppose that is all that can be asked of any newspaper article.'

Danny rummaged in his bag and withdrew the can of pepper-spray.

'I brought this back for you,' he said.

She smiled. 'You can keep it. They're not worth much half empty.'

Danny gave a hollow laugh. 'You have no idea how much that one was worth to me, Carmen. You really haven't.'

Danny was sitting on the patio of his house, drinking wine and playing guitar. He wasn't going to work today. It was always like this when he finished a big story: after the rush of publication he faced the comedown. He felt restless and tired.

According to that morning's papers, historians allied to the left were demanding access to the archive in El Cerrón in order to search for the documents they were convinced would reveal where the Republican bodies were buried.

Some things in Spain would never change.

At midday the postman arrived. He brought a single letter. The return address on the back of the envelope indicated it had come from the University of Málaga.

Danny opened the letter and read it on the patio.

'Dear Danny, re your question regarding your grandparents' experiences in 1937:

'I've looked into the matter you mentioned in your email. Given the highly personal nature of the matter, I have chosen to respond via conventional mail so that you will have a physical copy of the documents I have discovered.'

Danny sat for a long time with the photocopies folded in front of him on the plastic table. He smoked two cigarettes, looking towards the distant Sierra Nevada. Squinting, he could see the first white-frosting on the mountain peaks. The air smelt fresh and clean, the way it does in Spain when the wind draws the deep cold down from the sierras. Then he read the rest of the letter.

'As you'll see from the prison records, your grandfather was arrested on August 2nd, 1936 and was released on November 13th. The second set of documents relate to the Committee for Public Safety, as the ad-hoc justice department in Málaga was known. Your grandfather was "questioned" by them on three separate occasions. This is pure speculation on my part, but other documents I have seen relating to this body indicate that their methods of "questioning" could be extremely brutal.

'You seemed quite worried in your email about the possibility that your grandfather could have revealed the names of other people, but I think you should bear this in mind: if your grandfather did give them names, it was because they beat them out of him, and it took them three attempts to get them.

'I hope this gives you some degree of closure.'

Danny looked through the photocopies of the documents. Then he took his cigarette lighter, held the folded pages up and began to burn them from a corner. In a matter of seconds the flame licked upwards, engulfing the whole of the paper.

Danny dropped them and watched as the pages sizzled on the wet concrete.

He'd had enough of History for the time being.

Then he went inside and dialled Marsha's number.

A NOTE TO THE READER

First of all, thank you for reading my book. As a father, brother and son, *Stolen Lives* was an extremely difficult book to write and research, as the subject matter disgusted me: the theft and sale of babies and children seems to me the most abhorrent of crimes to which human beings can sink - worse in many ways than murder, as the possibility for emotional closure is so difficult to achieve when one suspects that somewhere out there in the vast world is a blood relative that may be lost to the rightful family forever. And yet the scandal of the *niños robados* (the Stolen Children) happened, and happened on a vast scale, beginning in 1939 and continuing until 1987 – a full 12 years after the end of the Franco dictatorship; and it only stopped when a Spanish magazine obtained photos of a dead baby - swaddled as if new born - in a freezer at a prestigious doctor's surgery and was brave enough to publish and make Spanish society aware of the terrible truth.

Despite the impact of this magazine article, the true scale of the scandal was not realised until the advent of the internet, when Spaniards began to create forums in order to search for lost relatives. It is now estimated that more than 300,000 people are affected directly by the scandal – a huge number when one bears in mind that Spain's population is around 45 million (so roughly one person in 150). As is nearly always the way with human history, it was the poor and the poorly educated who suffered most. It is an eternal blot on the institution of the Catholic church in Spain that priests and nuns participated so gladly in this deception; and an even greater blot that they profited financially from their actions.

What really made the book difficult to write, though, were the memories it stirred in me: while working as a journalist, I had interviewed a family that was affected by the scandal. It was one of the most harrowing experiences of my life, as the pain of the family was an almost tangible thing. When I finished the two-hour interview, I went outside, sat in my car, and cried my eyes out: I had recently become a father, and the sense of empathy was immense. I had nightmares for weeks after, in which my own precious and defenceless bundle was snatched from her crib and sold to some faceless, nameless stranger. But painful as the experience of that interview was, it taught me a valuable lesson: good journalism can only be written by journalists who allow themselves to connect with the subject matter. And thus was born my alter-ego, Danny Sanchez – he is hard-bitten and cynical, as are most experienced journalists; but Danny is also tenacious, mainly because he is driven by the fact he *cares,* cares in the way that I learned to care about the people whom I interviewed and reported upon in my 10 years as a journalist.

Whether the story is any good is not for me to decide; but I am immensely proud of what the story *reveals* about both Spanish society and humanity in general. It is important that secrets like these are dragged out into the harsh and merciless light of truth by any means possible – partly so that families can potentially be reunited; partly because their recurrence cannot be permitted by any sane and civilized society.

If you would like more information on me and/or the real-life inspirations for Stolen Lives, you can find them on my blog: **www.matthewpritchard.co.uk.** I would also appreciate it enormously if you would review my book anywhere you think appropriate: reviews on **Goodreads** and **Amazon** would be especially appreciated. Matthew Pritchard.

Sapere Books is an exciting new publisher of brilliant fiction and popular history.

To find out more about our latest releases and our monthly bargain books visit our website: **saperebooks.com**

Printed by Amazon Italia Logistica S.r.l.
Torrazza Piemonte (TO), Italy

16731893R00162